Photo credit: Teresa Cannon

Cheryl Adam spent her childhood in rural Australia where her love of storytelling began. In adulthood, she travelled widely and lived overseas including in Zambia (then Northern Rhodesia), Kenya, South Africa, Norway, Jersey, England and Sweden. She has been evicted, kidnapped, abandoned, made homeless and discriminated against in her foreign adventures and this helped develop her deep empathy for the plight of immigrant women.

In the 1960s, she was deported from Kenya and arrived as an unwanted guest in Sweden. She later moved to South Africa for thirteen years before returning to Australia. After her husband's stroke, she took up study, completing a Masters in Fine Arts at Monash University. In 2018 at the age of 74, her first novel *Lillian's Eden* was published. *Out of Eden* followed in 2021 and *Africa's Eden* is the final volume of the Eden trilogy.

T0274942

Other books by Cheryl Adam

Lillian's Eden
Out of Eden

AFRICA'S EDEN

Cheryl Adam

First published by Spinifex Press, 2022

Spinifex Press Pty Ltd
PO Box 5270, North Geelong, VIC 3215, Australia
PO Box 105, Mission Beach, QLD 4852, Australia

women@spinifexpress.com.au
www.spinifexpress.com.au

Copyright © Cheryl Adam, 2022

The moral right of the author has been asserted.

All rights reserved. Without limiting the rights under copyright
reserved above, no part of this publication may be reproduced, stored
in or introduced into a retrieval system, or transmitted, in any form
or by any means (electronic, mechanical, photocopying, recording or
otherwise) without prior written permission of both the copyright
owner and the above publisher of the book.

Copyright for educational purposes
Information in this book may be reproduced in whole or part for
study or training purposes, subject to acknowledgement of the
source and providing no commercial usage or sale of material occurs.
Where copies of part or whole of the book are made under part VB
of the Copyright Act, the law requires that prescribed procedures be
followed. For information contact the Copyright Agency Limited.

Edited by Pauline Hopkins, Renate Klein and Susan Hawthorne
Cover design by Deb Snibson, MAPG
Cover photo by Pierrette Paroz
Typesetting by Helen Christie, Blue Wren Books
Typeset in Berling
Printed by McPherson's Printing Group

A catalogue record for this
book is available from the
National Library of Australia

ISBN: 9781925950489 (paperback)
ISBN: 9781925950496 (ebook)

MIX
Paper from
responsible sources
FSC® C001695

To Joey and Colin, never forgotten.

1

A Move

Maureen clutched the aerogramme and stared at the only thing that mattered in her life – Henry Bernard. He pulled himself up on the arm of the chair, took a few unsure steps and then waddled towards Maureen's aunt, mouth open with the thrill of his new achievement. Her aunt folded him in her arms and Maureen's chest tightened, jealous that it wasn't her he had run to, even though she was grateful he was surrounded by love.

She chided herself for feeling jealous. Her aunt, Audrey, had taken care of them since Maureen and her baby arrived in England six months ago. Sweden was now a slim book pressed into the top shelf of bad memories. A song on the radio caught her attention. Simon and Garfunkel's latest hit, *Bookends*. The words settled in her gut and a sob caught in her throat. Aunt Audrey looked up, eyebrows raised.

"I need to talk to you," Maureen said. Her aunt nodded and put Henry down.

"After dinner."

A week ago, Aunt Audrey had asked if she could adopt Henry Bernard. *He is not to know you are his mother*, she'd said at the time. *Not while he's young, anyway. You would have to move out of course but you could see him regularly.* Aunt Audrey had fostered a baby for two years in Australia and had lost him to his grandmother, so Maureen understood her fear, but what she had said unsettled Maureen. The realisation that she couldn't stay with her aunt forever and that she had to make a home of her own. How was she going to do that when England was so expensive and she didn't want to return to Australia?

Her aunt's house in Staines was small for two young cousins, her aunt, uncle, herself, and Henry. And there were too many mothers! As wonderful as Audrey was, Maureen didn't feel in control of her own life. It was a bit like being under Matron's gaze in the home for unmarried mothers where she'd lived in Gothenburg. But beggars can't be choosers, and she was a beggar.

Twisting the fake wedding ring around her finger, Maureen thought about the lie she had told her colleagues at work – that she was a widow, husband killed in a motor accident in Gothenburg. Problem was she didn't know how widows behaved. Perhaps she laughed too much because they had begun to ask a lot of questions. And the manager was getting too friendly, holding her gaze a bit too long, winking, visiting the canteen when she did, leaning across her at the sink. It made her feel uncomfortable, got her antenna up.

There was also his wife whose smile would pass over her when she visited the office. That offended Maureen. As if she'd be interested in her podgy old husband. She was twenty-four, he was at least twenty plus years older. Did he think she was easy because she was on her own with a child? The single blokes who called in from the building sites who had asked her out always did a double take when she said she'd have to ask her aunt to babysit. Some found excuses. How was she going to get her freedom back? Travelling around Europe, working holiday seasons in hotels, wasn't possible with a child. It was 1967 and her dream of travelling the world had been stymied, but her craving for adventure hadn't.

She turned the aerogramme in her hands with the offer it held. It wouldn't be like last time, she thought. This man she knew. He had fished her from the passenger seat of a wrecked car after an accident when she was in Kenya and he had visited her in hospital bringing a bunch of roses. When she had recovered, they had gone out together for eight months. That was before she ended up in Sweden and all the shit that followed. She'd dumped Pete two months after she'd left Kenya. Pete was eight years older than her, full of fun, kind and generous, tall, and handsome to boot, but he had wanted to settle down and at nineteen she hadn't seen the world. Leaving him hadn't been up to her in the end. She had overstayed her visa and the Kenyan Government had given her a departure date.

While she was in Sweden, Pete had left Kenya and moved to South Africa. She didn't know anything about South Africa except that it had big gold mines. The letters had begun when she wrote telling him what had become of her since she had left him in Kenya. She really liked Pete and hated that she'd hurt him. In a moment of nostalgia, she thought he might feel better if he knew her boyfriend had left her pregnant and homeless in Sweden because his parents had disapproved of her. It would be a bit of retribution for Pete. But he'd answered and asked her to keep writing. Over the months his letters had become warmer and now there was this one. *I'll look after you. No strings attached. I'm sharing a house with old friends from Kenya, lots of room. There's plenty of office work in Johannesburg. You can employ a nanny to look after the little one while you work.* She remembered how Pete's niece and nephews loved him and how he had played with them. She imagined having a nanny and how easy that would make her life.

Maureen watched Henry Bernard stagger between the chairs, laughing his little head off. He would be fine. Matron had said children were adaptable.

She didn't have enough money for her fare to Johannesburg yet, but she would soon. Maybe her Eden was in Africa?

"If anything goes wrong you can always come back," her aunt said, as she hugged Maureen goodbye at Heathrow airport. Henry put his arms up straining towards her from his pram.

"Mum, Mum," he said. Audrey smothered his head with kisses and turned away, face wet. Henry Bernard was eighteen months old; he'd spent a year with her. He craned his head around the pram, reaching towards Audrey and crying as they went through the gate to board their Johannesburg bound plane.

It had been a long trip, her child had hardly slept, Maureen was exhausted and full of apprehension. She checked her reflection in the hand-mirror. There were smudges under her eyes, her hair was a mess. The French roll she'd paid so much for had come undone. Removing the pins, she pulled a comb through the tangle. So much for wanting to look her best for Pete. She'd left him as a perky blonde with a short elfin haircut, Vidal Sassoon's latest, and now her hair was back to dark brown and long. He hadn't seen her in four years. She should have gone back to her blonde look and been the girl he'd fallen in love with, but the upkeep was too expensive.

A man at the immigration desk with a face as hard as his rubber stamp flicked through her Australian passport then looked at the child in her arms and hit her with his eyes.

"You are not married? No job, no money, no return ticket?" His eyebrows met the crease above his nose.

"My fiancé is meeting me here. I am staying with him." Fiancé sounded better than friend. The man tapped the desk with his fingers. He called out in Afrikaans and had a loud conversation with a woman in a blue uniform. She came over and held her arms out to Henry. He shrank away. She tried to coax him into her arms.

"What are you doing? He doesn't like strangers." Maureen tightened her grip. The woman stared at her blank faced. "He must come with me," she said. Foreign hands took hold of her child. Henry Bernard screamed and pushed his face into Maureen's neck, scrunching the front of her blouse in his fists.

"Why are you trying to take him?" Maureen held onto her child, heart pounding.

"You must go to the front and speak to your fiancé. He must sign guarantor for you, but you can only stay three weeks. A South African citizen must sign you into the country. Without a guarantor you will have to return to England on the next flight. I will hold the child while you go and speak to him."

The woman yanked screaming Henry Bernard into her arms and walked into a viewing room. Maureen was about to follow when the man with the stamp gripped her elbow and steered her towards a horde of people queued at the arrival gate. Frantic, she looked back and saw Henry Bernard fighting in the arms of the woman, watching her go, face red from screaming. Everything inside her shook. In a panic, she searched the faces of the crowd and saw Pete's head above the throng. He waved an arm.

Her relief was enormous. Turning to the man next to her, she pointed, "I see him." She waved her arms and was about to rush towards the barrier when a hand clapped on her shoulder holding her back.

"You will speak from here. You cannot go through the gate." The crowd was noisy. Maureen had to shout.

"You have to go guarantor for me. I need a citizen to sign me in because I'm an unmarried mother with no means of support." The crowd quietened; many eyes turned towards her. Blood rushed to Maureen's cheeks; her whole body felt hot.

"I'm not a citizen, I'm a resident. I'll have to get a friend," he yelled back, then disappeared into the crowd. Sticky with perspiration, not just from the heat but gnawing anxiety, Maureen watched for Pete's return, worried he might rethink and not come back at all.

An hour passed. The waiting crowd had dispersed. The plane back to England would take off soon and she might be on board. At least she had Henry Bernard in her arms again, although a guard sat next to her. She heard a whistle. Remembering it from old, she looked up, to see Pete and another man approaching the immigration desk. Sick with relief, she jumped up. There was a loud exchange of Afrikaans. The guard motioned Maureen to follow him. She met Pete at the desk, eyes anxious, no kiss, four years, and Henry Bernard between them. They were like strangers.

Humiliated by the airport debacle, Maureen thanked Pete's friend, Damien, for going guarantor for her and wondered what he must be thinking of Pete's new girlfriend. She would be sharing his house along with Pete. What did Pete think? Was he already having regrets? She held Henry Bernard on her knee in the front seat of the car while Damien drove and Pete sat in the back.

"I've never been arrested before," she laughed, trying to pass off the awkwardness she felt, making light of her situation to cover up another mad impulsive decision she'd made. It wasn't just herself she'd put at risk coming to Africa but also the future of her child. Mad!

They arrived at Damien's house to be greeted by his wife Hannah and their ten-year-old son. Hannah welcomed Maureen like an old friend. After a relaxing glass of wine, Maureen fell asleep on the couch with Henry Bernard sprawled on her lap and only woke when he stirred. She sat up and gazed around, puzzled at the sunshine that bathed the strange room. At first, she thought she was dreaming then she remembered her ordeal and where she was. Pete sat across from her, reading. He put the book down and grinned.

"Sleeping beauty is awake at last." He pointed to Henry Bernard. "The little chap looks hot in that jersey." She looked at the red sweaty face of her child, blonde curls damp against his forehead. Of course, she was in Africa, it was hot. She felt hot herself. She removed his jumper and checked his nappy which was sodden.

"I'll have to change him." How weird she felt, disconnected.

"The girl can do it." He shouted towards the door. "Ruth." A smiling, young black girl came into the room.

"Boss?"

"Ruth, this is Henry Bernard, take him and change him for the madam." The young girl went over to Henry Bernard and held out her arms.

"Come Henry." Shrinking back, he clung to Maureen's blouse and buried his face in her chest.

"He doesn't know her. I'll change him." Maureen frowned; she didn't want someone taking over her child. Pete's eyes widened. He had arranged for Ruth to look after the child.

"Ruth is Hannah's nanny; she's looked after her boy. I just thought as she's here all the time he'd get used to her. You will need a nanny if you get a job." Pete didn't understand why Maureen looked so annoyed.

Picking up Henry Bernard, Maureen lay him on the couch and removed his nappy. She wanted to be seen as a competent mother, in charge of her own life. They hadn't started a relationship yet. If this didn't work out with Pete, it would mean returning to Australia. But she didn't want it to come to that. "Thanks, I'll work it out. I just need time to catch my breath."

Pete shuffled his feet and flashed her a look of concern. It was obvious he regretted opening his mouth. She knew he cared. He'd admitted to still loving her in his letters, before she came to South Africa, but she needed him to take things slowly if their relationship was to be a success.

The weeks flew by and they were getting on well, more relaxed in each other's company. Henry Bernard had warmed to Pete. He put his arms up for a horsey ride on Pete's shoulders. Watching them together, Maureen wasn't regretting her decision to come to South Africa. She had a job, arranged by Pete. Secretary to the manager of a small commercial airline based at the airport where Pete worked as an aircraft technician. They drove to work together every morning and Hannah's maid, Ruth, was looking after Henry Bernard, who seemed happy with her. For the first time since his birth, Maureen was starting to feel settled.

Then a letter arrived from Immigration. She opened the letter, and her life went sideways. Her visa had expired. Pete had said they would forget about her like they had about his friend who'd been in Johannesburg for four years on an expired visa. But Immigration had given her three days to book her return trip to England and she was to notify them of her departure time. It was because she was an unmarried mother with no means of support. An immigration risk. How unfair it was but she couldn't argue her case. She rubbed a hand across her eyes and replaced the letter in the envelope. Henry Bernard pulled a wooden duck across the floor on a piece of string. Maureen sat and watched him. Pete noticed how quiet she was.

"What's up?"

"I have to go back to England," she handed the letter to Pete and gave him a defeated smile.

He gnawed his lip as he read the letter. Then took her hand.

"There's only one way to do this," he said. "We should get married. They can't turf you out if you're married to a resident?"

"You don't have to marry me, Pete. I didn't come here to get married." She didn't want him to feel obligated to marry her and she didn't feel she was ready for marriage.

"I want to marry you. I love you and the little chap. If you want to stay in Jo'burg, it's the only way." It wasn't how Maureen wanted to do things. She loved Pete for the great friend he was. Would it be wrong to marry him without being in love with him? She knew he would be great for Henry Bernard, but marriage?

Maureen consulted Hannah. "I think you're good together and Pete loves you. He'll make a good Dad. It's not a bad start and if it doesn't work out so what? Divorce won't damn you to hell like in the old days." So, marriage would be her refuge. She would phone her mother to let her know about her decision to get married.

Maureen worked out the time difference – it should be 6.30 a.m. in Australia, her mother would be out of bed. She booked the call.

Lillian covered the telephone receiver and slapped at Eric's hand as he tried to pull her towards the kitchen.

"It's Maureen calling from Africa, and I can't hear her. Go away, I'll be with you in a minute." She turned back to the phone, "Maureen, sorry pet. You said you were getting married?"

"Kitchen's on fire," Eric said. Lillian dropped the phone and ran to the kitchen. Smoke rose from a molten saucepan.

"What in God's name have you been doing?"

"Boiling an egg," Eric mumbled. Lillian grabbed a tea towel, lifted the saucepan off the hot plate and put it in the sink. It sizzled and spat. Bits of shell had adhered to the bottom.

"There's no egg in it," she growled. His finger pointed to the ceiling. Lillian looked up. The ceiling was splattered with egg yolk. She pulled out a chair, climbed on it and wiped at the ceiling with the tea towel. The egg was stuck like paint to a canvas.

"I told you not to cook anything. What were you thinking?" she shouted, rushing back to the telephone. It was a stupid question. Since his stroke, Eric acted on impulse and lived on snatches of memory. Their neighbour had complained about him peeping in their windows. Lillian knew it was because he sometimes thought his aunt Maggie still lived next door. He used to check that she wasn't burning the money she'd buried in the garden. Before, the snails had eaten the numbers and made it worthless.

"Hello, Maureen. So sorry love, your father just blew up an egg … No, it's nothing pet, he's always doing something. No one can help, dear, least of all you, so don't feel guilty. I'm just sorry you didn't choose to come home to Australia instead of going to Africa. Now you're getting married I'm scared I won't see you for a long time." She listened to Maureen promise she would return and felt sorry she hadn't been more enthusiastic about her news. She wanted her to be happy, and Pete sounded like a good man.

"Congratulations from all of us. You know we want you to have a good life. One day I might meet my grandson. Have a lovely wedding." Lillian put the phone down and wiped away a tear with the tea towel she still held and then went back to scrub the kitchen ceiling. What was she going to do with Eric? They were divorced for God's sake!

2

Mirabelle Fosdick

The celebrant reviewed the form in his hand. Maureen and Pete stood before him, both looking startled. Hannah held her stopwatch to the ready, she had heard that registrar marriages were fast. A clearing of the throat and the celebrant began.

"Do you take Peter Millar to be your husband? "

"I do."

"Do you take Maureen McKinley to be your wife?"

"I do."

"You are now married in the eyes of the law. Sign the document on the table," he pointed to a small table with a white lace cloth, the only decoration in the drab room, then turned to a man standing by the door. "Please call the next couple."

Maureen and Pete moved to the table, signed the document, and wrote 24th April 1968 next to it. Hannah witnessed their signatures. It was the last time her name would be Maureen

McKinley. When they left the registry office Hannah held the stopwatch out for Maureen to see.

"One minute?" Her eyes popped. That was all the time it had taken for her to become legal and respectable? She had never pictured herself as a bride in a white dress and she wasn't, dressed in a burnt orange suit. The jacket fitted into her waist and had a silver chain belt, the skirt was a straight stylish mini that showed off her legs. She wore an emerald-green cowboy hat with matching green sling backs. She liked how she looked, not too serious. Hannah aimed her Kodak and Maureen smiled like a bride in a white dress. They climbed into two cars and went to a Spanish restaurant for lunch to celebrate.

Hannah, Damien and Pete's best mate, Chris, who had moved from Kenya with him and worked at the same airport, raised their glasses, and toasted the bridal couple. A waiter with a steaming pan of paella arrived at the table along with two musicians dressed like matadors. The musicians filled the restaurant with the sound of Spanish guitars. On the small stage a Spanish dancer clicked castanets and pummelled the floor with black high heels. It was a merry occasion. Maureen felt happy, Pete was beaming. The wine flowed.

Hannah leant towards her husband, Damien. "I'll give it three months."

A month down the track and Maureen was trying to avoid Damien. He was accidentally brushing her breasts as he walked past her or pinching her bum in fun. She had laughed it off in case she was mistaking his attentions but, in her heart, she knew she was kidding herself. He meant it. She had put up with these unwanted attentions from men for years and had even been accused of encouraging them.

It was Saturday. Pete worked Saturday mornings and Hannah was doing the weekly shopping which left Damien and Maureen in the house alone. Henry Bernard was sleeping, and Maureen was curled on the sofa with a book while Damien sat back with one arm along the couch, observing her.

"You're very sexy," Damien said, touching her shoulder with his hand. Maureen didn't look up, pretending to be engrossed in her book. The next moment her book was in his hand stretched above his head. She folded her arms.

"Come on Damien, give it back."

"I'll give it back for a kiss," he gave her a rakish smile. "No one's home, just you and me. Come on, I know you're up for it." Why did he think that? She had never encouraged him. Or had he read her defensive laughter as a come on? There was a squeal from the other room, Maureen pushed Damien away.

"I'm not up for anything. I'm married. Pete's your friend. I'm going to check on Henry Bernard." She fled. Should she tell Pete? No, it would cause a scene and spoil Pete and Damien's friendship. They had known each other since boarding school in Nairobi. Besides, Damien had gone guarantor for her, and he and Hannah had welcomed her into their home without having met her. She stayed in the bedroom playing with Henry Bernard until Pete came home. At dinner, Maureen pretended not to notice the worried looks Damien cast in her direction. Let him sweat, she thought. By the time Pete was ready for bed, Maureen had an idea.

"Why don't we find a place of our own to rent nearer the airport? It takes an hour to get to work from here and I want to get home in time for Henry Bernard's bath and dinner." Her workday was 8 a.m. to 2 p.m., which meant sitting around until Pete knocked off at 4.30 p.m.

"I only get to see him for an hour in the evening. I want us to be a family in our own place."

Three weeks later, Pete found a one-bedroom Spanish-styled villa for rent. It was in an area between Alexander, a black township, and Sandton, an upper-class suburb, closer to Grand Central Airport where they both worked.

Maureen held Henry Bernard in her arms while Pete knocked on the landlady's door. A stout black woman in a blue pinafore dress, with a matching blue cap over short wire grey hair, opened the door. Her broad face was a mass of wrinkles. A thick pink lip poked forward.

"Is the madam in?" Pete asked.

"Madam!" The maid shouted over her shoulder eyes squinting at Maureen and Pete. She turned away and shuffled off as a tall, wide-hipped, big-bosomed woman in her sixties strode towards them.

"What can I do for you?" the woman said.

"We've come about the villa you have for rent," Pete replied as the woman's eyes took note of them. "My name's Peter Millar and this is my wife, Maureen." It was the first time she had been introduced to anybody as Pete's wife and it felt odd.

"Mirabelle Fosdick." They shook hands. Mirabelle led them out to her verandah, where she seated them under a blaze of purple bougainvillea. An expanse of lawn rolled down to a fishpond.

"Tea?" Mirabelle's eyebrows questioned. Maureen looked to Pete for an answer, aware this was an interview.

"Thank you, that would be nice," Pete said. Mirabelle rang a silver bell on the table. The maid who had greeted them at the door ambled onto the verandah and drooped in front of her.

"Madam?"

"Bring us some tea please, Doris." Doris muttered under her breath and shuffled down the verandah, disappearing through French doors.

"This is the original farmhouse and over there are the villas."

Her hand swept towards a brush fence and a collection of orange-tiled roofs on the other side. She wriggled her backside into her chair, happy to have a captive audience. "They were the stables. I built the villas after my husband died. I didn't have any plans, used the existing structures, and added on. There's a two-storey house at the bottom of the plot that used to be a barn and hayloft, it's now divided into two flats. A single male tenant occupies the downstairs. He's one of the gentle types, if you know what I mean." She gave a coy look. "Upstairs is a German couple. They are musicians and art teachers at the Rudolph Steiner school. There's also the chicken coop under construction." She gazed into the distance.

"It's becoming too much for me to manage and I've been thinking of moving to Rhodesia. That's where my brother lives. I won't sell but I'm on the lookout for someone to keep an eye on the upkeep of the place. There's a gardener and maid to pay and rents to collect." Her lips pursed and she eyed Pete. "Whoever does that job will get their place rent free."

A packed wooden tray was plonked on the table next to her. Doris straightened, breathing heavily. Maureen smiled up at her. Doris scowled back.

"Thank you, Doris." The maid rocked her large frame out of the room. Watching the maid leave, Maureen felt a surge of sympathy. She looked too old to be working. Her hostess lifted a large china teapot filling three cups and handed them around. "No biscuits I'm afraid, cook only bakes on Tuesdays.

She continued, "Doris will keep her job here if I leave. She's in her seventies and too old to get another job. She cleans the villas." Mirabelle Fosdick stared at Pete. "You remind me of my son. He was a tall strapping fellow like you. Killed by a hippo on a river safari." Tea slopped in her saucer as she lifted her cup.

Pete cleared his throat. "My brother is a game ranger in

Kenya, he's had a few close calls with hippos. I'm sorry to hear about your son."

"That's terrible, Mrs Fosdick. I'm so sorry," Maureen said, horrified to think of anyone being killed by a hippo. She had only heard of people being killed by lions. She had seen lions up close, walked in a yard where they roamed free. Pete's brother, Mick, worked for George Adamson. He'd known Elsa the lion and worked on the film set of *Born Free*. He had once invited her and Pete to a barbeque on the film set. She had met Virginia McKenna and had tied herself in knots when the star had tried to converse with her. It had been embarrassing, but she had only been nineteen then. She wondered how a hippo would kill someone. Tear them to pieces like a lion?

"Call me Mirabelle, please. You have an accent?" Mirabelle aimed her large frame towards Maureen. "Canada?"

"Australia."

"Antipodean. Australians aren't popular in South Africa. The Afrikaners think with their similar history that they should have supported the Boers not the British. Of course, Australia is still on the side of the British government and boycotting the breakaway rebel government of Ian Smith." Mirabelle's chin lifted and she sniffed. Maureen wasn't sure if that was a mark against her or not. She didn't know anything about African politics, only what Pete told her.

"Most deaths in the wild are caused by buffalo, you know. My son was silly to camp by the river. Born in Africa, he should have known better. He's buried in Rhodesia." Her voice rang with longing. Maureen commiserated. She knew what it was like to be in a foreign country far from family, although Rhodesia was just a few hours' drive away, not across the ocean like Australia.

With their tea finished, Mirabelle showed them the villa for rent. According to Mirabelle it was furnished. Two lounge chairs, a bed, two stools at the kitchen bench, hot plates for cooking and a small fridge filled a space meant for one. The lounge was so small it was a squeeze between the lounge chairs that sat opposite each other. In the bedroom there was just enough room at the end of the double bed for a cot, but it would do.

There was no discussion between Pete and Maureen. It was like a silent pact had been made even before they had seen the villa. This was to be the beginning of their marriage. They hadn't asked questions of each other about their feelings or hopes, they'd just married and that was that. Pete and Maureen shook hands with Mirabelle Fosdick and Pete handed over a cheque for the rent.

When they broke the news to Damien and Hannah there were no hard feelings. Damien and Hannah had been wondering how to ask Pete and Maureen to leave anyway, because they had family members arriving from Kenya. One week later, Maureen and Pete moved into their villa.

The day after their move, Beauty, Doris's granddaughter, arrived on Maureen's doorstep.

"Have you any work, Madam?" The girl, about fourteen years old, stood with her hands clasped in front of her tired school uniform. Maureen had never interviewed anyone for a job and Pete wasn't home. What should she do? Opening the door wide, she stepped to the side.

"Come in." The girl sidled past Maureen, eyes to the floor. "Sit down." Maureen motioned her towards an armchair. Startled, the girl looked at the chair and back at Maureen.

"No, Madam. I can stand."

"You can sit down if you want?" The girl shook her head. An awkward moment was relieved by Henry Bernard running into the room. Stopping short, he stared at Beauty. She tweaked her fingers at him and smiled. Henry Bernard laughed.

"This is Henry Bernard." She noticed the girl frown. His name was a bit of a mouthful for people who didn't always speak English, and Maureen had often heard black people call him Henry. Even Pete had started calling him Henry. She would drop the Bernard to make it easier. "You can call him Henry. Why don't you take Henry outside and play with him while I make a cup of tea?" It would give Maureen a chance to observe them together. Beauty offered her hand to Henry who took it and pulled the relieved girl outside.

From the window, Maureen watched them play while she made tea. Her child was shrieking with laughter. She poured two cups of tea and a glass of milk for her son and put them on the tray with the sugar bowl and spoons and went outside. Maureen put the tray on a chair by the door then held a cup out to Beauty. The girl stepped back and put her hand up.

"No, Madam."

"You don't want a cup of tea?"

Beauty dug a hole in the earth with her toe. "Yes, but that cup is the same as yours, Madam."

"It's what I give all my visitors," Maureen said, surprised.

"What do you give your girls, Madam?" Maureen's eyes flicked from the girl to the cup. Were there special cups for maids? She had never taken any notice of what Hannah's maid had drunk from.

"If you want a different cup, I will buy one, but this is all I have. Please." She held the cup and saucer out to Beauty. Eyes averted, the maid took the cup, leaving Maureen with the saucer.

"I have a tin cup, Madam. This one I could break." She gulped her tea.

"I start work at eight o'clock in the morning. Can you be here at half past seven in the morning?"

Beauty's face lit up. Maureen took the empty cup from the beaming girl, aware it was an easy job for her with only one child to care for. Even so, Maureen would pay her the going rate of twenty rand per month, the same as maids who had more responsibilities and would supply the usual food: a ten pound bag of mealie meal, jam, fish, tea, sugar, and powdered milk.

"I will see the madam tomorrow." Beauty skipped through the gate.

The following morning, Beauty had to restrain a screaming Henry as Maureen, full of guilt, left for work.

3

Lessons

There were four villas in the shared courtyard, and it didn't take long for Maureen to get to know the neighbours. She found them friendly and interesting. Paul, a young writer, lived with his sister Emma in the adjoining unit to Maureen's. Then there was Gloria, her mother and three-year old Rossie. Next to Gloria's villa, in their twenties, were Phillipe, and Tommy.

Rossie and Henry started to play together in the courtyard. Maureen encouraged their play, inviting Rossie in for fruit and orange juice. His mother never reciprocated with Henry. In fact, Maureen hardly saw her in the mornings. But Rossie had become a regular visitor, knocking on Maureen's door at 7 a.m. It had begun to get Pete's goat.

The small hand was insistent on the door. Pete rolled out of bed. "It's Sunday, for Christ's sake! What's wrong with his bloody mother?" He pulled the door open and frowned down at the child.

"Go home, Rossie, it's too early to play. Henry hasn't had breakfast." Pete closed the door. "I'm going to have a word with his mother," he said climbing back into bed.

"No, you can't. We live too close to make trouble and Henry might lose his playmate. I'll talk to Rossie."

"It's on your head, then."

Maureen let it ride for another week, sending Rossie home before she went to work in the morning, but he was always there when she returned from work in the afternoon.

"What's Rossie still doing here?" Pete enquired. He'd gotten home late, and it was dark already.

"I wanted to see how long it would take until they missed him but according to Beauty, he's been here all day. His granny hasn't even checked on him and Beauty isn't paid to look after another child. It's not fair on her."

"The mother's a good time girl," Pete said.

"She might have an evening job. Telephone exchange, nurse or something." Pete shook his head. Rossie's mum often gave him the eye. It embarrassed him. Maureen grabbed Rossie's hand, annoyed with Pete for being so judgmental of their neighbours.

"I'll take him home. Maybe someone's sick." She walked him across the courtyard and knocked on the door. The grandmother opened the door and put her hand on the wall to steady herself.

"Rossie," she slurred. The smell of spirits on her breath was strong.

"Is his mother home? He hasn't had dinner."

"She's out escorting. Come on, Rossie, I've got some chicken for you." Maureen gave Rossie a gentle push and he went inside. His granny shut the door.

"Well?" Pete said when she returned.

"The grandmother was drunk, and his mother is escorting someone."

"Told you she was a whore."

"No, she's an escort. They show out of town businessmen around and escort them to functions," Maureen said. Pete looked at her in disbelief.

"Don't get too involved with them," he warned. Her hackles rose. God, he was always warning her about something. If it wasn't the neighbours, it was the black maid and gardener. "They'll take advantage of you," he'd said, after he had seen her helping Beauty peg nappies on the line.

Maureen didn't listen to his advice about the black people. She wasn't used to servants and thought they were paid too little for the work they were expected to do. Why shouldn't she be friends with them? But Pete's words kept grating in her ears. *They can't be your friends. It's not fair on them.*

Yet for all Pete's warnings, Maureen noticed how the blacks lined up to get a job with him if he needed a worker and how he helped them with their problems, even those who didn't work for him. He warned them if the police were doing pass checks, hating the way the police treated them. He enjoyed their company, laughing and joking with them, attempting to speak Xhosa or Zulu. In Kenya, Pete had spoken Swahili before English because his mother had been too sick to care for him and he'd always had an Ayah to look after him. Although he had been brought up a racist, he liked black people. It was all too complex for Maureen. She felt her way along the barbed wire fence that was Africa, learning as she went.

The aero club party was in full swing when Pete and Maureen arrived and within minutes Maureen found herself ringed by

23

Pete's friends. A glass of cane spirit and orange juice was thrust into her hands by one of the pilots. "You must try, it's a South African drink, tastes like cordial," he said. Maureen sipped tentatively. It seemed fine, tasting like freshly squeezed oranges. She swallowed it down, eager to please. Her glass was kept full by Pete's attentive friends while Pete sat on the sidelines entertaining with his jokes.

The Rolling Stones were on the record player and Maureen was rock and rolling with Pete's friend, Chris. He spun her around. Problem was she couldn't stop spinning even when the record had stopped. Crashing across the room, she knocked into a table and fell on the floor. On her hands and knees, unable to stand, she spewed on the floor.

"Mop," someone yelled. Pete helped her to her feet.

"Time to go," he called out to his hostess, his arm supporting Maureen to the door.

"I'm sick." Everything was revolving, her head, her stomach.

"You've been drinking cane spirit, it's lethal." Pete bundled her into the car and headed for home.

"Stop!" Maureen shrieked. Pete jammed on the brakes thinking she was going to vomit.

"You're driving on the roof," she said. Her brain was muddled and upside down.

"Jesus! Are you going to be sorry in the morning." He drove slower, easing around the corners, regretting he hadn't kept an eye on her. South Africans liked to ply the innocent with cane spirit.

In the morning she felt like an elephant had stamped on her head. Hanging her head over the bed she heaved into a bucket of stale vomit, but there was nothing left in her stomach. Henry came and stood by her bed. Pete had given him breakfast before he had left for an urgent job at the airport. Maureen called for the nanny, but nobody came as it was Sunday. She tried to sit up.

The room spun and she had to lie down again. Her mouth was parched. She reached out to Henry.

"Can you get mummy a glass of water?" It was a long shot for a two-year-old as the child couldn't reach the kitchen sink. Henry rushed off. Minutes later, he returned with a cup of water. Amazed at her son, Maureen drank it.

"Did you climb on the stool to get the water, Henry?"

"No, I got it out of the toilet." The water came up Maureen's throat and went back down again. Her stomach needed it more than the bucket.

"Get your car and play on the end of the bed until Daddy comes home. Mummy's too sick to play with you."

Pete brought home a box of fried chicken from the Pickin' chicken drive-through for lunch. Nauseated by the smell, Maureen buried her face in the pillow while Henry chomped his lunch on the end of her bed.

Two days later Maureen returned to work to discover her hangover was famous.

"All newcomers get the cane spirit treatment," one of the pilots said. "We've never heard of a reaction like yours, though. Pete told us you drove home on the roof and drank water from the toilet." The office staff hooted with laughter. Maureen lowered her head, embarrassed.

"You're not a good singer, by the way." Singer? Pete hadn't told her she'd been singing. "And you owe Hazel a birthday cake." Maureen stared at the pilot. What was he talking about?

"You put your hand in the cake when you danced into the food table," he explained. Pete hadn't told her that either. She was mortified. They would never invite her to a party again. Oh, God. She was the laughing stock of the airport. It was a great start to meeting Pete's friends. What must they think of her?

"I'm having a braai next weekend if you and Pete would

like to come?" The bookkeeper called out. "It's beer and wine, though, no cane spirit." The office staff laughed.

They had been living in their villa for three months when Pete came rushing through the door, late back from work.

"Come and look at this." He grabbed Maureen's hand and led her outside. Her heart pumped at the urgency in his voice. Had somebody been robbed, attacked? It was dark. What was she supposed to see?

"Over there, in the doorway." Pete's whisper was as loud as an average voice. Maureen looked across at the villa occupied by two men. Phillipe was standing in the doorway, smoking a cigarette with the hall light behind him and security light above him, wearing a nylon shortie nightie, with a fluffy edge, his manhood visible in the light.

"He's a poof!" Pete said, incredulous. He'd shared a beer with him. Maureen stifled a laugh. Phillipe was a fascinating sight, but he wasn't the first man she had seen in women's clothing. What was more interesting was Pete's reaction – she was still getting to know her husband.

"I wonder if old Mirabelle knows?" Pete hissed.

"They were here before us, so she probably does," Maureen whispered. They went back inside, and Maureen poured Pete a brandy and lemonade. "Good for shock," she said, laughing.

"What a bunch of oddballs," Pete said, shaking his head.

"I think they're interesting. Everyone's friendly and they're not oddballs. Paul's a writer and his sister goes to university." Pete didn't reply.

Weeks later, Paul turned up on her doorstep with a cardboard box in his arms. "I wonder if you'd mind looking after this," he said, in a low voice, looking behind to see if anyone was within earshot and thrusting the box in Maureen's arms. She looked at the box and then her neighbour and raised her eyebrows. "The police are raiding Rossie's mother's villa. She's been dealing in dagga."

"What's dagga?"

"Marijuana." They might come to our place so I thought you could hide this for me. The police would never suspect Pete." She could see the truth in what he was saying, Pete was straight talking, honest, and didn't abide fools. But what would he do in this situation? Probably tell Paul to bugger off! She gnawed the inside of her cheek, uncertain what to do.

"It's just for tonight. I'll pick it up in the morning." He scuttled off before she could object. Where could she put the damn thing? Not inside. If it was found, she wouldn't be able to plead innocent. She shoved it in her letterbox and went inside to put Henry to bed.

Dinner was ready by the time Pete arrived home. He sniffed the air, gave her a hug, and flopped into a chair.

"I'm bushed. What delights has my wife made for dinner?" The smile he gave her was full of love. She would tell him about the box after dinner.

"Lamb shank stew. It's one of my mother's recipes." Maureen dished up two plates, put them on trays and gave Pete one. She collected hers and settled in the lounge chair opposite him.

"I married a good cook," Pete said smacking his lips. He always showed his appreciation, it was one of the things Maureen loved about him. He was mopping up the last of his stew with a piece of bread when someone coughed in the doorway. The police uniform jammed Maureen's brain.

"Sorry to disturb you folks," a thick Afrikaans accent.

Pete put his tray on the floor and stood up. "Come in, officer. The policeman entered, eyes working the room.

"We is investigating some illegal activities. Drug dealings."

"Drugs?" Pete's head pulled back, shocked. Maureen's brain kicked in, she grabbed their trays and headed for the kitchen. Pete offered the policeman Maureen's vacant chair.

"Sit down, officer. Would you like a coffee?" The policeman assessed Pete, sat down and declined the coffee with a shake of his head. Maureen plugged the sink and turned on the water, making a noise with the plates so the policeman wouldn't talk to her. It was better Pete dealt with him. She wasn't good at lies, her cheeks always went red. Anyway, Pete wouldn't be lying because he didn't know what she had done.

The policeman and Pete discussed drugs, politics and the law while Maureen kept busy in the kitchen. After half an hour, the policeman, stood up.

"It's been nice talking to you. I'd appreciate you keeping an eye out for us."

"Sure will," Pete said, shaking the offered hand and seeing the policeman to the door. Maureen waved her tea towel at the departing guest and packed plates in the cupboard. Pete closed the door and turned wide eyes to Maureen.

"Well, what do you think of that? We have a poof, prostitute, and druggie, and you said they weren't oddballs. Told you." He sat down and patted his knee. Maureen sat on his knee and kissed his cheek.

"Just as well I didn't tell you what was hidden in the letterbox," she giggled before proceeding to tell him about the neighbour's visit. His mouth hung open.

"Bloody hell! We could have gone to gaol if they found us with that."

"You won't tell them, will you Pete?" Maureen didn't want her neighbours going to gaol.

"Are you kidding! You hid the bloody box. You're as guilty as they are. You can't mess with the police in this country even if you are white," he said, astounded at her recklessness.

After that night, Maureen started to notice the police. She hadn't noticed them in other countries she had lived in, but in South Africa they seemed to be everywhere, and even more in her neighbourhood because of the black township nearby. There wasn't a day that passed that she didn't see a black person being harassed by a policeman, showing their passes to prove their right to employment in the area. Often Maureen had seen them being bundled into police vans, even women with babies wrapped to their backs. She felt sorry for them. She mentioned it to Pete.

"It's tough, I know, but there are laws," he said.

"Well, I think it's wrong," Maureen snapped.

"You've only been here five minutes, Maureen. You don't understand Africa. My great-grandfather was born in the Seychelles, and I was born in Africa. I know these people." Pete had fought the Mau Mau in Kenya, seen atrocities. What he'd seen, he didn't tell her. She frowned.

"I had a black boyfriend in Australia. He was one of the West Indian cricket team doing a promotion for Coca-Cola at the same time I worked there. He had a university degree, you don't."

Pete stared at her, shocked. She put her hand on his arm and he shrank back.

"Don't. I have to think about this." He went off in his car and didn't come back for hours. She didn't ask where he'd been. He didn't touch her that night, or the next. A few days later, he put a bouquet of flowers in a vase. But they didn't broach the subject again nor discuss politics. Instead, Maureen listened to the conversations of his friends to try and understand the white South African way of thinking.

Everyone talked politics. They were all afraid no matter what their skin colour. The Afrikaners despised the English because of the Boer war. The Indians hated the English because they called them Coolies and had brought them to Africa to build the railways. The Indians looked down on the blacks because of their caste system. The blacks disliked the Indians because they were the merchants, ripping off the poor. The blacks hated all white people because of colonisation and Apartheid, and some black tribes hated other black tribes. And those of mixed race wore the scorn of everyone. It was a war zone. There were good people who stretched hands across barriers, but most people kept their heads down. Maureen couldn't get used to the bars at the windows and the prickles down her spine.

4

Juju

It was a few weeks after the marijuana raid and Maureen and Pete were on their way to the Snake Park for an outing. Henry sat in his car seat between them, making engine noises, his little foot resting on the steering wheel.

"Takes after me," Pete said, with a grin. Maureen gulped; Pete was sincere. Theirs was a new beginning, and Henry was his. He had never asked her about Henry's father, the Swede she'd met while working in a ski lodge in Norway and ditched Pete for.

"Look, little buddy, there's a Ford."

"Ford," said Henry, pointing. Pete chuckled. His hobby was cars, he had raced cars, driven in the East African Safari Rally. Maureen had spent many weekends having conversations with his feet while the rest of him lay under a car with a spanner in hand.

A siren wailed behind them. Pete swore and pulled to the side of the road. A policeman got off his motorbike and swaggered over to Maureen's window. He leaned in, ticket book in his hand and spoke in Afrikaans. Pete grimaced, answering in English.

"I didn't realise I was speeding, Officer."

The policeman patted his pockets, frowning. "Have you got a pen?"

Pete searched his pockets then leant across Maureen and opened the glove box, pretending to rummage through its contents.

"Sorry, Sir, I haven't."

"Fuck off copper," a small voice from the baby seat said. The air around them thickened. Maureen stared at her child open mouthed. Pete put his head down and snorted. The policeman pulled back from the car window, eyes bulging, lips a thin line, no pen to write a ticket.

"You better teach that kid manners, lady." He put his ticket book back in his pocket. "I'll let you off this time, but next time you keep in the limit, hey." He glowered at Henry, climbed on his motorbike, and roared off. Pete smacked his hand on the steering wheel and exploded with laughter.

"Where did he learn to say such a thing?" Maureen said, aghast. Pete wiped his tears, and patted Henry's foot.

"Good little buddy," he said.

The following Saturday, Pete took Henry to the airport and sat him in the cockpit of the plane he was working on. Henry fiddled with the controls pretending he was flying. One of Pete's black workers called out, "Fuck off cop" and keeled over laughing. Henry became known as 'The Little Boss' amongst Pete's workers and enjoyed many more Saturdays at the airport.

A note arrived for Maureen and Pete. It was from their landlady. Maureen opened it.

"Mirabelle wants to see us, Pete. She doesn't say why, just that we both must be present." She passed the note to Pete, anxious. "I hope she's not going to kick us out?"

"We haven't done anything to get kicked out, unless," he indicated Henry, "some little buddy's been swearing at her." Pete grinned. Maureen frowned.

"Don't encourage him, Pete."

"Let's go now and get it over with." They walked across the courtyard to Mirabelle's.

Doris clattered a tray of teacups down and Mirabelle waited for her to leave before speaking.

"I've decided it's time to move to Rhodesia and I need an overseer in my absence. "Hernandez Hideaway is habitable now." Mirabelle had Spanish names for all her villas and Hernandez was the chicken coop at the bottom of the property. "It's quite secluded so you wouldn't be intruded upon. No children will bother you." Mirabelle knew about Rossie. "You can have it rent free and furnished if you'd like to collect the rents and see to the staff for me."

Maureen's eyes lit up and she looked across at Pete. He was nodding, interested. Rent free meant they could save money! Although both of them worked, there was nothing much left in their kitty after payday. Maureen was sold on the idea even before Mirabelle invited them to inspect the chook coop.

They followed her down the hill to what resembled a bunker with a flat tin roof, stone floor and mud brick walls. The smell inside reminded Maureen of Eden's Curalo Lake at low tide. The lounge room was long and narrow with two steps down into a smaller area at the end. Pete looked around, lips pursed.

The bedroom was small with two single beds and a dressing table. Off the bedroom was an unfinished bathroom just big enough to fit a cot. The kitchen had a sink Maureen could only reach by standing on a box. A four-burner paraffin stove sat on a cupboard. No oven. The bathroom, lavatory and laundry were outdoors which didn't faze Maureen. She'd grown up in rural Australia with an outside lavatory.

"We'll need some cupboards."

"I have spare cupboards in my house you can have," Mirabelle offered. Maureen gave Pete a nod.

"We'll take it," said Pete. There was no signed agreement other than a shake of hands.

Mirabelle departed for Rhodesia after appointing new tenants for her house.

Shortly after her departure, the author and his sister left, and Maureen decided Pete should choose the tenants so she wouldn't be blamed if he didn't like them. He chose an Irish woman, Nora, and her friend Pauline, both in their thirties. Maureen asked them to dinner a week after they moved in. Nora made an apple pie for the occasion and won Pete's heart.

"Who put you onto the villa, Nora?" Pete had only pinned the advertisement for the villa on the aero club notice board at the airport.

"Gloria told us," Nora said.

Maureen's interest tweaked. "Gloria? Rossie's mum?"

"Yes, we work in the same place."

"What?" Pete looked at Nora in disbelief. Nora looked from Pete to Maureen, surprised. Maureen sucked in her cheeks to contain a grin, grateful that Pete had chosen the tenants.

"It's just that we had a spot of bother with the police a while back and they searched Gloria's villa," Maureen explained.

"Silly woman. She gambles and pays her debts selling dope," Nora said dismissively.

"She's an escort. You said you work at the same place?" Pete needed to get it right. There was a slight wail in his voice.

"I'm the receptionist, take the money. Pauline's the book-keeper." Pete turned unbelieving eyes towards Maureen. She picked up the bottle of wine and filled the women's glasses.

"Brandy, Pete?" She held up the bottle. He filled his mouth with Nora's pie and gave her a defeated nod.

After Nora and Pauline had left, Pete turned to Maureen with a look of disbelief. "She takes the money! She's the bloody madam!" The mouthful of wine Maureen had taken came up the back of her nose and she choked with laughter.

"You liked them, Pete."

"I know. But you can choose the next tenants," he said, shaking his head. Their visit had given Maureen an idea.

"Why don't we have a barbie? Invite all our friends now we have a nice garden, and the lounge is big enough. What do you think? We've always gone to their places for braais."

Most of their friends were Pete's and Maureen still felt like a curiosity amongst them. It was as though they were watching to see whether she was a genuine wife to Pete or just using him for her own ends. There were always questions. "How long have you and Pete known each other? How long have you been in South Africa? Where were you before?" She didn't avoid the questions. She had gotten used to explaining herself in Sweden and England and to her parents. But she never went into detail with his friends, for Henry and Pete's sake more than her own. She would like to show Pete's friends that she and Pete had a normal marriage and entertaining was how it worked in South Africa. Parties and braais even brought the Afrikaners and English South Africans together. It was something Maureen felt she needed to do to validate herself. Pete nodded.

"That's a good idea. I can borrow some fold-out chairs from the aero club. We can string up lights." They put the word out for the last Sunday of the month.

When their guests had arrived and been settled with drinks, Maureen gave a friend a tour of their villa.

"You can't be serious!" Corona's eyes swivelled around the lounge. She was the wife of Pete's friend from Kenya. "Pete must earn the same as my husband so why on earth would you live in this dump? Only poor whites live like this."

Maureen's enthusiasm died. She hadn't given a thought to what anyone would think of their house. Yes, their friends all had two storey or Dutch-style houses with swimming pools on acreage, but that hadn't bothered her. Her life with Pete was turning out all right and she wanted that to be the focus.

"We have an agreement with the owner to look after the property for a year," Maureen said. "Pete's going to fix it up." She had lived in worse, but she wasn't going to mention that. Corona pushed a cigarette into her black holder.

"I'd expect more from my husband than this."

"We haven't been married long. It's a start and I'm fine with it. Let's go and have a wine."

After their guests had gone, Maureen told Pete what Corona had said. He looked around their lounge. The turquoise, blue and black Casa Pupa rug with its knotted edge brightened the room. The furniture was brown leather but now they had some African art on the walls the room looked homely and colourful.

"It looks good, don't worry what Corona says. She spends more money on her hair than she pays her housemaid, and her house looks boring." He draped an arm around her shoulders. It was as romantic as he could get.

The days rolled over to rent collection day. Maureen and Pete had had an argument over who would do it and Maureen lost. She knocked on Mirabelle's door that now contained a family from Rhodesia.

"I've come for the rent," Maureen said to a maid she hadn't seen before, surprised it wasn't Mirabelle's maid, Doris. The maid went off to get her madam. A young English woman, Jane, came to the door carrying an envelope. Maureen had only met her once.

"Hello, Jane, I'm here for the rent. I see you have a new maid. Where's Doris?"

"I caught her stealing and told her not to come back to my house. She's stolen from the other tenants too, so have a word with them, they don't want her either." She handed Maureen the envelope with the rent. Nora was her next call so she would ask her about Doris.

"It's true," said Nora. "I haven't had her in my place for a couple of weeks. She hangs around the courtyard getting drunk on home brew."

"Bugger!"

Maureen thought about Mirabelle's request to keep Doris employed. She would have to contact Mirabelle's accountant since the staff decisions had to go through him. After a long telephone conversation with the accountant, Maureen's instructions were to fire Doris. Firing someone wasn't something she'd ever done before.

"Can you do it, Pete?"

"Your job is the maid and rents. Mine's the gardener and repairs. Maids don't like a boss to fire them, they work for the madam. That's you," Pete said. "I'll get the gardener to arrange a meeting for you and Doris.

Maureen's insides cringed when she saw Doris waiting for her. Doris wobbled in front of Maureen.

"You want me, Madam?"

"No one wants you to work for them, Doris. They say you have been stealing and you are drunk all the time, so you will have to go. I'll pay you two months' salary."

Doris's face darkened. She folded her arms, legs planted. "My madam said you can't fire me."

Maureen would lose her tenants if Doris stayed. She would have to lie. "I'm sorry, Doris. I telephoned Madam Mirabelle and told her I'm firing you. She's not coming back to live here, you know."

"You'll be sorry for this," Doris said.

Maureen watched her stamp away, feeling guilty and sorry because Doris was old. Where would she go? And what about Beauty? Would she leave because her grandmother had been fired? Maureen hoped not, Henry loved her.

She waited for Pete to come home and told him about her concerns. He shrugged. "Doris will go back to her homeland and her family will look after her. It's not your problem. She shouldn't be stealing. Beauty isn't going to leave. She knows she's on a good wicket. No other madam baths her children and hangs out the washing," Pete grinned, shaking his head at her.

When Maureen arrived home from work the next day, the new maid at Mirabelle's house came rushing down.

"Madam, there are bad things happening, you must come." Thinking there was a robbery or someone was ill, Maureen followed the maid. The maid's hand went up signalling Maureen to stop and then she ducked down behind a bush and flapped her hand at Maureen to do the same. Obeying, Maureen ducked down next to the excited girl. Hidden from view, they watched Doris in the courtyard. She was whirling, stamping, singing in a high monotonous tone. Her hand dipped into a cloth bag hanging from her waist and withdrew a handful of powder which she threw around the courtyard as she danced.

The maid next to Maureen moaned. "This is bad juju, Madam."

Maureen felt a tremor of apprehension. She'd grown up with a mother who read tea leaves. She should stop Doris. She made a move to get up, but the maid's hand grabbed her arm holding her back.

"You stay. She might make bad juju on you. You talk to the

38

boss first, Madam." It was a good idea. Pete would know what to do. They remained crouched behind the bush until Doris had gone before parting ways.

"Do you believe in black magic, Pete?" Maureen said, after telling him what she had seen.

He lay down his knife and fork and chewed his food thoughtfully. "The thing is, they believe it. It's their culture. I'll speak to my guys at work. They might know a witch doctor we can get to break the curse."

The fine hairs on Maureen's arms stood up. "Curse?"

"Yep. The workers will be afraid to stay in case of bad luck. Word will get around and no one will work for us."

"What about Beauty?"

"She'll wait to see what we do. Don't worry. Have a glass of wine. I've dealt with this stuff in Kenya."

"Tell me." Maureen leant forward, intrigued.

"I was managing a sisal plantation in Tanganyika and there was this special tree the Bantu put money under to keep the evil spirits away. I told them not to give their money to the tree, that someone was stealing it, that nothing would happen if they didn't put their money under the tree. But they wouldn't believe me. They said the tree spirits took it and continued leaving money under the tree.

"So I decided to prove to them that it wasn't the tree spirits taking the money and the next time they left money I picked it up and hid to see who would come to collect it. The Witch Doctor came. He hunted everywhere. He was pretty pissed off. He didn't see me.

"I waited until it was the next payday and gave the workers the offerings they had left under the tree as well as their normal salary. Then I told them what I had done.

"I said, 'See nothing happened to me or you. I saw the Witch Doctor take your money not the tree spirits.' Then they told me that the spirits can't hurt me because I'm a white man. They said, 'The spirits tell the Witch Doctor to get the money.' And the extra money I gave them they put back under the tree." Pete shrugged. "It's what they believe."

Two days later, Pete had the gardener and maids assemble in the courtyard. Maureen held Henry's hand and watched from Nora's window. Pete ushered a tall black man with fine features into the centre of the group and moved away. The man tied some bells around his ankles and from a pouch, produced feathers, twigs and a box of matches. Every eye was on him. He knelt and made a small fire with the twigs. He waved the feathers over the fire, danced around jingling the bells on his feet, singing and waving the feathers.

When he had finished, he scattered the charred twigs around the courtyard, lifted his hand and spoke to the group. There was a moment of silence and then a rush of excited voices. The workers dispersed, chatting and laughing. Everything was back to normal. Pete joined Maureen and Nora.

"Evil spirits are gone," he said. "Cost me ten rand."

"It was worth it." Maureen was relieved and amazed at what she had seen.

Nora nodded. "So much superstition. We only have leprechauns in Ireland," she said.

5

A Goat

A year had passed, and Maureen sat in the doctor's office absorbing the news. She was pregnant. At first, she was scared, remembering the 23-hour birth with Henry and then she thought it would be nice for Henry to have a little brother. She didn't think it was a girl.

"Pete, it's not food poisoning, I'm pregnant," Maureen said on her return from the doctor's. Pete's shoulders went back.

"Well, what do you know?" He stared at her grinning, surprised.

She frowned, looking around. "I don't know where we're going to put a baby."

"I could divide the lounge into two rooms and Henry can sleep in the smaller area and the baby move into his room." His room had only been made to accommodate a bath. Maureen surveyed the wall in the lounge – it was green with mould. The chicken coop wasn't an ideal place for a baby.

"We should paint the wall."

Pete nodded in agreement. "I've been thinking we should take a trip to Rhodesia to see Mum and Dad before you get too pregnant?"

Pete's mother and father, Annie and Clement, were living with Pete's aunt and uncle in Bulawayo. The last time Maureen had met them, she and Pete were going out in Nairobi, before she left for Europe, before Henry. Seeing them again wasn't something she was looking forward to. When Pete had told his mother they were getting married she had said, *don't marry her just because you feel sorry for her.* There was no chance he would have done that, but it had irked Maureen.

"Yes, we may as well." She had to meet them sometime.

The trip came around quickly and having put her reservations aside, Maureen was looking forward to it. She hadn't seen much of South Africa, being too busy with work and Henry. She let the neighbours know they were leaving and their villa would be empty for ten days.

"We are going to see lots of animals, Henry. Maybe an elephant." She made a trunk out of her arm and charged at him. He laughed and ran away.

"You won't see many in South Africa. Most are in the national parks, not much left in the wild," Pete said. "Should be plenty of zebra in Rhodesia but not sure about elephants."

"I don't care what we see, it will be fun." The love of travel was something they both had in common, and Pete loved to drive. Their marriage wasn't going to tie them down.

Pete packed a tin of water in case the car needed a top-up and a small drum of petrol. He put Henry's car seat in the front between himself and Maureen, checked the windscreen wipers and loaded their bags. Maureen put a basket of food on the back seat, and they were ready to go.

"All aboard," Pete yelled.

It was difficult to imagine that the narrow dirt road with its occasional strip of tar in the middle was the main highway to Rhodesia. They passed trucks, their open backs loaded with Africans – men, women and children, standing room only – and clouded them in dust as they went.

"They must be choking," Maureen said.

"If we don't get in front we'll be choking in dust and it will take us all day to get to the border."

"Look, giraffe." Pete slowed down. Ahead was a group of giraffes ambling unconcerned across the road. He stopped the car and waited for them to cross. They were just a few feet away, their car shrunken by the size of the graceful creatures. Henry leapt up and down in the car, while Maureen and Pete watched, overcome by the glory of nature.

They spent the night at the border hotel. The rambling thatched roof dwelling was surrounded by pink bougainvillea and beautiful gardens. The porter, wearing a white cotton uniform and a red fez, came to take their bags. He ushered them through thick wooden brass studded doors and into an entrance hall where two kudu heads were mounted on the wall. They went through an archway and into a huge lounge. Zebra skins were scattered across the stone floor. Black beams crossed under a high thatched roof. The hotel smelled of hay and gardenias. Their bedroom looked out onto the lush garden and a pair of peacocks scratching in the lawn.

"Gosh, it's gorgeous," Maureen said. This was the honeymoon they had never had.

"It's up for sale. Shall we buy it?" Pete joked. Rhodesia was a renegade country, boycotted by Britain. Its only ally was South

Africa. It wasn't a safe country and people were leaving en masse. They had drinks at the bar before retiring for the night.

Breakfast was a gourmet's delight and Pete stuffed himself, farting for the next two hours of their journey.

When they arrived at Pete's relatives' house, Maureen's gut tensed at the sight of his family lined up on the verandah ready to greet them. His mother rushed to the car, arms wide. Pete gave her a hug. Maureen lifted Henry from his car seat and put him on the ground. Pete's mother smiled at the child, gave Maureen an appraising look and a hesitant hug.

"Welcome, Maureen," Annie said. She was a stocky woman with kind eyes. She bent down to Henry. "Want to come and see the ducks while Mummy and Pete, eh, Daddy unload the suitcases?"

"Ducks?" He smiled up at her. She took his hand and led him off to see the ducks. Maureen let her breath go. So far so good.

At dinner, Pete told his family Maureen was pregnant. Slaps on the back, teasing and congratulations followed his announcement. Maureen was pleased at how happy Pete looked. His cousins poured a round of beers while the women moved to the verandah and fussed over Maureen, bringing her a cup of tea and filling her with their horror birthing tales. She wanted to put her fingers in her ears, but they were including her in the family, so she suffered their stories until it was a polite time to excuse herself and go to bed.

Sightseeing tours around Bulawayo took up their mornings and in the afternoons Maureen and Pete stayed at the house with Annie and Clement, mindful they wouldn't see them for a long while after this visit. A farewell family braai was held two days before they were due to leave. Pete's four cousins and their families came – it was a fun affair until Cousin Ruth, a pastor's wife, summoned Pete and Maureen aside.

"We can't keep your mother and father any longer. It's your

duty as a son to take them to live with you. I know you have been paying for their upkeep while they've been here" – Maureen's eyes widened, that must be why they never had any savings – "but my parents want to have their house to themselves again."

Dumbstruck, Maureen looked at Pete. Where would they put them in the chicken coop with hardly enough room for themselves and a baby on the way?

"You must take them back with you." She waved a hand towards his cousins. "We've all agreed."

Panicked, Maureen clutched Pete's hand, not caring how desperate she looked. When she'd married Pete, she hadn't reckoned on his parents living with them. She had left her aunt in England and chosen Africa to be in control of her own life. Africa was to be her refuge. Was she always going to have someone looking over her shoulder?

"What about your sister and brother, Pete? Couldn't they go to them?"

He shook his head. "My parents can't go back to Kenya. They gave up their citizenship when they left. Besides, they would have to prove financial independence even if they stay with family."

The pastor's wife stood arms folded.

"Where are they going to sleep? We've no room," Maureen wailed. Clouds were gathering on her horizon.

The car was packed tight with Pete's parents in the back seat next to their belongings and Maureen, Henry and Pete in the front. The car juddered over corrugations making conversation impossible as they clattered towards the South African border.

Suddenly a goat came out of the bush and ran in front of their car. Pete stood on the brakes. There was a loud thump and the animal was flung in the air landing on the side of the road where it lay bleating.

"Fuck!" Pete leapt out of the car and checked the damage. "It's broken the headlight and crumpled the front. Shit!"

The goat bleated pitifully, flopping, unable to get up. Maureen didn't give a bugger about the car; the animal was in agony. "Leave the bloody car and help the goat. It's hurt," she yelled.

Pete booted the car wheel and went over to the goat. "It's back's broken, it'll die. The blacks will eat it." He glared at the goat and stomped back to the car.

"You can't leave it in pain. Kill it." Maureen started to cry.

Henry threw himself around his car seat. "The goat! The goat!" he screamed.

"Oh, for God's sake," Annie tutted from the back seat.

"The bloody goat's damaged Pete's car," Clement said, frowning. Maureen turned on her father-in-law. "I don't give a shit about the bloody car." She saw his lips squeeze together and his eyes look past her. Pete opened the car boot and searched for a spanner big enough to bonk the goat on the head. There wasn't one.

A black man emerged from the scrub and stood at a distance from the goat. Others joined him.

Pete went back to the goat and grabbed it around the throat, squeezing for all he was worth. When the goat's eyes rolled, and its tongue hung out, he let go. The goat bleated and kicked.

"Shit!" He tried again squeezing with all his strength and let go when he thought it was dead, but the goat raised its head and bleated. Pete sat back on his haunches covering his face with his hands.

"You real mad at that goat, Boss," the black man observed, shaking his head. His friends ringed Pete.

Pete jumped to his feet and shouted at the group now grown to six people and a child. "You kill the bloody thing." He strode to the car, got in and started the motor. A few silent miles passed beneath the wheels.

The South African border post was a small brick building. Outside stood a large, uniformed man with a big gun. His hand went up as they approached the road barrier. They made ready with their passports and were ushered inside. A big Afrikaner with a shrewd eye flicked through Maureen's passport with tight lips. Hard blue eyes raised to her brown ones.

"Where is your visa?"

"My visa?" Maureen said, looking blank.

"That is what I said, lady."

Maureen turned to Pete, confused. "This is my husband. I don't need a visa."

"You, and ..." the border cop flicked a page on Maureen's passport and jabbed a finger at the photo of Henry, "the little Okie here are Australians. You need a visa for South Africa."

Pete stepped forward and spoke in Afrikaans. The uniformed man answered, his face stony. Pete's neck reddened. His voice got louder. The border policeman's jaw came forward. Pete changed to English.

"It's Sunday. My wife can't stay here until Immigration opens on Monday, she's pregnant! You didn't stop us when we crossed the border to Rhodesia a week ago. How come we weren't informed then that my wife required a visa to get back into South Africa? I'll be taking this up with Immigration."

A pen tapped Maureen's passport. The air was rigid between Pete and the official. "This time I'll blind my eye. But this passport says she is a Miss, not a Mrs, and not a resident in this country. She will need a visa if she leaves next time." He whacked the entry stamp down and snapped the passport closed. "Lady," he said, shoving the passport towards her, "you are lucky today."

She picked it up with a damp hand, vowing to get a new Australian passport with a changed surname.

47

It was a squeeze for all of them in the chicken coop. Pete used a wardrobe to divide the lounge creating a makeshift bedroom for Clement and Annie. Annie told Maureen she didn't cook.

That meant four adults and a child she had to cook for on a paraffin stove as well as working at the airport and collecting rents. Life in Africa wasn't Eden.

Annie and Clement stayed out of her way as much as they could. Annie sat in the lounge room and knitted for the coming baby while Pete hung out with his father outside. Maureen felt like the odd one out. Other than her bedroom there was nowhere she could be alone. Having given up work a week before, she was missing her friends.

In the privacy of her bedroom Maureen posed side-on in front of the mirror. Her stomach was enormous. Pete stood behind her and gave her belly a rub.

"Everyone's asleep. Let's have a cuddle," he said. They tried gentle sex; Pete nervous. And then it happened. A gush of water.

"You've wet the bed!" Pete leapt to the floor.

"My waters have broken. The baby's coming!"

"Oh, God! Mum!" Pete shouted.

Maureen rolled herself in a sheet and Annie came running.

"We have to get her to hospital."

Maureen felt a crushing pain build in her abdomen. She clutched her stomach and groaned. "Don't wake Henry, leave him here with your father," she said.

Between Pete and his mother, they managed to help Maureen into the back seat of the car. Annie got in the front next to Pete. As another pain raked through her, she gritted her teeth and groaned, panting the way Matron had taught her in Sweden.

"Those pains are close," Annie said. Pete trod on the accelerator, the wheels spun, and they roared down the dirt road. The hospital was forty minutes away. One more mile before they hit

48

tarmac. Maureen bounced all over the seat groaning, while Annie calmed her son.

On reaching the hospital, Pete helped Maureen out of the car and up the steps. The hospital lights were blinding, voices clamoured. A nurse assisted Maureen into a wheelchair and directed Pete to the admissions desk while she whisked Maureen down the passage towards the delivery ward. After filling in documents, Pete left in a confused state to drive his mother home. He didn't say goodbye and Maureen was too busy to notice.

Six hours later, on 22 May 1970, Liam arrived and Maureen burst with love. His hair stood on end, his hands little fists. He was searching for her nipple the moment he was in her arms. It had been an easy birth after Henry. She fell into a contented sleep.

6

The In-laws

From the time Maureen had brought the baby home from the hospital, Clement and Annie couldn't keep their hands off him. Pete hardly got a look in. The baby's every waking minute, Clement was rocking the pram. One squark and Annie was picking him up. Maureen had had to share Henry with a matron in a home for unmarried mothers and then her aunt who had wanted to adopt him, and now she had three more people. When would she have her baby to herself? She moaned to Pete about his parents always hanging over the pram, but he laughed it off.

"You can't blame them; he is their grandchild."

Maureen's resentment grew. She didn't have any privacy and there wasn't a place she could get away from Annie and Clement. In the lounge they sat on the couch outside her bedroom door and watched her breastfeed through her dressing table mirror until she realised and closed her door.

They were all sitting in the lounge room with dinner trays on their knees when Annie put her fork down.

"Why don't you go back to work, Maureen? I can look after the baby and the nanny can do the housework." The offer was well meant but Maureen felt this had already been discussed between Pete and his parents. She took a slow breath to calm herself. If it wasn't for the extra expense of having Annie and Clement, she wouldn't have to consider going to work. She and Pete would be able to manage on his salary, at least until Liam was one year old.

"Why not?" Pete said, oblivious to Maureen's grinding teeth. "Dad can handle collecting the rent and Mum can keep an eye on the maid."

Maureen concentrated on her plate. She didn't have an excuse; her milk had dried up through stress and Liam was on the bottle. She nailed Pete with a look and picked up her tray. Her options were shrinking. "I suppose I don't have much choice." She left for the kitchen to the sound of scraping plates.

A week later, Maureen started a half-day job at Rennie's Air, an Air Safari company. She enjoyed the work and making new friends but resented going home to see Liam in Annie's arms and Henry with the nanny, forgotten. Her irritation caused an atmosphere in the house. She tried not to feel resentful, telling herself her children were lucky to have people around who loved them. She was being jealous and petty. As much as she remonstrated with herself, she couldn't overcome her feelings towards Annie and Clement. She didn't want them in her house. But they had nowhere else to go, no money. Pete even bought their cigarettes. Maureen's resentment built and her vision of a happy marriage clouded.

Liam developed croup and after numerous emergency visits from the doctor, they were told the house was too damp and unhealthy for a baby. "If you want him to see another winter you should move out of here," the doctor had said. It was grim news.

"We have to save every cent we can. I'm going to apply for a pension for your parents," Maureen said. The accountant at work had suggested she try.

"My dad was born in the Seychelles and Mum left South Africa when she was eighteen. They won't get one. Perhaps you could work full-time?" suggested Pete.

Was he kidding? Maureen rounded on him. "Or maybe we could move into one of the other villas when it becomes vacant? Squash up a bit more. Or maybe you could get your sister or brother to help us support your parents?" she snapped. They had rarely argued in the short time they had been married. Pete didn't sulk. If something annoyed him, it was said and then forgotten. When she was cranky, he usually teased her out of her moods, acting the idiot. There was plenty of laughter in their marriage.

"I'll see if I can make the place less damp," he said, and stomped off. It wasn't the solution Maureen wanted.

Two weeks had passed since their argument. Liam's croup had settled down for the time being and Maureen was getting more sleep. She was changing Liam on the bed, a safety pin between her lips when a car horn tooted outside. She heard Clement get off the couch and call out to Annie.

"That's Pete with his new car." New car? Maureen snatched Liam off the bed and rushed outside. Annie and Clement stood next to a black car. Pete got out of the car. Patted the roof. Looked across at Maureen, misreading her horror for a look of surprise.

"Bought it from a friend," Pete said, standing back admiring the Peugeot. He opened the passenger door for Henry. "Daddy's new car," Pete grinned.

"It's in great condition," Clement said, walking around the sparkling vehicle, washed at the airport.

Maureen steamed, all her bloody savings. "You didn't tell me you were buying a car!" she fired at him. Why hadn't he discussed it with her first? "We're saving for a house!" There hadn't been anything wrong with their old car.

"It was a good deal," Clement said, in defence of his son.

How did his father know how much it cost? Maureen stormed inside, slamming the door behind her. Pete followed her into the bedroom.

"It's a reliable car and will last us a long time. It belonged to one of the pilots. Our old car needed a new clutch, handbrake. You know that."

"I don't care what it needed. You didn't ask me. You worked it out with your parents in secret. How do you think that makes me feel?"

"I said a while back there was a good car for sale."

"You didn't say you were going to buy the bloody thing!" Maureen hissed; aware his parents were within hearing distance. "And I didn't expect you to sneak behind my back." She glared at Pete. "It's me you're married to. I feel like an outsider with them around. I don't want them here any more." Angry tears ran down her face. She swiped at them. "You know what!? I'm pregnant and I want to be on my own with this baby." She sat on the bed, put her face in her hands and cried.

Pete stood hands in pockets, frowning at his feet. "How did you get pregnant?"

Maureen glowered at him. "Your mother said I couldn't fall pregnant while I was breastfeeding but obviously it was an old wives' tale! You believed it too." She put it back on him.

Pete was silent. His mother had left school when she was twelve and had a lot of strange beliefs.

"How are we going to live here with three children and your parents? We have to move from this damp place, it's unhealthy. And you go and buy a bloody car!" Pete dropped on the bed next to Maureen and draped an awkward arm around her shoulder. She shrugged him off.

"I didn't know you were pregnant," he said in a soft voice. She had known for a week but wanted to get used to the idea before breaking the news to Pete. She wanted to share something with him for once without his parents knowing everything. She felt stupid for believing her mother-in-law.

"Why don't you go and visit Jackie and Ben in Durban for a few days?" Pete said. Maureen had met Jackie and her husband, Ben, in Kenya. They had moved to South Africa before Pete. "You can take the new car." He looked at her hopefully.

Pete was an open book. She knew he thought driving the car might change her mind about it. It wouldn't, but getting away from them all was enticing. The next day she phoned Jackie and after the call asked her boss for time off. The following day she was on her way to Durban with Henry and Liam.

It was a relief to be at Jackie's place. She felt free, her mothering not judged, her familiarity with the servants not questioned, away from her resentment of Pete for sharing more of his time with his parents than her. Jackie was a good listener.

"Tell him you're not returning until they leave," Jackie said pushing the phone into Maureen's hand. It was two days into her stay, and they were on their third glass of wine.

Maureen took the phone and called Pete. "I'm not coming home until your parents leave," she said.

There was a sigh on the end of the phone. One to feel sorry for.

"Pete?" Her guilt surged. Poor Pete having to tell his parents to leave. "Contact your brother and tell him it's his turn to look after them." His brother had just moved to Salisbury.

"I'll call you tomorrow night," Pete said. He hung up. She was suddenly sober, regretting her impulsive action.

"That was so mean of me."

"Come on. You were hardly married and they came to live with you. You can't afford them. You need a house. They have other children who should be helping." What Jackie said was true, but it was difficult for her in-laws. They were good people and loved the children. It wasn't their fault they had nothing. Her father-in-law had lost his job when Kenya gained its independence and Pete had financed them ever since. That was another thing he hadn't shared with her.

She didn't want her marriage to fail but if it did, which it could if his parents didn't move out of her home, she would leave Africa. Henry was on her passport and baby Liam was registered as an Australian citizen. Most whites in South Africa had a second passport as an escape route, afraid of what would happen if the black leader, Mandela, was released from prison.

Two months after her holiday in Durban, Pete drove his parents to Salisbury in Rhodesia to live with his brother. With her in-laws gone, Nora started visiting again, keeping her up-to-date with the escort agency and Maureen would pop into Nora's for a coffee. The air lifted around her and the villa expanded. So did time. With fewer people to cook for, shop and run around after, she began painting, filling the walls with Australian landscapes to help her homesickness. And her savings account began to grow.

7

A Request from Eden

Lillian finished her letter to Maureen, placed it in the envelope, licked the seal, then put on the stamp and airmail sticker. She needed a holiday. Looking after Eric had become too demanding and she was exhausted. The CWA women were a help, taking him for drives around town to give her a break, but it wasn't enough. Yesterday he had mortified her in the Coles supermarket in Bega. Standing next to the nuts, he had filled his face with handfuls and the manager had come over and said he was going to charge him with shoplifting. And Eric said he would be happy to pay if the manager could weigh them. Lillian had disappeared up an aisle and left them to it.

Last week, when things had gotten too much for her, she'd broken down in front of Splinter who had offered to keep an eye on her father so Lillian could go away for a couple of weeks. But with her mother dead and her sister living in England, there was nowhere in Australia she wanted to go. And she had never spent the money she'd saved to bring Maureen home from Sweden years ago, which was enough to get her to Africa. Putting the letter in her handbag she called down the hall.

"I'm going to the post office, Eric. Is there anything you want?"

Eric wobbled towards her and held up his pipe. "It's empty." His face brightened. "Can I come with you?"

A surge of annoyance snatched at Lillian. Couldn't she walk out of the door for five minutes without him? She frowned at the wreck of a man, then sighed. "Come on then."

They walked at a snail's pace so he could keep his hand on her shoulder, too vain to use a walking stick. After the post office they went to the paper shop and bought his plug of tobacco. Lillian hesitated outside the butcher shop. She needed some mince but didn't want to go inside with Eric. George the butcher hailed her from the shop window. She'd delayed too long. "Wait here, Eric, I need some mince." Eric's eyes narrowed in thought then his jaw came forward and he pushed open the shop's door and wobbled inside. There was a vague recollection of George and Lillian having a fling. The memory was hazy, like the rest of the past. George pulled up the knife sharpener attached to his tool belt and stroked his cleaver across the steel.

"How's it going, Eric?"

Not giving Eric time to reply, Lillian called out, "I'd like a pound of mince please, George." There was a nervous edge to her voice.

"Cooking that nice bolognaise recipe I taught you?" George said, shooting a malicious grin in Eric's direction, making Lillian regret she hadn't listened to her instincts and taken Eric home first.

She gave George an anxious look. It wasn't that she didn't have feelings for George. They had remained friends and he still gave her a discount on a leg of lamb, but after her divorce all she wanted was to enjoy her freedom and not be subordinate to a man again. Not being forced to have sex had been a welcome relief.

During their marriage, Eric had been very demanding. No foreplay, just hopped on and off, whereas George had been gentle and for the first time with a man, Lillian experienced an orgasm. Had George come along a few years after her divorce, who knows? She might have accepted his marriage proposal, although there were a few things about him that annoyed her.

The main irritation was the way he referred to his penis as a saveloy. She hated the image and wouldn't look at his penis because of it. Nor had she eaten a saveloy since. Automatically, her gaze went to the tray of saveloys in the display case and she quickly looked away. George put the wrapped mince on the counter. "Slaughtered this cow a week ago, no fat in my mince." He gave her a wink.

Her cheeks turned scarlet. She knew he was doing this for Eric's benefit; George hated him for the way he had treated her. But Eric didn't have all his faculties so what was the point when it only embarrassed her? She reached out to pick up the mince when a hand came under her arm and squeezed her breast.

"No milk in this cow," Eric returned. Lillian whirled and shoved Eric. He fell back, hit the wall, and slid to the floor. He looked up, confused.

George came around the counter and helped him up off the floor. "Steady on your feet, sport," he said, giving Lillian an apologetic look. "The floor can get slippery, but I can't put sawdust here because the wind blows it everywhere when customers come in." His explanation was for the benefit of a customer who had just entered the shop. Shaken, Eric leant on Lillian to steady himself.

She wanted to cry with frustration. How long would she have to put up with this? They were divorced – he shouldn't be her responsibility. He gagged waiting for the swing of the room to settle and clutched her hand like a child. She sighed, accepting her lot. If she didn't look after Eric, her children would have to, which meant Splinter. Johnny was long gone to some outback region in Australia. At least she was in control these days, and it wasn't Eric dictating.

A customer held the door open for her while she helped Eric negotiate the step onto the pavement. Pulling him by the sleeve to cross the road, she walked in front of a parked car a man was about to get into. He looked at them and smiled.

"G'day, Eric, where are you off to mate?"

Caught in the moment Eric's brow wrinkled, and he chewed on his empty pipe. Lillian guessed he was struggling to remember the man's name. The fellow's face softened.

"It's Smokey, mate. Well, only you call me that. Remember, I've got the farm near your old place, before you had the stroke." Eric's jaw came forward and he nodded.

"Some snake took my farm because I was sick, Smokey. He'll be roadkill when I catch the mongrel." He shook his head to clear the fogged years.

Lillian realised it was time she intervened. She didn't want Eric remembering it was her who had sold the farm to help support Maureen in Sweden. "Nice to meet you, Mr ...?

"Bell, Jonathan Bell, Mrs ..." He laughed and shook his head. "Sorry, I don't know Eric's surname. We've met at the club a few times and he gives me advice on farming. I'm afraid I'm a bit of a novice at it."

"It's Lillian McKinley. We're divorced. It was something she liked to remind Eric of because after his stroke she'd had to take care of him as he had nowhere else to go. Her eyes challenged Jonathan Bell. Divorcees were viewed as fast women, which was ridiculous. The only way she was fast was how quick she could get away from men in general.

Eric's face lit up. "I'm going to the Fisherman's Club to watch the horses on television." Lillian was about to correct him when Smokey jumped in.

"I'm going up there myself if you want a lift?" He turned to Lillian. "I can drop him home later.

"That's good of you, Mr Bell," she said, restraining the urge to run before he changed his mind.

"Jonathan, and we won't be long."

"There's no hurry getting him back, take all the afternoon." Without a goodbye to Eric, she rushed home to her book, a block of chocolate and dreams of a holiday in Africa, while Smokey helped Eric into his car.

They had met when Smokey had picked Eric up hitchhiking to his farm in Towamba. He'd learned about Eric's stroke and the loss of his farm after making a few enquiries at the Fisherman's Club and felt sorry for him. He had taken him to his own farm after meeting him at the club a few times and then it became apparent that Eric knew a lot more about farming than Melbourne-born Smokey. Farming was a part of Eric's brain that was still intact. And Smokey, recently returned from Vietnam and suffering from flashbacks, found the only thing that settled his nerves was the dope he grew at the farm he'd bought. Eric – none the wiser about Smokey's new strain of tobacco – had recently saved his crop.

"Before we go to the club would you like to pop out to the farm with me and have a drive of the ute?" Smokey had been letting him drive the ute around the farm to help him gain his confidence. His plan was to get Eric's licence back.

8

Hospital Check-up

Maureen opened the letter from her mother and felt a rush of excitement at her mother's decision to come for a holiday in Africa. It would take six weeks to get an Australian passport, Maureen calculated. That would be close to the time she gave birth. She thought about Pete's parents. It wasn't long since they had left, and she would have liked more time with just Pete and the children. Their marriage always seemed to be a crush of people, but she hadn't seen her mother since she'd left Australia and no one in her family had met her children. She spoke to Pete.

"Mum wants to visit us. She's asked me to write a letter saying I need her help with the children while I have the baby. It's so she can flash it around town and not look cold-hearted leaving a man who's had a stroke." Pete's eyebrows rose.

"Small town," she said. "She will be here when we move into

our new house." It was a big house. They wouldn't be on top of each other like they had been with Pete's parents.

The area where they had bought was called Halfway House because it was halfway between Pretoria and Johannesburg and had been a rest stop for the ox wagons in the old days. It occurred to Maureen that South Africa was halfway between Sweden and Eden and wondered if it was an omen. Time was a swirl of events until her mother arrived.

Maureen squeezed her mother as tight as her eight-month pregnancy would allow. They pulled apart, wet-eyed and smiling. Maureen turned to Pete who was holding one-year-old Liam.

"This is Pete, Mum." He smiled.

"Please to meet you at last, Mrs McKinley."

"Call me Lillian," her mother said. Her hand went to Liam's plump little leg and gave it a squeeze. "You look a healthy boy." Liam jumped up and down in his father's arms.

Maureen ruffled Henry's hair, "and this is Henry Bernard. Say hello to your nanna, Henry Bernard."

"Hello, Nanna," Henry said, pressing into his mother's leg.

"Henry Bernard is a bit of a mouthful I'm going to call you Henry. Hello, Henry."

"We all call him Henry. It was only in Sweden his name was used correctly. They are more formal." She gave her mother a level look, letting her know that she wasn't going to ignore what had happened to her in Sweden. She had kept Henry despite her mother's advice to have an abortion and had left Sweden within six months of his birth to make sure the welfare department wouldn't take him from her for not being able to support him. "Anyway, it works better with our names." Maureen smiled down at Henry and smoothed his hair.

Lillian's head tilted to the side as she appraised her daughter. "I don't like your hairstyle," she said.

Maureen's hand went to her pigtails. She had had to rush to get ready for the airport. Her smile faltered. She wasn't the eighteen-year-old who had waved goodbye to her mother from the deck of a ship bound for England. The years between them was ink on paper and now they would have to get to know each other.

Pete loaded the bags in the boot of the car.

"We live in a chook pen, Mum, so don't expect too much. Just reminding you it's not fancy." She had explained the situation in her letters. "We won't be in it for long though. We're moving into our new house after the baby's born. It's near the airport where we work and halfway between Pretoria and Johannesburg. It's on five acres, Spanish style, with a swimming pool, servants' quarters and a flat that Pete's going to renovate. You'll love it." Maureen couldn't keep the excitement out of her voice."

They drove past a black township, avoiding a worm-riddled dog. A group of children were racing cars made from wire with bottle-top wheels. They ran behind their cars using a long wire handle the length of a golf stick to steer them.

"Don't black children wear shoes?"

"They can't afford them, Mum."

Lillian looked at the squash of brick buildings that lined the dirt streets. There were no trees or gardens. Once they had passed the black township, the scene changed to lush gardens and beautiful homes, more like the Africa she had read about. The contrast was jarring.

Pete parked outside the half-submerged mud brick rectangle that was their home and Lillian's eyes widened. She thought Maureen had been pulling her leg about living in a converted chook pen. It was nothing like the other villas on the property.

A stooped old black man abandoned the lawnmower he had been pushing and walked over to the maid standing in the doorway. She was dressed in a pink apron and headscarf for the occasion. They stared at the madam's mother.

Maureen was the first out of the car, opening Lillian's door and helping her out before reaching for Liam. The young black girl ran over to collect Liam.

"This is, Beauty, Mum. She helps with the children while I'm at work. Beauty this is Missus Lillian, my mother."

Lillian put her arms around Beauty and gave her a hug. Beauty stiffened, not knowing what to do in the white woman's embrace. Removing Liam from Maureen's arms, Pete handed him to Beauty.

"Take Liam, Beauty, and give him a drink."

"Yes, Boss." Relieved, the girl grabbed Liam and disappeared into the villa. Maureen leant towards her mother whispering in her ear.

"Mum, you can't be too familiar with the servants. It's not allowed here, and it makes them feel uncomfortable." It had taken Maureen three years to understand that black people didn't want familiarity from whites. They didn't trust them. From Maureen's perspective it was understandable, and she had shocked Pete when she told him if she was a black person in this country, she would be a terrorist.

"They get a free education, and no one starves," he had replied.

Entering the villa, Lillian looked around, surprised at how bright and colourful it was. At the end of the lounge Maureen drew back a heavy curtain and stepped down into a small room.

"You're in the dungeon, Mum. A single bed, chair and wardrobe took up what had been part of the lounge room. Further down was another curtained off section that was Henry's room. "Lavatory and bathroom is outside and kitchen's through the arch." It was a mishmash of nooks and crannies. "We won't be here for long, so pretend you're camping."

"I'll be fine," Lillian reassured. She'd lived in a sawmill.

"Tomorrow I have an appointment at the hospital and if you're not too tired from the flight can you come with me? It's in the city. We can have a look around the shops after."

Lillian's eyes lit up. She didn't get to the city much. Eden was halfway between Sydney and Melbourne, a seven-hour car trip on a winding and sometimes dirt road that often made her carsick. "That would be lovely, Bubs."

Maureen's insides warmed at the use of her childhood name. She settled her mother and went into the kitchen to prepare a meal.

The car had needed a service, so Pete left Maureen with his VW twin-cab Kombi, a battered old thing he had bought to carry his spray-painting equipment. It was a clamber for Maureen to heave herself into the driver's seat. "I won't be able to get in this much longer," she said. Her stomach looked like she was carrying a beach ball under her maternity dress. Her mother pulled herself up and swung into the seat next to her. It took Maureen a few attempts to get the Kombi started. The battery was nearly flat and there was no handbrake, so she heeled and toed between brakes and accelerator before it jerked forward and roared off to the city.

She found a park in front of the hospital. It was on a hill and good for push starting the Kombi if necessary. Arms linked, mother and daughter went into the hospital.

There were a lot of empty chairs and only a few women in the waiting room. Maureen announced her arrival at the reception desk, and they sat down. Taking stock of the room, Lillian leant over and whispered.

"There aren't any black women here."

"It's a white hospital, Mum. Black people have their own hospitals."

"Why?"

"It's called Apartheid. Everything is separate, schools, hospitals, sports, beaches."

"That seems a shame."

"It is, but don't talk about it to Pete. I'm sick of arguing over it." A nurse appeared with a clipboard and called out her name. Maureen stood. "I won't be long, Mum."

Lillian browsed some magazines and tried to make sense of the accents and Afrikaans language, as she listened to the women around her. The faceless interior of the hospital and white clientele in miniskirts wasn't the Africa she imagined. She had expected to see black women in bright kaftans and beads. The black women who came into the waiting room wore blue uniforms, down-at-heel shoes and carried a mop and bucket. No one seemed to notice them and nurses walked past without a look or greeting. Catching the eye of one of the cleaners, she smiled. The cleaner gave her a huge smile back.

Maureen returned. "All good, doctor said mother and baby are healthy. Let's go shopping."

They climbed into the Kombi. Maureen turned the key and tapped the accelerator. Nothing. She tried again. Nothing.

"Bugger, I'll have to give it a push."

"Want me to?"

"No, Mum, I'm used to it. But you could get out to lighten the weight. Bloody Pete had better get a new battery, I'm sick of this." Her mother got out of the Kombi and stood on the pavement while Maureen held the steering wheel with one hand and pushed the door frame with the other. It took a while before she could budge the vehicle. It started to roll forward, and Maureen, still holding the steering wheel, put her foot up on the running board and tried to heave herself inside. The vehicle gathered speed as it descended the hill. Gripping the steering wheel, she pounded along next to it, one foot on the running board, the other on the road. At the bottom of the hill was a roundabout and the Kombi was picking up pace. There was no time to check for cars.

Using all her strength and gripping the steering wheel, she hauled herself up and into the driver's seat, turned the key and tapped the accelerator. The motor stuttered and came to life just as she was approaching the roundabout. A car coming from her right and having right of way kept its pace. Maureen stamped on the brakes locking the wheels and smoked past the other vehicle missing it by a hair's breadth. She pulled the Kombi to the side of the road, slipped it into neutral and, keeping the engine revving, sagged over the wheel, hands trembling.

In the rear-view mirror, she saw her mother at the top of the hill waiting for her return. She hooted the horn and waved her to come down. Her mother waved back but didn't move.

"Shit!" There was nowhere to turn. She'd have to reverse up the stuffing hill. An urge to pee hit her – all the excitement had been too much for the baby pressing on her bladder. There was nowhere to go, and she couldn't leave the car with the engine running and no brakes. The only thing available was her handbag. Maureen emptied its contents on the seat, pulled up her dress, and while keeping her feet on the brake and accelerator, eased her knickers down. She slapped the open bag between her legs and let her bladder go. The relief was orgasmic. Winding down the window she poured the pee from her bag into the street before wrestling her knickers up. And then whacking the Kombi into reverse, she hung out the window and backed through the roundabout and up the hill.

Her mother climbed in the Kombi. "You took a bit of a risk with that car. Why didn't you jump in the driving seat earlier and not leave it so late?"

"I couldn't get in. It was rolling too fast. Can you put my things in your handbag, Mum? I had to pee in mine. And I'm afraid we can't go shopping in this thing because I'm scared if I turn the engine off, I won't be able to start it again." Lillian's face dropped as she had been looking forward to shopping.

Maureen drove to Pete's hangar. "Where's the boss?" she shouted, clambering out of the Kombi.

Pete came out of his hangar, wiping paint off his hands. "What's up?"

"This bloody thing is what's up," she shouted, not giving a bugger who could hear and banging the driver's door in fury.

Lillian sat in the cab full of admiration for her daughter. She would have been too scared to speak to Maureen's father like that during her marriage.

"The battery is rooted, and I had to push start it down the hospital hill. Only just got inside the cab before I reached the roundabout at the bottom and nearly hit an oncoming car. If you don't get a new battery, I'm going to shove a match in the petrol tank." She glared up at Pete, hands on hips.

His face pinched with concern. "Sorry. I thought it was charged."

"I couldn't take Mum shopping."

"Sorry, Lillian."

"She could have been killed," Lillian said, thrilled to add her bit to help Maureen.

Pete looked more devastated. "You can take the Peugeot home and I'll get a lift." He looked at her stomach, eyes scared. "Are you all right?"

"Seem to be, but I could give birth tonight, so don't go to sleep." She snatched the car keys from Pete and drove home, satisfied she'd put the wind up him.

9

Durban

Two weeks later number three arrived with the cord around his neck and no doctor available, only one midwife and her student.

"Don't push. We only have two minutes to get that cord off before he chokes."

Maureen's body shook as she fought the demands of her body while she counted the seconds in her head.

He was dark blue when he finally rested in her arms. And once again she fell in love just the same as she had with her other two when they were born.

Pete arrived at the hospital when all the drama was over and peeked at his son, then drew back startled.

"Why is he so dark skinned?"

"Because his father is the gardener, what do you think!"

The nurse attending Maureen was quick to hop in. "The

cord around his neck restricted his oxygen, he'll lighten up."
She understood Pete's concern.

The following day, the nurses voted him the most placid
baby in the nursery and the best on the breast. He had a mop of
black hair and enormous brown eyes but there was something
that didn't fit. Maureen gazed at the bundle she cuddled and
frowned.

"Pete, he doesn't look like a Bruce. I don't think that name
suits him."

"What about Pierre?" Pete liked French names. It was his
heritage.

"No. It doesn't work with our names." They tried a few more
names but nothing seemed to fit the little fellow. A nurse came
in and rang a bell, visiting hours were over.

"Let's sleep on it," Pete said. He gave her a peck and left her
rocking the nameless creature in her arms.

A short time after Pete had left the hospital, a name dropped
into her mind, one she'd never considered. "You are Gerard."
She tried it on the nurse when she came to fetch him.

"That's a good name. I think it means spear or mighty
weapon," she said. Maureen hadn't considered the meanings
of names. She had named Henry Bernard after two wonderful
people that had helped her in Sweden, and Liam was a name she
had always liked.

When visiting hours finally arrived the following morning,
Pete bounced through the maternity ward doors with a grin
on his face. He had thought of a name – it had come to him
when he was driving home from the hospital the previous day.
He dropped into the chair next to her bed. "Guess what? I've
thought of a name," he said.

Maureen's eyebrows rose. "Me too. I thought of it after you
left the hospital yesterday." They stared at each other in silence.

"You go first," Pete said.

"Gerard." Maureen watched for his reaction. Pete shot back in his chair.

"That's nuts! It's the same name I thought of! How's that possible? I've never thought of that name before, don't even know anyone called Gerard."

"We must have thought about it at the same time," Maureen said. It was prophetic. The nurse brought their baby in and lay him in Maureen's arms. Pete leant over and placed his finger in the tiny hand.

"Hello Gerard," he said. The baby's face reddened, he pulled his legs up and farted. Pete threw his head back and laughed. "I hope that's not what he thinks of his name."

"The nurse said the name Gerard means mighty weapon and he looks strong." She didn't doubt the nurse.

"That seals the deal," Pete said. "He's Gerard."

A week later Maureen arrived home from hospital. Everyone jammed around the carrycot on the bed. "Meet your Nanna, Gerard," she said. Her mother pulled the blanket away from his face to get a better look.

"Hello Gerry," Lillian said.

"He's not Gerry, Mum. He's Gerard, a Gerry is a piddle pot. You're not to call him that."

"All right, I was only kidding."

Maureen found it easier having her mother around her children than she had her in-laws. She could tell her mother what to do and not worry about hurting her feelings like she had with Annie. And she knew her mother would be returning to Australia, so there wasn't that threat of permanence. Also, nothing worried her because she was in a state of excitement – they were moving.

Maureen danced through her new house, its big rooms,

and archways, yelling with glee, "My house, my house!" Lillian followed eyes shining, remembering how she'd felt moving into the house Aunt Maggie had given her.

Pete came inside, his pockets bulging, hands full of granadillas and unloaded them onto the table. "There's a quarter of an acre of them. We've also got peaches, apricots, figs, guavas, mulberries, and grapes. And I've been looking at the flat next to the carport. All it needs is a coat of paint, a bath and toilet and we could rent it out." Pete beamed at Maureen's mother. "You've brought us good luck, Lillian."

Maureen squeezed his arm, happy that Pete and her mother had liked each other from the moment they'd met, a love of books being their common ground.

"What are you going to name your house?" Lillian asked.

Pete and Maureen turned to each other; they hadn't thought of naming their house. Maureen's brow creased. "What about calling it Eden after my hometown?"

Pete's face screwed up. "This is the high veld, open grassland, middle of South Africa, not a lush, beautiful landscape by the sea. How about 'Bahati'? It means luck in Swahili."

Lillian clapped her hands. "It's your lucky house." The name sounded exotic; this was Africa. Bahati won.

"I've checked the servant's quarters, they don't have any electricity but there's a long drop near them, so they have a lavatory." Pete wasn't concerned, he'd seen worse. He had assigned George, one of his workers from the airport, to be their gardener, and Maureen had employed a new maid, Maria, at the request of a work colleague who was moving to Cape Town.

Maria was nearly blind with cataracts on both eyes, but she was always cheerful, loved children and could manage housework. She also had a pass that allowed her to work in the area, whereas Beauty didn't have any pass and Maureen had been warned about the police in Halfway House. They were tough on passes for the blacks and fines were high, both for the employer and employee, the latter usually serving a gaol sentence. So Beauty had to go.

Maureen showed her mother to her room, taking pleasure in her delight at its size, the view of the jacaranda tree and open veld from the window. Her mother had slaved over wood stoves, run after people all her life. Sitting on the bed she watched her unpack a paint box full of oil paints and brushes.

"I'm going to paint a picture of your house," her mother said. "I want the whole town to see it."

"I've organised a trip for us to Durban during the school holidays. You'll love it, Mum. We'll be staying with Pete's old friends from Kenya." Lillian beamed, she'd read books about the Zulu wars and couldn't wait to visit Natal.

Four weeks later the car was packed and ready to leave for Durban. Prone to car sickness, Lillian occupied the front seat next to Pete while Maureen sat in the back with the children. They weren't long into their journey when there was a request to stop.

"Henry wants to pee, Pete."

"He can hold on until we stop for petrol." Pete checked the rear vision mirror and looked at Henry squirming on the seat. He didn't seem too desperate.

Maureen sighed. It was always a battle getting Pete to stop.

"Mummy, I need a pee," Henry begged.

"I want a pee too," Liam said.

"Come on, Pete, stop the car."

"It's not much further," he said.

Maureen leaned over the back seat, felt under their suitcases and pulled out a piddle pot.

"Here," she held it out for Henry, who pulled his shorts down and did a pee, then it was Liam's turn.

"Mum, do you need a pee?"

Her mother laughed.

"Pete never stops the car so make sure you go when we get to the petrol station." Maureen was peeved. She wound the window down and emptied the piddle into the wind. Brakes screeched, Maureen looked back, the car behind had its wipers on. Lucky it was just a pee.

A meerkat lookout stood on a fence post. Pete slowed for Lillian to take a photograph but didn't stop.

Durban was lush and green, humid after Johannesburg's dry air. The thick bush was a tangle of flowering vines. Pete pulled to the side of the road and parked under a tree so Liam, a bad traveller, could vomit. Maureen shoved him out of the car door just in time. Monkeys chatted in the trees overhead, some swung down and sat on a branch close to the car and watched Liam. Maureen finished wiping him down and got into the car. A vervet monkey jumped onto the bonnet and grabbed the windscreen wipers. Pete cursed and sprayed the window with water. It let go and bounced on the bonnet. Pete banged his hand on the window and hooted the horn to scare it away but all it did was turn its back to him and press a pair of bright blue balls against the windscreen. Everyone squealed.

"Why don't you get out and shoo it away?" Lillian asked.

"Not on your life, they bite and carry disease." On cue the monkey grinned, its long incisors warning them to stay in the car. Another monkey joined it. They pressed their faces to the window inspecting their caged audience. Then turned, showing their bums in contempt.

"Look! That one's bum is blue and pink," Henry said, awed. The animal stretched a finger and mined its anus.

"It's picking poo," squealed Liam, clapping his hands. "Is that its dickie?"

A mother landed on the bonnet with a baby clinging to its underside. Shrieks of wonder and appreciation filled the car. It was a National Geographic event. Blinded by monkeys, Pete edged the car forward as far as he dared, wheels inches from the edge of the road and an incline. He braked and blasted the horn to get rid of the hitchhikers, but they rode the bonnet for a couple of kilometres before jumping off and leaping for the trees.

"Well, fancy that," Lillian said, ecstatic.

"Bastards scratched my car," frowned Pete.

"Bastards," repeated Henry and Liam.

Turning into Jackie's driveway, Pete tooted the horn. Kids rushed from the house with shrieks of welcome. Liam and Henry leapt from the car and they all disappeared around the side of the house. Lillian lifted the carrycot out while Maureen and Pete hugged Jackie and Ben.

The house was federation style with bay windows and a bull nose verandah, like Lillian's home in Eden. It was on an acre and a distance from the city.

Maureen introduced her mother. "Jackie, this is my mum, Lillian. Mum this is Jackie." They pecked cheeks.

After everyone had been shown their sleeping quarters they collected around the table for a cup of coffee and planned where to take Lillian. It was decided that they visit the Hluhluwe-iMfolozi game park.

It was hot and humid, and the car windows had to be kept up to keep the biting flies out. They parked by a river and watched the hippos' heads rise like tree stumps in the river. The animals were the length of their car.

Maureen told her mother the story of Mirabelle Fosdick's son being taken by a hippo. Hearing the story, Lillian decided nothing would make her get out of the car to take a photo. They left the game park before the sun reached its zenith and the children their limit being cramped in a car.

On the way back to Jackie's, they drove through a Zulu village where people wore their traditional attire, beaded necklaces, hair ornaments and colourful sarongs. Pete gave Lillian a history lesson on the Zulus he so admired for being formidable opponents of the British. Lillian was enchanted. Apartheid wasn't so obvious in Durban and she felt more comfortable.

By the time they arrived home, Lillian had a headache brought on by all the travel, heat, flies, and squabbling children. She excused herself and went to lie down leaving Maureen, Jackie and the men having drinks on the verandah under the stars.

At breakfast it was decided they'd spend the day around the house to give Lillian recovery time and a play day for the children. Pete helped Jackie's husband fix a car in his shed and Maureen lazed with a book. When they congregated around the kitchen table for afternoon tea, the bantam cockerels came inside to peck cake crumbs off the kitchen floor. Lillian, closest to the cockerels, got up to shoo them out.

"Leave them. They're a damn nuisance, but they won't be in here long," Jackie said. Brutus, the family bulldog waddled into the kitchen. He was a randy bugger, and mounting a cockerel wasn't beyond him. An opportunity was offered by the rooster's engagement with a crumb. Brutus straddled the cockerel. Wings flapped, the bird screeched, rose into the air and landed on the dog's head. Its spurs dug in. Fur flew, the dog yelped and roared around in circles with the bird attached to its head. Blood spattered from Brutus. Everyone jumped to their feet. Ben grabbed the dog and dragged it into the hallway while Jackie swung a broom at the offending bird driving it out into the yard. The dog's face was covered in blood. Ben examined him.

"He needs stitches. We'll have to get him to the vet."

Twenty-five stitches later, Brutus returned home. But unrepentant, he tried his luck with the cockerel again and Jackie had to shut him in the bedroom.

Brutus lost his testicles at the vet and the cockerel was banished to the chicken coop before Maureen and Pete left Durban.

"What will you remember most about our trip, Mum?" Maureen asked on the drive back to Johannesburg.

"Blue balls and Brutus," Lillian replied. They all laughed.

"Your trip to Zambia isn't too far off." Her mother's eldest brother lived in Zambia and he had arranged for her to spend a few weeks with him. Maureen had also booked a tour of Victoria Falls and the game park for her mother. It was her way of apologising for not returning to Australia when her mother had tried so hard to help her get back.

10

The Party

Maureen decided to have a housewarming party while her mother was in Zambia on tour. They invited work colleagues, the airport crowd, Kenyan friends and Joey and Des. Joey was the only friend Maureen had made outside of Pete's clique. They had met through the local school. Joey's son Colin was Henry's friend.

The house was perfect for a party. It had two lounge rooms at right angles to each other that led out to a swimming pool and braai area. Pete filled one lounge room with chairs he'd borrowed from the aero club and cleared the other room for dancing.

A heap of people turned up, word had gotten around, and Pete couldn't remember who he'd asked and who he hadn't. With curry and rice on the table, Neil Diamond on the stereo and liquor flowing, everyone was having a great time.

Maureen was slicing more bananas into the fruit salad she'd made for dessert when she heard angry voices shouting outside the kitchen window. Bloody George, drunk and causing problems, she thought, walking over to the window to see what was going on.

Joey was sitting on the edge of the porch under the light, her face in her hands. Des was shouting, pacing, waving his arms. Joey lifted her head to say something and suddenly Des whirled and kicked her in the side of the face. The knife Maureen was holding dropped to the floor. She grabbed Pete who was getting beers from the fridge.

"Help Joey!" Maureen cried, pulling him towards the window. Des had Joey by the hair, his fist raised. Pete raced out and threw himself on top of Des. They rolled on the ground. Des broke free and ran for his car. Pete held Joey while she sobbed in his arms. An engine roared, wheels spun, and the car lurched forward. Pete leapt onto the porch pulling Joey with him. The car braked to a stop, its bumper touching the porch. Des got out.

"Get Colin, we're going," he snarled.

"Come on, Des. You're drunk. You shouldn't be driving. Come in and have a coffee and settle down." Behind Pete's shield of calmness, he clearly wanted to belt the daylights out of the brute.

A finger stabbed towards Joey, who stood behind Pete hand pressed to her face, blood dripping through her fingers.

"She's drunk, should keep her mouth shut. Accused me of sleazing over the air hostess in there." His face was bloated, eyes bloodshot. "I'm not going to tell you again, get Colin." He made to step forward.

Panic gripped Maureen and she tugged Joey's arm and pulled her into the kitchen, placing herself between husband and wife.

"Colin is asleep, why not pick him up in the morning?" Maureen said, desperate for Joey to stay under their protection.

Des crowded her back into the kitchen and stood over her, jaw thrust forward, eyes slits. Pete laid a warning hand on his shoulder.

This snarling animal was a new Des, not the thoughtful husband and loving father he had presented.

"I'll get Colin," Joey whispered. She headed down the hall towards the boy's bedroom.

Maureen followed pleading. "Joey, why not leave Colin here? Des is too drunk to drive. You might have an accident."

Joey shook her blonde ponytail. She was a tall, slender, pretty woman. "We'll be fine," she looked gaunt and white, eyes staring without registering what was around her.

Maureen had seen that same look on her mother's face when she was a child. Not about to give up, she tried again. "You don't have to go, Joey. I can open the couch into a bed, and you and Des can sleep in the lounge. Please stay here."

"No, it's better if we leave. You don't understand. Des will be fine tomorrow." Joey woke Colin and led the stumbling boy to the car. There was nothing Maureen could do but watch them. Des did a wheelie in the driveway and roared onto the road leaving a spray of dirt behind him. Sickened, Maureen turned to Pete standing next to her.

"I'm so scared for Joey." She would never have guessed Des was a wife beater. Always the charmer when he visited, bringing sweets or cake for the children, although he'd never won Liam over no matter how hard he tried. Liam wouldn't go near him, asking Des to leave his sweet on the table and then getting it when Des left the room. His reaction to Des had embarrassed Maureen because he wasn't a shy child. When Maureen had quizzed Liam, he said he didn't like Des's eyes. There was something the child saw that adults didn't.

"He's plastered, but he hasn't got far to go so they should be all right," Pete said.

"He kicked her in the face. She isn't drunk. She's been drinking lemonade all night." Maureen was glad her mother was in Zambia. There had been domestic violence in her own life.

"We can't do anything about it. Joey has made her decision and from the way she reacted it looks like this has happened before." Pete draped an arm across her shoulders. "Come on, we have guests." They went back to their party full of misgivings. Thanks to the loud music no one had witnessed the drama other than them, but the fun had gone out of the night for Maureen and Pete and they wanted their guests to leave.

In bed, thoughts of Joey plagued her. Had she gotten home okay? There was no family to help her – her mother had been killed in a car accident when she was three and her father was murdered when she was nine. The children had been split up; her brother sent to an uncle in Rhodesia and she was brought up by her grandmother in the poor white district of Johannesburg. Poor whites were underprivileged white people who lived on the fringes of coloured townships. They were looked down upon by all races, a margin above the coloureds but despised by them because they were white. She had told Maureen that she and Des had met at a dance. He was from a wealthy family and Joey couldn't believe he had been interested in her.

In the morning Maureen woke with a thumping headache, still worried about Joey. She cursed not having a telephone. It was on her to-do list to harangue the telephone department until she got results. Having to wait six months to get the telephone connected was ridiculous. If they had an Afrikaans surname the phone would be connected in a week, a friend had told her, but she guessed it was more about who you knew.

Leaving George and Maria to clean up last night's mess, Maureen drove to Joey's to reassure herself she'd made it home all right. Des's car was in the driveway intact. She decided not to go up to the house in case her presence angered Des. She didn't want to make it more difficult for Joey. At least Joey was safe.

There had been no word from Joey all week and Maureen resisted the temptation to visit, instead waiting for her to feel comfortable enough to contact her. Two weeks passed and then Joey and Des arrived on Maureen's doorstep.

Looking sheepish, Des held out a bottle of wine and a box of chocolates. Taking the offerings Maureen levelled him with a gaze. He lowered his eyes, a mess of guilt.

Joey stood tall. "Des has something he wants to say." Joey gave Colin a gentle push. "Go and play with Henry."

Colin scooted off and Joey nodded to Des. Pete arrived to see who was at the door and stood behind Maureen, stiff-faced. Des hung his head and cleared his throat.

"Look, I'm sorry about the party. I don't know what came over me. I'm not supposed to drink, doctor's orders. I don't know why I did. Alcohol turns me into another person." Des looked like he was about to cry. Neither Maureen or Pete said anything and then Maureen caught the appeal in Joey's eyes and stood aside.

"Well, come in and we'll have a cup of tea." She called out to Maria to make a pot of tea, not wanting to miss out on Des's apology. She was suspicious of him now and doubted the feeling would ever go away, despite Des's obvious remorse and desperation for their forgiveness. Over a cup of tea, he told them a story about his twelve-year-old self when he lived on a farm and his uncle had a frontier store, selling goods to the blacks.

"One kaffir was a loudmouth. My uncle hated him. He caught him stealing but the kaffir denied it. Then one day my uncle had to go to Jo'burg to the stores and asked me to go with him.

We were waiting for the train when my uncle saw the kaffir who had stolen from his shop. He told me to stand on one side of him and when the crowd had grown, and the train was close, to push him when he said go. We stood either side of the kaffir and the train was putting on its brakes. He yelled, 'Go!' and we pushed him in front of the train. Killed him." Des had a sip of tea and looked around the gaping faces while Joey looked at the floor.

Maureen stared at Des in horror. He didn't seem sorry. Why would he tell anyone this? It sounded like a boast.

"Your uncle should have been horse-whipped and thrown into gaol," Pete said, aghast.

Des shrugged. "I was a kid, did what my uncle said. A fortune teller once told me I'd end up in gaol."

Seeing the disbelief on Maureen's face, he changed the subject. "Look, I came over not just to say sorry about my behaviour but to ask if you'd like to come with Joey and me to my parents farm in Nelspruit. We're going there in the school holidays next month. You could come for a few days?" There was an awkward silence. Maureen shot Pete a look. He was staring into the distance.

Des leant forward opening his hands. "I'd like to make up for my behaviour." He put his arm around his wife. "Joey's giving me another chance and I hope you will too."

Joey stared at Maureen, a silent plea in her eyes. One side of her face was blue and swollen, and her eye dark ringed despite heavy makeup. He'd fractured her cheekbone.

"I've asked my folks," Des said, "and they're keen to have you. You'll love it there. Bring your mother, Maureen, there's lots of game on the property. Buck, monkeys, she'd enjoy it." His smile was disarming.

Joey clasped Maureen's hand and gave it a tight squeeze. "Please," she said.

For her friend, Maureen would go. "I'll ask Mum when she

gets back from Victoria Falls. She's on a bus tour and she might not want to do another car trip." The excuse would give Maureen time to convince Pete.

Two hours later they waved Des and Joey off and went inside for a discussion. "Joey needs us to go. I want to help her."

"The man's a pig and you shouldn't get involved," Pete said.

"I won't, but Mum would love it. It's only three days?" she pleaded.

"Well, I guess so." Pete wanted his mother-in-law to enjoy her African trip. Maureen gave him a hug. Neither of them would forgive Des.

The farm in Nelspruit was serene and beautiful, forests, hills, flowers, idyllic. The house was a rambling colonial home with wide verandahs for entertaining. Buck grazed close to the house and monkeys observed them from the trees. Maureen's mother was enchanted. It was the Africa she had come to see and Des, the handsome, perfect host, drove her everywhere. Maureen put Des's actions aside. There was no mention of the party or the story he had told, and the weekend passed without incident, but inwardly Maureen remained vigilant.

The night before they left, Maureen asked Joey to help her buy curtain material for the picture windows that occupied one wall of their lounge and faced the road.

"I feel so exposed. Anyone who drives past can see right into our house."

"We could go to Vrededorp. They'll have cheap material," Joey said. She knew the area well; it was the poor white district. Maureen saw Des frown.

"When do you think you'll do that, Joey?" His voice was soft. Joey stiffened.

"You can check your plans, Des, and I can do it if you have nothing on?" Maureen didn't miss the concern in her voice.

Des strung out his reply, watching Joey's agitation. "I'll look at the calendar when we get home," he said smiling. His eyes connected with Maureen's. Not wanting him to read her loathing, she looked away.

Two months later, Joey and Maureen sat cross-legged on the turquoise, purple and black Casa Pupa rug in Maureen's lounge admiring the purple curtains Joey had made.

"Who said purple wouldn't look good with black and orange furniture?" The women at work had looked shocked when Maureen discussed her colour scheme. "The curtains make the room look cheerful. Thanks, Joey, they look great."

"Jersey isn't curtain material so they might drop a little," Joey said.

"When that happens, I'll take them up." Maureen clinked Joey's glass. She looked at the coronet of bubbles in her glass and, unable to contain herself any longer, leant forward and peered at her friend. Beneath Joey's unusually thick makeup was a large bruise on her forehead. Joey put her hand up to cover it and Maureen sat back. "Things okay with you and Des?"

Joey's eyes filled with tears, she swallowed and lowered her hand. "It's only when he drinks. He doesn't mean to. There's something I do that aggravates him. He tries hard to make up for it afterwards, just can't help himself. He blames having only found out he was adopted when we got married. His birth certificate was false. Turns out his father was a manic depressive, and his aunt is his actual mother." Scared at her disclosure, she looked at Maureen. "Please don't tell anyone, I'd hate him to find out that I'd told you."

"I won't, cross my heart." She wouldn't do that to her desperate friend. Living away from Australia for so long, her friends were her family. "It's not really an excuse for hurting you though, Joey. No man should hurt his wife, or any woman. Pete wouldn't hurt me." They had never had a real fight – arguments, yes, but no screaming matches. It was hard to stay annoyed with Pete because he would act the fool to get her laughing if he saw she was annoyed. "Has he ever beaten Colin? I mean, really beaten him not strapped his legs a couple of times?"

"When he was two, he threw him against the wall because he was screaming at us fighting. Des blamed me for that. Colin is a very good child around his father." Maureen didn't need convincing of that.

"Joey, if ever you leave Des you can come and stay with us you know." Their conversation ended when the kids bounded into the room.

After she had waved Joey off, she leant against the big jacaranda tree in the driveway. It was in full bloom and buzzing with bees. There would be more bruises on Joey, of that Maureen was sure. She wanted Joey to leave Des, if not for herself then for Colin. A child shouldn't have to live with that fear and tension. Maureen had always watched her father's moods when she was a child. There had been a poet inside her mother, a thinker that had been demolished by her father along with her confidence, until Aunt Maggie had saved her. Joey didn't have an Aunt Maggie and Maureen knew she couldn't be one for her.

A shriek up the road caught her attention. The neighbour's dogs were barking and snarling, hurling their bodies at a wire fence as two women with babies wrapped to their backs ran past the property. Maureen watched their panic and cursed the huge animals, trained security dogs, vicious beasts taught to terrorise the blacks. The dogs made her think of Des. When the women

86

had safely passed, she went inside to contemplate her own marriage.

How lucky she was to have a man who loved her, who wasn't a big drinker and preferred to be with his family rather than go to the aero club and hang out with friends. He had put her needs before his parents and taken them to Salisbury to live with his brother. He didn't fawn all over her or force himself on her in any way. He praised her and boasted about her cooking skills to his friends. He never mentioned her past. To him, it was a closed book, and he was as proud of Henry as he was of Liam and Gerard, often laughing at Henry's antics and likening him to one of his family members or himself. Thinking about her marriage Maureen realised she respected and had a deep regard for Pete.

A few months later, Joey and Des moved to Germiston, a suburb near the gold mines on the other side of Johannesburg from Maureen, which meant she and Joey didn't see much of each other. Maureen couldn't help feeling Des had moved across town to distance Joey from her friends.

11

Splinter's Phone Call

Madam, I have to leave you." Maria stood in front of Maureen, eyes to the floor.

"Why? Do you want more money?"

"No, Madam. Missus Jane has moved back from the Cape and she asked me to work for her again. She has a new house now. I want to be with Mathew."

Maria had brought Mathew up, carried him on her back as a baby while his mother worked. She had been with Jane's family for six years. Maureen had too many children, and Maria's eyesight was getting worse. She didn't know when the children were outside, couldn't see them in the distance and it would be worse after Nanna went back to Australia. Nanna helped her with the children, was her eyes. Maria liked the madam's mother.

"I'm sorry you are leaving me, Maria." Maureen was peed off with her friend Jane. She had employed Maria at Jane's request and now she wanted her back. "If you know of a nice girl who needs a job, please ask her to come and see me."

"I have good girl for you Madam. She can see good." Maureen's heart squeezed. Poor Maria, she had taken her to the doctor to see if anything could be done about her eyesight, but the doctor had said there was nothing they could do. Maria had just nodded at the news and tried to make Maureen feel better by telling her it was all right, that she would hire a child to lead her around when she was old.

"Tomorrow I will bring your new girl." Maria turned her back and began filling the sink with hot water. There was no argument, she was leaving.

When Maria had finished for the day and gone to her room, Maureen told Lillian the news.

"That's a shame, she's such a nice woman. I'll give her the oil painting I did of her. She asked me to paint her with two good eyes." Maureen's eyebrows rose, unaware her mother had been painting Maria's portrait.

"I did it when you were at work. I helped with the ironing and made the children's beds while she cleaned the bathroom and floors. With two of us cleaning, Maria had time to sit for me. Wait here and I'll get it." Proud of her painting and keen for Maureen to see it, Lillian hurried down the hall to her bedroom.

Maureen smiled, understanding how her mother would help the maid. She had done the same when she first arrived in South Africa and rather than seeing Maria on her knees scrubbing their sheets in the bathtub, she had bought a washing machine with a mangle. But Maria had been too scared to use the machine and Maureen had ended up doing the washing. Pete had piddled himself laughing. "You have a dog and bark yourself," he'd said, quoting an African saying. She wondered what he would say if he knew her mother had been helping the maid so she could paint her portrait.

"Here it is. What do you think?" Lillian held up the portrait of a laughing Maria with clear eyes that looked out from the canvas. It made Maureen feel happy and sad. Happy for the pleasure she saw in Maria's unclouded eyes, the gentleness in her face and sad for the woman's future.

"It's beautiful, Mum. I think she will love it." Maria would never have had a white woman do something like that for her before. Maureen gave her mother a hug.

The following morning Maria brought Dorcas to the door. She was beautiful, with fine features, tall, slim, and neatly dressed. Her eyes held Maureen's.

"Good morning, Madam, my name is Dorcas, I believe you are looking for a girl?" Her English was good. Maureen liked her instantly.

She caught sight of George hovering in the background, scowling. He signalled with his head for her to come over. Henry stood next to him. What was wrong now? Ignoring George, she focused on Dorcas.

"Come in, Dorcas. Maria can tell you about the job and show you around the house."

Henry ran inside after her. "Mummy, George wants you to talk to him." Maureen sighed and left Maria with Dorcas to go and see what George wanted.

As she approached, George shook his head at her. "It is no good getting that girl, Madam, she is a cheeky one. I can find better."

"I'm going to give her a try, George."

"The boss won't like it." He folded his arms. Maureen's nostrils flared. The bloody nerve of him suggesting he could influence Pete not to employ Dorcas and that Pete would listen and have the final say.

"I employ the maids, not the boss. Now you go and kill all the vegetables and lose the chickens like you always do." She stamped off. How dare he threaten her with Pete. Bugger George. Dorcas was her choice, and she could stay. Maureen later found out from Maria that Dorcas had rebuffed George's amorous attentions.

"Madam! The telephone!" Dorcas called down the hall. Maureen checked the clock by her bed. It was 7 a.m. Who would call this early? She grabbed her dressing-gown and, half-awake, stumbled into the lounge and picked up the phone.

"Hello, Maureen, it's Louise. I need to speak to Mum, it's urgent." The telephone line crackled. "Don't take long. This call costs a fortune."

"Right, I'll get her." Her sister sounded desperate. Maureen trotted down the hall and opened her mother's bedroom door. "Are you awake, Mum? Splinter is on the phone."

"Who?"

"Splinter, Australia. She says it's urgent."

"God, hope it's not the little one." Lillian didn't bother with her dressing gown, dashing off to the phone in her nightie. Maureen followed to listen in.

"Hello Louise, it's Mum, what's wrong?" A minute passed, Lillian's face clamped down, both her hands gripped the phone. "What can I do about that here?" Maureen rounded her eyes and held her hand out for the phone. Lillian shook her head.

Maureen watched her mother put the phone down. "What's going on with Splinter, Mum? Is anything wrong with Dad?" Her mother gave her a pensive look.

"Don't think I'm being cold-hearted about your dad, but I don't see why he has to be my responsibility. Apparently he's missing, and Splinter wants me to come home. As if I would know where he was." She frowned. "I love it here. It's the first time I've felt free of other people's expectations. I want to stay in Africa with you. I wouldn't be any trouble." There was desperation in her voice.

Maureen felt herself pull back. She didn't want her mother living with her – not that her mother was a problem, she just wanted to have her family to herself. In some ways she was still finding her way with Pete and Apartheid. She didn't want a third person on the scene regardless of where her loyalties lay.

"No Mum. I made Pete send his parents away and it would be unfair to Pete if I said you can live with us. Besides, I want to move back to Australia. I don't want the children to grow up here. Henry would have to go into the army. I have friends who have lost their sons fighting in Angola and their parents didn't even know the South African army was in Angola." It was the first time she had realised that was her main reason for wanting to move. She'd already spoken to Pete about emigrating to Australia and he hadn't been averse to the idea, but he wanted to see it before making up his mind. She was saving every cent for a holiday.

"You have a wonderful life here, Maureen. Servants, a big house, friends, a good job. You wouldn't have that in Australia. Imagine how hard it would be with three children in Australia."

"It was harder in Sweden, but I managed," Maureen said.

Lillian couldn't argue with that. "I'd like to stay a couple more months if you don't mind?"

Maureen nodded in agreement, and then thought of Splinter's reaction at having to look after her father longer.

12

Eden Dilemma

Splinter was of a mind to phone her mother again. The last time she had phoned she was in a panic thinking her father was missing. She had begged her to come home, told her she couldn't work, look after a child, and keep her eye on him. He was a bloody pest, constantly nicking the car keys and going for drives without a licence. If she had known her mother was going to stay away so long, she wouldn't have offered to look after him.

He had buggered off a few times since, sometimes was gone for a whole day, leaving her to worry that he'd had an accident on some godforsaken back road and then he would chug up the drive with a grin on his face. Her brown eyes flashed thinking about it.

She flung the door open and pushed up the window, ignoring the squadron of flies that zoomed into the kitchen. Then she squirted half a bottle of her expensive Coles 4711 perfume adding to the already heavy scent of fly spray that filled the air. But nothing she did seemed to get rid of the clogging smell of her father's pipe. She knew he had chopped up the last of his plug tobacco and vowed not to buy him any more. She didn't mind him having the occasional cigarette, but he wasn't going to stink her house out with his pipe.

The empty pipe chomped between Eric's teeth as he sat at the end of the kitchen table glowering. "Where's Mum?" he demanded.

"I've told you a dozen times, Dad, she's in Africa visiting Bubs, Maureen, your daughter," she snapped, seeing her father frown. "She'll be back soon." She had better be, Splinter thought.

"Where's the car keys?" Her father asked as if reading her mind.

"You can't have them; your licence was suspended after your stroke. You'll have to have another test." And it's not going to be in my car, she mumbled under her breath. Eric pushed his chair back and staggered to the door, his right side weakened since the stroke.

"I'm going out." Happy to get rid of him, Splinter didn't ask where he was going, presuming he would head back to her mother's house. Well, good riddance. She'd call by and check on him tomorrow.

He stood at the front gate gazing up the road.

Not having the car was a big problem for Eric. How could he help his friend with his farm if he couldn't drive out there? It was nearly harvesting time. It was possible Smokey might be up at the club and could have more of that tobacco Eric had been tending for him. He wondered how the crop was going. He hadn't inspected it in a while, not since Splinter started hiding the keys to her car. He could just make the walk up to the club if he held onto the fence rails.

"G'day, Eric." Smokey gave a good-natured smile, collected his beer from the bar and assisted a near collapsing Eric to a chair. "You look a bit shot, mate."

Eric held out his pipe. "Have you got any of that tobacco you grow, Smokey?"

Smokey's eyes darted towards the bar. "Not here, mate. Plenty at the farm if you want to come back with me. The plants are doing great since I dug those gullies you suggested. Saves a lot of watering time."

"I'd like to see the plants. Need some tobacco. Splinter won't buy any and Mum's away. Took my chequebook." He patted his pockets, frowning.

"You won't need your chequebook, mate. Tobacco is free. Car's out the back. I've arranged a driving test for you next week. How about I pick you up from your house next Monday?"

Eric's driving test was going well. The testing officer commended him for his quick reflexes as he swerved past a sheep in the middle of the road. "I'm told you were a submariner. I served on subs at the end of the war." Eric knew he had his licence in the bag. Navy blokes stuck together. "I think we can go back to the station now."

Smokey collected him from the Fisherman's Club the following day and drove him to his farm where the ute waited. "I've got a job for you, mate."

Eric whistled his way along the road, happy to be behind the wheel, thrilled that he'd been asked to drop Smokey's crop off in Wollongong. It was for the war effort, Smokey had explained, as there were a lot of Vietnam vets who had problems with their nerves and needed tobacco. "But if anyone asks what's in the sack tell them it's hay," he'd instructed.

Hankering for a smoke, Eric pulled to the side of the road and parked under the shade of a gum tree to light his pipe. The last of his plug was gone and he only had the small amount of tobacco Smokey had given him a while back. He packed his pipe, pressing it down with his thumb and lit the mound. His lips curled back from the first intake of smoke, and he coughed until his eyes watered. Smokey's tobacco needed a lot of improvement. It tasted foul, stank and was as rough as the handful of grass he'd had to wipe his arse on an hour ago. The grass had left him with an itch that was difficult to get to while he was driving. He regretted having eaten the bag of plums.

He got out of Smokey's unregistered ute, had a pee, then settled back behind the wheel. A few more miles and a couple more puffs on his pipe and he stopped noticing the tobacco's roughness or his itchy bum. A mob of roos hopped across the road in front of him, slowing him down. Something about the way they hopped tickled his fancy and he laughed and kept laughing as he drove, wiping away the tears with the sleeve of his shirt.

Nowra was the next town, and not normally a big eater, Eric was still feeling hungry even though he'd eaten the lamb and chutney sandwiches Smokey had made him and finished off a tin of condensed milk as well as the plums. The thought of a pie and sauce was tantalising. Maybe he had worms?

Church bells rang as he entered the main street, reminding him it was Sunday, and he removed his hat out of respect while keeping an eye out for a café. The two he passed were closed as were the shops. The town was deserted. Then he saw the Pizza Hut. The bloody wogs were everywhere but it seemed to be the only place open. Normally he didn't touch wog food, but the picture of the pizza in the window looked a bit like bubble and squeak with tomato sauce and he liked bubble and squeak.

Magpies chortled around the door hoping for some crumbs as he went inside. A short woman wearing an apron over a black dress, her plump cheeks pink from the heat of the pizza oven, smiled up at Eric.

"You wanta pizza? We make own tomato sauce." Eric moved his pipe to the other side of his mouth. He could taste garlic. It was in the air. Revolting stuff. He could always tell garlic eaters – they sweated it. Still, the flat round dough the woman had spread with tomato sauce and was now grating cheese over, looked appetising. He could feel the saliva build in his mouth. "I'll have one of those, please." He pointed to the pizza, and she pointed to the bench that ran down the side of the wall. While he sat waiting for his pizza, he sucked up the remains of the tobacco in his pipe and noticed his heart racing, and that his mouth was dry.

"You … wanta … some … salami?" The woman's voice sounded slow and a distance off. He snorted a reply. She shrugged, threw a few pieces of salami on the pizza then placed it on a long-handled paddle and put it in the oven, closing the oven door. The cake on the counter caught Eric's eye, it was a beauty, getting more delicious as he stared at it. He pointed to the cake. "I'll have a piece of that." She nodded and cut him a slice.

"Tiramisu."

"Terror … miss … you," he repeated, stumbling to the counter, disorientated. After ten minutes of dreamtime and devouring the cake, Eric left the café with his pizza. He sat in the ute and ate the pizza, smacking his lips after each bite and loving wog food. When he'd finished his meal, he drove along the road at ten kilometres an hour, admiring the bush, the smell of eucalyptus, the sound of kookaburras and the clear blue sky, oblivious to the car horns blasting behind him. The frustrated driver of a police car drew alongside Eric, lights whirling and motioned for him to pull over.

The policeman settled his cap on his head, collected his book of tickets and walked over to Eric and tapped on his window. Eric wound the window down. "You're driving too slow. This is a highway. Are you looking for something or someone, sir?"

"I'm not sure," Eric said, brow wrinkling. The policeman's eyes narrowed. Lowering his head, he peered in Eric's window, coughed and pulled back.

"Jeez!"

"Tobacco. It stinks doesn't it? Not as good as my plug of champion." Eric shook his head at how far his taste buds had sunk.

"It smells illegal to me. Show me your licence." Eager to show off his new licence, Eric removed his wallet from the glove box, rifled through old receipts and proudly handed it over. The policeman made a note of the number, handed it back and checked the registration sticker on the windscreen. Satisfied, he pulled out his book of tickets. "This vehicle is unregistered. I'm afraid you'll have to leave it here and come with me." He opened Eric's door and motioned him to get out. Eric's knees felt a bit wonky. He put a hand on the ute to steady himself. The eye of the law cast over the sack in the back. "What's in the sack?" Eric scratched his head, frowning.

"Cattle feed," he replied, not being able to remember what Smokey had told him.

"I'll lock it in the ute so no one steals it and I'll take that pipe and have its contents checked." Eric's hand clamped over his pipe.

"You can't have it." It was a precious object that always occupied a pocket on his body. It helped him remember things.

"I'm afraid that's not an option." The policeman went to take the pipe from Eric's hand. Eric took a swipe at him, missed, and landed on the ground. The pipe rolled under the policeman's

98

boot. They stared at the disintegrated meerschaum pipe bowl and its ash remains, now a smudge in the air riding on a breeze towards the unknown.

"You broke my pipe," Eric wailed, scrabbling in the dirt to save the pieces. Not an unkind man, the policeman helped Eric to his feet. He wouldn't charge him with assault – it was obvious the fellow was mentally unstable. He called up the station on his two-way radio and ordered a tow truck for the ute, then helped Eric into the back seat of the police car.

Splinter looked relieved at the sight of the policeman standing at her front door and her father in the police car with an officer by his side. He gave her a victory signal from the back seat.

"You found my dad. Thank heavens! I was so worried." He hadn't returned after their argument over the car keys and Splinter had thought he'd gone back to her mother's place. Checking on him two days later, she found his bed hadn't been slept in and the kitchen was tidy. No dirty teacups in the sink and her father loved his cuppa. That set off the alarm bells and she had phoned the police station to report him missing.

This policeman, she noted, wasn't local. All business, the officer regarded her with a stern expression.

"I have come to inform you that your father is under arrest."

"What?" She looked at the officer, incredulous.

"It's a serious matter, but it seems he has a medical condition that affects his memory and can't explain the stolen ute or the contraband he was carrying. We would like you to come to the police station to assist us with our enquiries."

"Jesus Christ! What stolen ute?" Splinter never swore, in her head occasionally, but not out loud. What had her father been up to? "He's had a stroke. I reported him missing. He hasn't got a licence – it's been suspended." Frowning, the policeman looked at his notes, reading carefully.

"It seems he sat a test, and his licence has been renewed." Splinter gawked at him, speechless. Olivia came through the gate, her schoolbag on her back and joined her mother at the door. She looked at her mother's confounded face. The policeman stepped away from the door.

"Please be kind enough to come to the station as soon as possible." He walked back to the car and got in. Her father waved as the police car left. Splinter slammed the front door and raced down the hall. *Shit! Shit! Shit!* It was too much to expect her to deal with her father; her mother had to come home NOW. The call was booked to South Africa without considering the time difference. When her mother answered it was three o'clock in the morning.

"You have to come home," she shrieked down the phone. "Dad's in gaol and I'm pregnant!" She wasn't, but that was the reason Lillian went to Africa so it might get her back to Eden.

An hour later she was at the police station, sitting in front of a desk looking dumbfounded.

"You don't know anyone called Smokey?"

"Never heard of him," said Splinter.

"We've traced the ute your father was driving, and it seems it was stolen in Melbourne two years ago. Know anything about that?" Dazed, Splinter opened and closed her mouth. They couldn't be talking about her father, none of this was possible!

The policeman continued, "Who was he meeting in Wollongong?"

Wollongong? Her lips formed the word, but no sound came out. The officer tapped his pencil on the table.

"What about the contraband? Or cattle feed as your father calls it." His questions slapped at her brain. Where had her father been going when she had thought he was up at the Fisherman's Club?

"I don't know anything about anything. My mother is in Africa and I just visit him to check if he's all right." The officer made a note and put his pencil down.

"Seeing he is low risk, we will allow him to go home but you must keep him under surveillance at all times until his court case comes up."

"I can't keep him under surveillance, I work and have a child to look after. Also I'm pregnant." A tear trickled down her cheek and she fished for a handkerchief in her handbag.

The policeman pursed his lips, looking thoughtful. "Well, we could keep him in gaol until his court case."

A glint appeared in Splinter's eyes. Behind bars was a good place for him. He could stay in gaol until her mother came home. She nodded and signed the document that was pushed towards her.

Eric spent three weeks in prison before the judge arrived in Eden to hear his case. He hadn't minded his stay, sharing his cell with the odd drunk and bashing the ear of the officer at the desk about this and that. Unfortunately, his incessant yacking had got on the officer's nerves and he had been told to shut up or he'd accidently get shot. It was a relief for the policeman when the trial started.

Jonathan Bell – Dinga to his Vietnam buddies or Smokey, as only Eric called him – stood before the judge, clean shaven, short hair, parted to the side with a slick of Brylcream and war medals shining on his suit coat. The long hair, chest length beard and drooping moustache had gone. He looked like the schoolteacher he had been before the call up for Vietnam. Eric didn't recognise him until he spoke.

Jonathan Bell shook his head. He had no idea who the Smokey character was, but he had met up with Eric McKinley in the pub, like the bartender had told the police. He was aware Eric had had a stroke and felt sorry for him so decided to lend a hand fixing up an old ute Eric had found. And at Eric's request, he helped to arrange a driving test for him so he could get his licence back. To his knowledge, Eric had found the ute in the bush near a property he had owned prior to his stroke. Jonathan Bell had no idea who owned the ute or anything about the sugar bag full of marijuana or why Eric was driving it to Wollongong.

He turned towards Eric and gave him a sympathetic smile. "Mr McKinley often gets mixed up with his thoughts, but he's never mentioned anything criminal. Look at the man. He even has difficulty walking."

Eric gripped the arms of his chair and staggered to his feet, to confirm the story. He would never dob on a mate.

Not being able to get any sense out of Eric about where he was going to drop the marijuana and for whom, the judge ruled Eric had been taken advantage of by an unscrupulous character. He found him guilty of driving an unregistered vehicle, suspended his licence for six months and put him on a good behaviour bond for one year. The ute was impounded and Eric was left in Splinter's charge until his ex-wife, Lillian, returned from South Africa.

13

A Zulu Maiden

Maureen felt sad for her mother. She knew how much Lillian wanted to stay with her in South Africa, but Splinter had sounded piteous on the phone. Eric was a scandal in the town. It wasn't hard to see how that would impact Splinter – Eden loved its scandals. Eyes and whispers would follow her everywhere. Her mother dreaded going back.

They stood at the Johannesburg Airport with arms around each other. It was nine months since Lillian had arrived and apart from wiping her oil paint brushes on Maureen's bedroom curtains, they hadn't had a harsh word between them.

A panic of kisses followed the announcement to board the flight to Cape Town. Lillian had decided to take her time to get back home and return by sea. She was flying to Cape Town where the ship was docked that would take her back to Australia.

She hugged her grandchildren, lingering over Gerard. He put his arms up to her and she blinked back tears.

"Write and tell me how it goes on board the ship. We'll come and see you in Australia, Mum." Maureen swallowed the lump in her throat. How long until that would be she didn't know but determination was something she didn't lack. One day they would all live in Australia permanently. There was the final flurry of hands as her mother disappeared behind the departure door. Maureen put Gerard in the stroller.

"Nanna has gone. It's time for us to go home." She tried to keep her voice light for the children's sakes. Liam hung onto her hand and Henry held the side of the stroller as Maureen steered them misty eyed through the crowd.

The visit had left her even more homesick for Australia and the children missed their Nanna. A few weeks on and baby Gerard was still crawling into his grandmother's bedroom looking for her in the morning and Henry had stopped eating his pumpkin again.

The constant daily demands of life in South Africa soon got in the way of Maureen's homesickness. If the kids weren't sick, there was always some debacle going on with the servants and today it was George's turn. Hat in hand, he stood on the porch looking forlorn.

"I need money, Madam, for my mother's funeral. She has died."

"Oh, George, that's sad. I'm so sorry." Maureen thought how awful it would be if her mother or father died while she was in Africa. "I'll see how much I've got, George. You might have to wait for Boss Pete to come home if I haven't enough."

"What you have will be enough, Madam." George turned his big sorrowful eyes on her. "We won't wait for the boss." Maureen went through her purse and found thirty rand; it was a month's salary for George. He reached for the money with one hand, the other clasped around his wrist as was the custom and took the money from Maureen. "I will be back next week," he said.

"Tell your family I am sorry you have lost your mother."

George nodded. Eyes downcast, he dragged his feet back to his room.

At dinner, Maureen remembered George. "I've given George four days off Pete, his mother died. He asked if I could pay for the funeral, so I gave him thirty rand." Pete lay his knife and fork down and looked at her askance.

"What? We've buried her twice now! His mother died last year, and I paid for her funeral." He shook his head. "He's put one over you because he knows you miss your mother and you're a soft touch. Bloody scoundrel."

Along with his irritation, Maureen detected a touch of admiration in Pete's voice. George had been with Pete since before their marriage. His addiction to alcohol and marijuana made him unreliable at the airport, hence Pete had appointed him as their gardener. He wasn't a good gardener – chooks disappeared, as did most of the fruit off their trees, yet Pete kept him on. "No one else will employ him," he had said, when Maureen complained about the missing chooks. She wasn't the only soft touch.

Weeks later, George shouted for Maureen from the kitchen door.

"Come quick, Liam has a snake!" The spoon fell out of Maureen's hand as she abandoned Gerard in his highchair.

"You left him with a snake?" Maureen screamed at George as she tore after him. "Why didn't you pick him up?" There was no reply from George.

They ran through the long grass towards the servant's quarters. Liam was squatting in the grass, naked except for a vest. He hated wearing clothes and Maureen didn't mind him shedding them – it had helped with his potty training.

Hearing his mother, Liam looked up. "Snake, Mummy." His hand was around the tail of a cobra stuck up an irrigation pipe.

Maureen rushed at him, scooping him up in her arms, her breath coming in gasps. "You mustn't touch snakes, Liam, they bite." She turned on George.

"Why didn't you take him away? You left him with the snake to call me? Are you mad? I'm going to tell the boss. You should find another job!" She was so angry she could hardly get the words out.

"Where's his nanny, Madam? I want you to see she's a bad nanny, you should get another nanny." George had been making trouble for Dorcas for a long time. She had refused to sleep with him.

"I will speak to Dorcas, but if Liam had been bitten, it would have been your fault for not saving him."

Maureen felt guilty. She should have kept her eye on Liam while Dorcas was busy cleaning the bedrooms. That was something Maureen and Dorcas had relied on her mother to do. She missed her. It was hard keeping an eye on the whereabouts of children on five acres. She needed a nanny to help with the children while she was at work. Dorcas could find someone for her. But the extra cost meant it would take longer to save for their trip to Australia.

A young, well-built Zulu girl knocked on Maureen's door. "Gele," she said tapping her heart. Then with a lot of hand signals to make up for her lack of English and Afrikaans, she indicated she wanted to look after the children. Thinking she'd been sent by Dorcas, Maureen called Henry who appeared with his soccer ball tucked under his arm. Gele grabbed it from him, beckoning Henry and Maureen to come outside. She dribbled the ball with great dexterity, weaving between them. She kicked the ball at an overturned bucket, clapped her hands and laughed. Henry picked up the ball and threw it to Maureen; the next minute Maureen was flat on her back in the dirt. Gele held up the ball in triumph, then seeing her winded madam on the ground and realising what she had done, threw it to Henry. Moaning apologies in Zulu, Gele helped Maureen off the ground and brushed the dirt off her with a vigorous hand. She stared at Maureen round-eyed and anxious. To placate the girl, Maureen motioned her inside and gathered the children. She would try the eager applicant out.

Dorcas was furious. "She is a Durban girl, Zulu, not from here, Madam. You should not employ her. You can't understand her, and she doesn't understand you. She is fifteen, Madam. Stupid!" Maureen wasn't sure if she meant Gele was stupid or herself. She had an urge to giggle at the look of indignation on Dorcas's face.

"I'll give her a try, Dorcas. If she isn't any good, I will let her go."

Dorcas lifted her chin. "I will not help her, Madam. You must show her what to do." If Joey had heard this African girl speaking to her like that, she would have gone bananas. The norm was that Blacks were supposed to show reverence. All her friends had told her she was hopeless with maids.

Training Gele without the help of Dorcas was difficult. She used sign language and gave practical demonstrations showing her how to bath the children and watch them in the garden or in the pool. She didn't care that Gele got in the pool with them, nor did she mention allowing her in the pool to her friends. They would have forbidden their own children from swimming in the pool with a black person.

Maureen decided to extend Gele's knowledge and train her for house duties in case Dorcas got sick or left for some reason.

She'd start by showing her how to serve at a dinner party. She was hosting one next week.

Maureen set up the dining room table for make-believe guests and put out serving dishes on the kitchen bench. She stood in the kitchen with the bell and with an attentive Gele by her side.

"When I ring the bell," Maureen lifted the bell and dinged it, pointed to Gele, "you bring in the food." To demonstrate, Maureen picked up a serving dish, signalled the girl to follow her and carried it into the dining room, placing it on the sideboard. She looked at Gele and raised her eyebrows. A big smile and intelligent eyes said she understood. Maureen handed her the dish and sent her to the kitchen, then sat at the table and dinged the bell. Giggling, Gele came in with the dish and put it on the sideboard. Maureen clapped.

"You must be clean, wear good clothes." Maureen pretended to wash under her arms and put on a dress, then smoothing her hands down the front, she twirled in front of a pretend mirror, gave herself a nod of approval. She received a round of applause and then Gele pretended to put on a dress and sauntered past Maureen. Maureen gave her a clap. She showed her the kitchen clock, changed the hands to seven and tapped the glass. Gele nodded. Maureen held up her hand and counted five fingers, "Sunday." It was Dorcas's weekend off so there wouldn't be any problems. The girl's face lit up.

"Sunday," she repeated, beaming at Maureen. Her enthusiasm made Maureen smile. May her critics suffer heartburn, she thought.

The guests were all seated at the table, Maureen had the serving bowls with curry and rice in the oven, chapattis, and side dishes on the table. She dinged the silver bell. Gele was a buxom girl –

she waltzed in with a casserole dish full of curry, dressed in her best. Every eye widened, every mouth loosened. On her head was a Zulu headdress made of coloured beads in geometrical designs. Around her neck hung a beaded breastplate that reached down to her large bare breasts, with matching bracelets on her arms. Her bead skirt didn't cover her abundant bum. Bands of coloured beads ringed her ankles. She was bare footed. Maureen was bowled over by her beauty. There was total silence at the table and then a guest whistled in appreciation. Maureen stood up.

"This is Gele, everybody. She's a Zulu." Around the table, white hands waved. And in unison, everyone greeted her. She had broken all protocols, making Maureen's dinner party a raging success. Pete laughed himself onto the floor after the guests had left.

"You can really pick them. What a shame your mother missed this. She would have loved it."

14

Eden Bound

T he ship had hardly left Cape Town when Lillian fell ill with trembling chills and a massive headache. Taking herself to the ship's doctor, he questioned her on where she had been and then took a blood sample. Instead of sending her back to her cabin, he put her in hospital. A day later the diagnosis came back: malaria. Lillian struggled for the rest of her trip until arriving in Sydney.

Splinter and her children were there to greet her at the docks. Neither were looking like the robust women that had parted nine months before. Splinter hurried her mother through immigration and baggage and packed her in the car for the seven-hour drive to Eden.

"You've no idea what he's been like," she said to her mother.

Lillian gave a wry smile, certain she knew exactly what Eric had been like.

"He never listens to me. I had to go and live in the house with him after the court case to make sure he didn't wander off to God knows where. I still don't know where he met the people who set him up with the marijuana. The police asked me to be vigilant in case he remembers. It's been a nightmare. The whole town still talks about it. I hate going up the street."

Lillian leaned back in her seat and closed her eyes, feeling sorry for Splinter and guilty for taking her time returning, but she didn't want to think of Eric and what was ahead of her. She still felt wonky from the sea trip and her bout of malaria.

"Maureen has a beautiful house and a maid to take care of the kids. South Africa is so interesting. You never know what's going to greet you from one day to the next. I could have lived there."

"Well, you tried." Splinter said, a little snap to her voice.

"I loved the black people, but I was scared. Pete and Maureen are too – they're saving for a holiday to see if Pete wants to move to Australia. You would like Pete. He's full of fun. I didn't know what to expect not having seen a photo of him. He's six foot two and handsome. I suppose I had imagined him as an ordinary looking fellow because their marriage began as a convenience. We'll have to make his holiday as good as possible, so he'll want to immigrate." A spasm of shivers hit her, and she hugged her body, rocking forward in her seat.

"Are you all right?"

"Malaria. I caught it when I was staying in Northern Rhodesia with your uncle. I was in hospital on the ship for most of the journey home. The doctor said I could continue to get the occasional shivers."

Splinter turned to look at her mother. There was a yellow tinge to her skin; she looked haggard, older than when she'd left Australia.

"We'll stop for lunch at the pub in Batemans Bay. My treat,"

Splinter said. "We can look at the shops. A walk around might do you good." Lillian cast her eye towards Splinter's flat stomach.

"How's the pregnancy?"

There was an awkward silence. Splinter cleared her throat. "I'm sorry, Mum. I was desperate to get you home."

"It's fine, love. I understand. Tell me about your father."

Uninterrupted, Splinter talked until their lunch stop, while Lillian nodded, her mind deciphering, seeing Eric's every move. He was good at finding shady people. Her brow wrinkled, as she tried to catch a thought. There was something she knew but couldn't quite ping. It would come to her once she had rested.

Eric gave her a wide-eyed grin when she walked into the kitchen. Nothing had changed – spilt sugar and rings from slopped teacups marked the kitchen table. Flies at the window, some on their back, legs stiff on the ledge. Beyond them was the sea view the only sparkle in the room.

Splinter unloaded the suitcases and carried them to Lillian's room, gave her a kiss goodbye and rushed for the door. Lillian didn't blame her for wanting to get away. She'd only just arrived and she felt like doing a runner.

"I'm going for a lie down, Eric." She would face the fridge and think about what they would have for tea later. She hadn't had to think about preparing meals and cooking for nine months.

A week later, Eric's scandal shifted to Lillian's return and the local newspaper welcomed back Lillian with a photograph of her standing next to Maria, holding up the oil painting she had given the maid. Maureen had taken the photo before Maria had left her employ. There was a paragraph on her trip to Africa. *Lillian McKinley, wife of Eric McKinley, recently found not guilty of transporting marijuana, has returned after an extended stay with her daughter, Maureen in Johannesburg, South Africa.* Lillian put the newspaper down, poured herself a sherry from Aunt Maggie's decanter and sat down to think.

Life returned to normal for Lillian: attending CWA meetings and seeing to Eric, checking where he was. She used the spies Splinter had cunningly set up while she was in Africa. Most were shop assistants and the bar staff at the club. All of them were eager to give Lillian their version of Eric's exploitation as well as praise for Jonathan Bell, the returned Vietnam soldier for his support of Eric, which got Lillian thinking she should make Mr Bell a thank you cake. She phoned Splinter to see if she would drive them to the gentleman's farm on Sunday.

Eric guided them down the turnoff to Jonathan Bell's farm. Splinter parked and Lillian got out with the cake, leaving Eric to heave himself off the passenger seat. Feeling awkward at arriving unannounced and not wishing to be an inconvenience, she was going to knock and put the cake in the gentleman's hands, thank him and leave. Jonathan Bell came around the side of his cabin having just finished weeding his plants and stopped. He pushed his battered slouch hat back on seeing his visitors, recognised Eric and took a step backwards. Seeing Jonathan's reaction, Lillian held out the cake tin.

"I'm sorry to intrude on you like this but I wanted to thank you for getting Eric out of trouble and I made you a cake as a token of our appreciation." Jonathan hesitated then ventured forward and took the cake. Lillian's eyes widened.

"Why! I remember you. I'm Lillian, we met outside the butcher's when you kindly drove Eric up to the Fisherman's Club and then brought him home. It was over a year ago?" He nodded in recognition.

"That's very kind of you, Lillian. you shouldn't have." He looked past her to Eric ambling towards him then recognised Splinter from the trial, standing by the car. Alarmed, he fished for an excuse to get rid of them in case Eric slipped up and said something incriminating. "I would ask you in but I'm off to Bega to buy some fertiliser for my tomatoes." He removed his hat and bashed it against his leg, to remove the dust and make it more respectable.

"Growing tomatoes? If you want a hand, I'm good with tomatoes. Better than tobacco," Eric giggled. Jonathan Bell blinked. The police were still making enquiries.

"That's good to know, mate. I'm afraid I must get to the farm supply shop. It's only open two hours on Sunday." He held his hand out to Lillian. "Thank you for coming and for the cake."

Lillian felt his apprehension. There was something not quite right. She shook his hand and smiled.

"Well, I just wanted to let you know how grateful we are for your support and for helping Eric with his driver's licence. I would have phoned but I don't have your number. We won't keep you any longer. Come on Eric, you can catch up with Mr Bell at the club sometime." She pulled on the sleeve of Eric's shirt, urging him towards the car.

"Cheerio, Smokey. See you at the club," Eric called, turning to leave. Smokey smiled and lifted his hat in response. Splinter's head came up. She put her hand up to stop her parents and planted herself in front of Jonathan Bell.

"You're Smokey? The man who sent my father to Wollongong in a stolen ute?" Her cheeks flushed with anger. Lillian looked from Splinter to the startled man holding a cake tin and recalled Eric calling him Smokey when they first met outside George the butcher's.

Jonathan cringed under Splinter's stare. "Look, I'm sorry, it was a big mistake. I was trying to help some mates who were affected by the war. Eric wanted his licence back and …" He opened his hands in apology.

"He's a good bloke," Eric said.

"A good bloke!" Splinter exploded. "He got you arrested. I was questioned by the police. I couldn't let you out of my sight until Mum came home. He is a criminal. I'll have to tell the police."

"Don't go to the police, please. I'm truly sorry. I didn't mean all this to happen."

"The police took my licence. Smokey gave me tobacco. You wouldn't buy me any tobacco," Eric said, agitated.

"He gave you marijuana, Dad."

"I only gave him a small amount as a thank you for helping me grow the plants," Smokey protested.

Lillian put her hand on Splinter's arm. "You're saying Eric helped you grow marijuana?"

Smokey looked at the ground. "The plants were dying. Eric revived them for me."

"You made him drive a stolen car." Splinter's voice rose to a squeal.

"Eric found it in the bush, and I fixed it up for him. If I hadn't forgotten to get it registered, he wouldn't have been caught." Seeing the outrage on Splinter's face, he threw his hands in the air. "I know I was wrong but what's the point in starting another trial?"

"My father was put in gaol. We were in *The Sydney Morning Herald* and on the news. The whole town lived off the scandal for weeks and then I was left to supervise my father's every move. My mother had to give up her holiday in Africa and you got away scot free. That's the point." She pushed her finger into his chest. "It's not bloody right."

Lillian put her hand on her daughter's arm. "I think we should go home and discuss our options while Mr Bell thinks about what action he should take." Foremost in Lillian's mind was that Eric had helped grow the marijuana and they had to think about the consequences of that.

"Please, let me know what you intend to do before you contact the police. I don't think I would survive being in gaol after Vietnam." He started to shake. Lillian saw the haunted look in his eyes, it wasn't for their benefit.

"We can arrange a meeting and I'll tell you what we decide. Come on, Eric." Lillian prodded him in the direction of the car.

"I want to stay with Smokey. I can sleep on the couch." Ignoring Eric, she motioned to Splinter to help her get him in the car. Eric began to struggle.

Smokey took his arm. "Another time, mate. I'll call by tomorrow and we'll finish our talk." He closed the car door and watched them drive off.

The day darkened for Smokey as he walked towards his front door. He was a tunnel rat again, smelling his own fear as he squeezed down a dark hole armed with a pistol, knife, and flashlight, his hand feeling along the wall for boobytraps, scorpions, snakes, not knowing what was waiting for him, while above him artillery pounded. He fished in his pocket and pulled out a joint, lighting it with shaking hands.

God, Lillian thought. What had she come back home to? Hardly off the ship and having to deal with this. Being in Africa with Maureen had been wonderful, free. On the ship coming home she'd had time to think about her life. Promised herself that she wouldn't allow anything to rob her of her independence again yet here she was, bound by her conscience to Eric, the bane of her life.

"He can't get away with this, Mum. You weren't here to know what I had to go through."

"I know, pet, but let's not be hasty. Dad did help him grow the marijuana." Her mind went to food. Tomorrow she would see if her grocer had a good curry powder, turmeric, coriander, fenugreek, chilli, and the other spices she had enjoyed in Africa. She would also buy spaghetti, oregano, and basil. Tonight would be the last time she would cater to Eric's tastes. He could like it or lump it.

"Why don't you sit on the verandah with your newspaper, Eric? It's lovely out there. I'll bring you a cup of tea and a slice of cake." She winked at Splinter. Once she got rid of him, they could talk.

After Splinter left, Lillian chopped up onion, the left-over lamb roast, left-over vegetables, added mashed potatoes and mixed in an egg. She made it into patties and rolled them in breadcrumbs ready to fry. Then she sat down with a glass of brandy to think what she should do about Jonathan Bell.

The following morning there was a knock at Lillian's front door. She opened it to the gaunt face of Jonathan Bell.

"Hello, Lillian." Solemn faced, Lillian ushered him in. He followed her past the goat heads on either side of the hall archway and down the hall into the lounge room. She seated him near a large brick fireplace and took the armchair opposite him. He hunched forward, aware his future lay in this woman's hands. They spoke for an hour and then Lillian put her cards on the table.

"I agree with my daughter that you shouldn't get off scot free, so I have a proposition for you."

"I haven't any money, only an army pension which isn't much," Jonathan said, anxious.

"I don't want money. What I would like is you to have Eric on weekends, to give me a break. He tells me he has stayed overnight at your place sometimes?" Jonathan's shoulders whipped back, flummoxed by the request. He sought an answer from the empty fireplace, the quince tree outside the window and the compost imbedded under his nails. He could do with some help tending the plants he was relocating further into the bush. He could give it a try for a couple of weekends until everything had settled down and then find excuses not to have Eric, like say friends are visiting.

"He'd have to sleep on the couch, and I only have one spare blanket." Lillian smiled.

"I have plenty of blankets, I'm sure we can make him comfortable." Jonathan Bell, alias Smokey, was a godsend.

15

Film Nights

Dorcas and George came to tell Maureen the bad news together. They stood with downcast eyes.

"Gele is gone, Madam. She was missing her Durban," Dorcas said.

"But I haven't paid her."

"It is good, Madam, she ate your food. I can do the housework and see to the children. You don't need another girl. George will watch them outside." Dorcas glared at George. He nodded his capabilities.

Disappointed Gele was gone and suspicious of the reason why, Maureen knew there was nothing she could do about it. Despite her misgivings, she gave in to keep the peace. Weeks later when she returned from work, she wished she had employed another nanny.

"God! Where are they?" Maureen shouted at Dorcas.

Dorcas wrung her hands. "We have searched everywhere, Madam." She went into a high-pitched wail. George swept his arms wide to indicate their five acres.

"Everywhere, Madam."

Maureen tore at her memory for some clue as to where the children might have gone. She felt sick. Then she remembered Liam telling her about frogs. They didn't have a pond or a place for frogs, so where had he seen or heard them? Why hadn't she listened and asked him about them?

"We must look for a place where there's water. You go that way, Dorcas, and George go to the neighbours up the road." They split up to search. Terror in her heart, Maureen climbed the wire fence into the plot next door and made her way through a field of pink and white cosmos, oblivious to the beauty. Then she heard a child's voice.

"Throw the stone Gerard. There's a froggy down there." She could have collapsed with relief. Maureen was about to call out when instinct warned her not to. She crept forward, parting the grass. Gerard was leaning over a hole the circumference of a tank with a stone in his hand and standing next to him was Liam. Maureen reached out and pulled her children back into her arms. They squealed with fright. She held them firmly and peered into the hole. It was a cement well that went down ten feet before reaching water. A flash of heat went through her body. If she or even Pete fell in, they wouldn't be able to get out, and only if there was someone within earshot who could fetch a rope. She sucked in a lungful of air, all the terrible things that could happen to her children flashing through her mind. Shaking, she gripped their hands and dragged the two small boys through the cosmos. Her fear turned to anger.

"There's a baddie down there, a Tokoloshe." Liam's legs moved faster – he knew what that was, Dorcas and George were always threatening him with the Tokoloshe gremlin. "You are

120

naughty boys. Never, never come here again. Do you hear me?" She stopped and slapped Liam's bare bum hard, leaving a red handprint on his white skin, then hoisted Gerard up onto her hip by his arm. She marched up the road with Liam in front, at a run.

"That well has to be closed. Get some tin and rocks and cover it until the boss can seal it off properly," she told George. It was time to collect Henry from school and she wasn't going to leave Liam and Gerard at home. She bundled them into the car and Maureen gave Dorcas her ultimatum.

"Dorcas, you find me a nanny, or I will, and I won't care what tribe she is from. Do you hear me?"

Dorcas lowered her eyes. "Yes, Madam."

When Evelina started work the next day, at first Maureen relaxed.

But then Maureen came home early to discover Gerard standing in the toilet bowl playing with the flusher, his legs white and wrinkled.

"I know he is safe there and he likes playing with water, Madam," Evelina said in her defence.

Gerard was weaned from the toilet bowl and Evelina given another chance. And then Maureen discovered the damage on her new silver high heels and on further investigation of her wardrobe, her clothes smelt of sweat and one dress, blue silk and prized, had a stain down the front. Evelina was her dress size, George and Dorcas, not. There were tears and denials, but Maureen fired her. She had only lasted three weeks.

Having servants was far more complicated than Maureen had imagined, and Pete was no help in that department. He'd just raise his eyebrows, go to work and tinker with his cars. It was the same with money – he never even looked at a bank statement. She paid the bills and saved what she could. And now it was a toss-up whether to hire another nanny or buy a new bed. Theirs had come with them from Mirabelle Fosdick's place and didn't accommodate a growing family, especially in the mornings.

"Watch where you're putting your foot," Pete yelled, hand over his testicles as Liam leaped over him to squeeze in between his parents. A fight broke out between Henry and Liam.

"We need a bigger bed," Pete moaned as he hoisted the boys off the double bed.

"Joey works for a bed manufacturer, I'll call her."

"I want a king size," Pete said excited.

"It will cost a fortune, we'll never get to Australia," Maureen groaned. Pete's hand sought hers under the blanket.

"Yes, we will. I promise."

After breakfast, Maureen called Joey. Yes! She could do them a deal with a reject king size that had been scuffed during storage, but Maureen would have to come to the factory to view it. A good excuse for them to catch up without Des around.

On approaching Joey's factory, Maureen's interest tweaked when she noticed the 'Films for Hire' store further down the road. She missed going to see a good film. The city was a distance away, too far to bother going to a theatre, and most of the films had fallen between the censor's scissors to the point they were hardly worth seeing. Also, under Apartheid, any films with black actors were banned. Even the film *Black Beauty* was banned just because of its name. Maureen wanted to see the film her aunt had raved over, *Guess Who's Coming to Dinner* with Sidney Poitier, but that would have to remain a dream until they went to Australia for a holiday. Unless she could hire it? She would visit the store after the mattress factory.

The thrill of seeing each other showed on their faces. Maureen wanted to give Joey a hug and kiss, but Joey flicked her eyes towards the manager's office. As far as the management was concerned, Maureen was just another customer and Joey the sales lady. Joey didn't want to let her boss know she'd tipped her friend off to the reject possibility. Rejects were usually offered to the black workers first.

Out of habit, Maureen scanned Joey's face for bruises. There were none she could see, but it concerned her how thin Joey was. She looked haggard. Once they were in the back of the factory, Maureen gave Joey's arm a squeeze.

"I've missed you and Henry's missed Colin. Why don't we organise an outing with the boys during the school holidays, take them to the Snake Park or somewhere?"

There was a pause before Joey answered. "Colin's off to school camp during the holidays." She looked past Maureen, "I'm coping for the moment but not sure how long I'll be able to keep this job. Des is working as a sales rep for a company nearby and he keeps coming in all the time and my boss has spoken to me about it, wants me to tell him he's taking up too much of my time."

Maureen pulled a face, wishing Des to hell. She wanted to see more of Joey. The only contact they'd had since her move was on the telephone and she had done all the calling. Joey always sounded guarded on the phone and Maureen assumed Des stayed within earshot.

"Pete and I are thinking of starting a home movie club if you and Des want to come?" The idea had just popped into Maureen's head.

Joey's face brightened. "That's a great idea, I would love to come."

"There's a film hire place down the road I'm going to check out before I go home."

Joeys' lips pursed. "I won't say anything to Des. Phone me at

123

home and speak to Des so he doesn't think we've talked about it."

A grunt escaped Maureen. How she would love to shake some sense into her friend. Joey wouldn't fart unless Des gave her permission. "We all miss you, Joey."

"Me too. If you like the mattress, I could arrange to come with the driver on the delivery. He's new so I can tell my boss I need to show him the way, then we can have a cup of tea and a gasbag." Joey grinned, eyes sparkling. They walked between a pile of stacked mattresses and Joey stopped, pointing to one that was set apart from the others. "That's it. There's hardly anything wrong with it."

Maureen threw herself onto the king-sized Sealy Posturepedic and bounced around. The bed was solid under her, no more rolling into Pete every time he turned over and plenty of room for the kids. "Pete will love this. Where do I pay?"

She followed Joey to the cashier and paid for the mattress. Joey walked her to the door, and they squeezed hands.

"Good luck with the film shop, and don't forget to phone me," Joey said.

The films on display in the shop were disappointing, mostly Disney or outdated. Maureen was about to leave when the fellow behind the counter walked over.

"Anything I can help you with, Miss?"

Maureen looked around to see if anyone was near them. "I was wondering if you had *Guess Who's Coming to Dinner?*" She said, trying to look angelic. The fellow put his hands in his pockets and scrutinised Maureen, then he walked over to the children's section and removed *Bambi* from the shelf. Hadn't he heard what she'd asked for? She frowned and he winked at her.

"I think you'll enjoy this one." He opened the cover and tapped his finger on the reel. A sticker read *Guess Who's Coming to Dinner.* The penny dropped; Maureen smiled.

"I'm sure the kids will love it. How much do you charge?"

"This one is fifteen rand for one night with the projector." It was expensive.

"I won't take it today because my husband will need instructions on how to use the projector." The fellow put *Bambi* back on the shelf.

"I will need your ID, and I'm open weekends. We have a good supply of the latest children's films, so you won't be disappointed." Another wink.

Maureen left the film hire shop in a state of excitement. The first thing she did when she got home was phone Joey. Des answered.

"Hello, Des, you live too far away, we miss you." His response was non-committal and she heard him call out to Joey. Undaunted, Maureen prattled on.

"Before you hand me over to Joey, I want tell you about a film club Pete and I are starting," she kept her voice light and cheerful. "It's once a week, Friday nights. Our first film is *Guess Who's Coming to Dinner* with Sidney Poitier. I'm only asking the people I can trust as the film has a black actor and of course it's banned, but I thought it would be fun and wondered if you and Joey are interested in coming?"

"Really?" He sounded surprised. "I'll see what we have planned, but that sounds interesting." Maureen listened to a mumble of voices in the distance and then Joey came to the phone.

"Hello, Maureen, what a nice surprise. Des has just told me about your film night. We would love to come but it depends on how late Des has to work so he said I can give you a call and let you know tomorrow." They discussed all the things they'd talked about at Joey's work so Des wouldn't know she'd been to the factory, promised to organise a get together for the children and sent each other kisses then hung up.

Two Fridays later, Pete borrowed chairs from the Aero Club and lined them up in the lounge. Paintings were moved off the large white wall that was to serve as the film screen and the projector was placed at the back of the room on a plinth.

The guests arrived, carrying their beers and chips, with promises to keep the club a secret. Des and Joey poked their heads through the door just as Pete loaded the first reel. Maureen hugged and kissed Des, inwardly recoiling, then kissed Joey, giving her their secret hand squeeze, and felt relieved when it was returned. Under strict orders from Maureen, Pete waved his hand at Des in greeting and turned back to the projector.

The film was a big hit. Des and Joey left before the beer flowed and the heated discussion started about the Immorality Act, brought on by *Guess Who's Coming to Dinner*. Maureen had never heard of the Immorality Act, but learned the act prohibited any liaison between a black man and a white woman. Gaol time was the consequence for both parties if caught breaking the law. Enlightened, Maureen decided never to mention the black boyfriend she'd had in Australia to any of her South African friends, especially when her morals had already been deemed questionable, having been an unmarried mother.

The club was the highlight of every attendee's week. As word leaked out, sometimes up to twenty people came. Everyone put in a rand to cover the cost of the film, but nobody put in for the brandy they sneaked from Pete's liquor cabinet. That irked Maureen. They didn't make money from film nights. In fact, it cost them to collect and deliver the film every week. Maureen pasted a notice on the liquor cabinet.

Please bring your own grog and don't drink Pete's!

All was going well until they received a visit from some unwanted guests. Pete was changing the reel when the police made their entrance. The local chemist and real estate agent disappeared through the back door and slid off to their cars, scared that if their names were exposed, it wouldn't look good for their businesses.

"Run the film," one of the police officers ordered, while helping himself to a bowl of potato chips.

Pete's face was impassive. "It's pretty boring," he said with a shrug.

"You will do it from the beginning!

"I'll have to rewind the first two reels. It could take a while," Pete said.

The police conferred in Afrikaans. "Put on the one you was going to watch," he said in a heavy accent. The final reel of *The Poseidon Adventure* came on. There was another discussion between the two police. This film hadn't breached the censors. Pete waited.

"It's enough," the one in charge said. "We will tell our informant there is nothing illegal, but we will be watching you." He nodded to Maureen, and they left the house.

"Bloody cops," Pete said, laughing. "He was telling the other cop he had already seen it and he didn't want to watch it again, that's why they decided to leave." Pete turned to the remaining friends that hadn't scuttled off. "I think that's the last of our film nights, fellas."

After their guests had gone, Pete and Maureen discussed who could have informed on them to the police. "It couldn't be anyone who comes here because they would be fined for attending," Pete said, frowning. "Anyway, we'd better keep our heads down and out of trouble in case they decide to check my worker's passes. We can't afford any fines."

16

Ephraim's Beating

They were in bed reading when Dorcas rushed into their bedroom, eyes wild, hands flapping.

"Boss, you must come quick, the neighbour is killing Ephraim!" Dorcas began to whimper and tear at her hair. Ephraim was her boyfriend and he worked for Pete at the airport.

"What the bloody hell?" Pete said, dropping his book.

Maureen jumped out of bed. "Let's wait for the boss in the kitchen while he gets dressed."

A minute later Pete was dressed and joined them in the kitchen. Dorcas began to babble.

"Ephraim was walking up the road. He was coming to see me. The two men next door came out of their house and started punching Ephraim. The dog bit him. They dragged him into the house. The neighbour's gardener saw it all and he ran to tell me. He said Ephraim was screaming inside the house." She clutched

Pete's hand. "Please Boss, you must go to Ephraim now," Dorcas choked, through tears.

"Fetch George, Dorcas. I want him to come with me."

"I'm here, Boss," George called from the doorway. He had followed Dorcas to the house.

"Get in the car," Pete said. Pete drove into the neighbour's driveway. "Stay in the car, George." Pete wanted a witness if anything went wrong. He got out of the car leaving the motor running and headlights on as two white men came out of the house dragging Ephraim's inert body between them. A slathering bull mastiff followed.

"What's going on here?" Pete called out. That's my boy you've got there."

The neighbour's chin jutted. "Thijs de Jong is my name and you is?"

"Your neighbour." Pete didn't want his name on the bastard's lips.

"Your kaffir is drunk. He was calling us bad names when he was passing my place. I ask him where he was going and he smart-mouthed me, man. We're taking him to the cops."

Pete stepped closer. He was a big man. The security dog growled.

In the light from the headlights, Pete could make out Ephraim's face. He was unrecognisable, smashed and bloody. His shirt hung in tatters exposing his chest and arms covered in blood. One leg of his pants was ripped open, and blood poured from wounds where the security dog had attacked him.

"You've beaten him senseless, you bastards. I'm going to follow you to the police station." Pete waited for them to close the back door of their car on Ephraim and get in. He reversed out. Then followed them down the dirt road to the main highway and had to stop at the intersection for an oncoming car, losing sight of them. When he arrived at the police station, Pete looked for his neighbour's car. It wasn't in the parking lot and there was no sign of Ephraim when he went into the station to make a report. The policeman on duty was the same one who had barged into his house on film night. He hadn't seen the neighbour or Ephraim. Pete made a statement.

"Perhaps they caught your boy stealing?" the officer said, not wanting to waste his time filling out a report on a kaffir.

"No, a boy saw it happen and I want them charged."

"I have to see the injured black first. He has to make the charge, not you." He put his pen down. "I suggest you goes home and has a sleep and thinks about it. Come back tomorrow. Maybe we hear from the neighbour then, hey?"

Pete ground his teeth and slammed the door as he left the station. On the drive home his headlights picked up what looked like a body lying on the side of the road. He pulled over and went to look. Ephraim lay in the gutter groaning.

"George, it's Ephraim, come and help me get him in the car." Between them they carried Ephraim to the car and lay him on the back seat. "Those fucking bastards," Pete stamped on the accelerator and sped to the nearest hospital. He screeched to a stop at the entrance, got out and with the help of George lifted Ephraim from the car. They carried him up the steps, through the hospital doors and placed him in a chair by the reception desk. An attendant came over and looked at Ephraim.

"You can't bring him here. This hospital is for whites only. He has to go to Baragwaneth hospital." Baragwaneth was on the other side of Johannesburg.

"He's nearly dead! He needs attention now. It will take an hour to get to the other hospital," Pete shouted.

A doctor came over and knelt next to Ephraim, lifted his eyelids, and listening to his heart with a stethoscope. He looked at Pete. "I'll get an ambulance to take him across town. I'm sorry," he said, "there's a lot of things that have to change in this country."

He spoke to the attendant and a stretcher materialised. Ephraim was loaded on. An ambulance arrived; it was a 'whites only' ambulance. Pete waited until Ephraim was inside the ambulance before he went back to his car. He'd go to the police in the morning, speak to the highest copper and report his neighbours.

Maureen gave Dorcas the day off so she could let Ephraim's family know what had happened to him and Pete paid his neighbour a call before going to the police.

The neighbour cracked his door and kept the chain on when he saw who his visitor was.

"You dumped my boy on the road."

"We was on our way to the police and the boy wanted to get out of the car. He said he was good so we let him go. Maybe a car hit him?" The neighbour shrugged at Pete.

"He couldn't get out of your car. He couldn't fucking walk! He was half dead. I found him on the side of the road where you dumped him, and I drove him to the hospital. I'm going to lay charges against you bastards."

"You do that, man. I've gotta get back to training my security dogs. Never know when you need them. Say, if you want a security dog, I got a good one here." The neighbour shut the door in Pete's face.

Pete made his report and waited for Ephraim's recovery. When he was eventually discharged six weeks later, he walked with a limp as the dog had torn the muscle from his thigh. He was left with a head injury from being beaten on the head with shamboks – African clubs – that caused him to have black-outs.

Ephraim showed Pete his wounds. There were holes in his arms, legs, and buttocks. The flesh on his side had been stitched from under his arm to his waist. His injuries made Pete sick to

131

his stomach. He took Ephraim to the police to sign a statement. Ephraim had been interviewed in hospital after Pete had laid the assault charge, but he was asked to tell his story again in the hope his brain damage had affected his memory.

"I was coming to see my girlfriend," Ephraim said. "This big dog came out of the house I was passing. It growled and bared its teeth. It was going to bite me." Sweat beaded on Ephraim's face and his body began to shake. "I yelled for the dog's boss. He and another boss came out and started hitting and kicking me. They dragged me into the house. They put me in a room, beat me with shamboks and set the dog on me. It tore my body. It was too much pain, Boss. Everything went dead and I can't remember more."

The policeman looked at Ephraim with troubled eyes. "Sign the statement," he said.

It was eight months before it came to court and the court case was held in the town of Krugersdorp, one and a half hour's drive away.

"The bastards are making it difficult, hoping I won't turn up," Pete told Maureen.

"You will go, won't you Pete?"

Pete's jaw came forward. "I'm not going to let those bastards get away with it."

Maureen put her hand on his arm, proud of him.

At the trial, the defence lawyer told the judge that Pete had a vendetta against his client, and that was the reason Pete was pursuing the case. Pete denied the accusation and told them he'd never met his neighbour before Ephraim's beating. When the neighbour was examined, he couldn't name Pete's wife and didn't know how many children they had, proving Pete to be correct.

Outside the courtroom, after the hearing, Pete caught up with his neighbour. "If I see your dog outside your gate, I will shoot it. And if I see you near my property or hear you've threatened any of my workers, I will beat your brains in, you scum."

The neighbour paled. He put his hands up. "Hey, man I didn't know he was your boy."

"I'd report you if I saw you do that to anyone," Pete said through clenched teeth.

When he arrived home after the court case, Pete stormed into his house. "You won't bloody believe it," he said to Maureen, incensed. "The bastard only got a twenty-five rand fine."

In the morning, Dorcas stood in front of Pete. "Thank you, Boss. I know you are disappointed with the fine. But they were made guilty and that's very good for us. Those neighbours are moving, Boss. They can't get workers." Dorcas gave a grim smile. There were other ways to get justice.

17

George's Story

Their new neighbours were from Czechoslovakia and they had an eight-year-old daughter, Marcella. She stood on the side of the road with a dog the size of a small pony and waved at the boys as Maureen passed her in the car. Maureen stopped the car and wound the window down.

"Tell your mother you can come to our place and play if she would like to bring you." Marcella ran off to her house and Maureen continued up the road.

"We don't want to play with girls," Henry grumbled.

"Don't be mean. Dorcas told me they only have one child so she must be lonely."

"I hope they're not another bunch of your oddballs," Pete said, when she mentioned the new couple and the child with the great dane dog.

The child arrived seated on the back of her dog. The dog

baulked at the cattle grid in the entrance and the child slid to the ground and led it across the grid, then remounted. Awed, the boys ran to meet her.

"Her name is Lola," she said patting the dog's head. "My name is Marcella." She was tall for her age. The dog's head was level with Gerard's. She sniffed Liam and sponged his face with a tongue the size of Pete's shoe.

Henry, Liam and Gerard led her around the back of the house where George was chipping away at some weeds. Sighting the dog, he squealed, dropped the spade and ran. The children laughed.

"It's all right, George, she won't bite," Liam called after the fleeing figure. Maureen came out to see what was going on. Marcella looked up at her, one hand on the dog's head. Maureen's eyes moved past the little girl, expecting to see her mother.

"Did you come on your own?" She wouldn't let her children walk the lonely road between their houses without supervision. There was a shebeen, an illegal bar, that sold native home brew from a caravan hidden in the trees and a lot of drunks hung around.

"No. Lola is with me." The dog gave a giant woof. No one would go near that, Maureen decided. Clever parents.

After two hours playing in the tree house, Marcella's mother arrived to fetch her. She was blonde and attractive, and almost six feet tall. The singlet she wore showed her square shoulders and muscular arms. Maureen offered her a coffee.

"No. We are going out; Marcella must come home now." She spoke with a heavy accent. She said something in Czech to her daughter and Marcella spoke to the dog. It sat and she climbed onto its back. The mother raised a large hand in farewell and Lola trotted off with Marcella, her mother striding behind.

Pete stood with his hands in his pockets, staring after them. "Looks like oddballs."

"Oddballs don't beat up black people," Maureen said.

"I wish we had a sister," Liam said admiringly.

Maureen knew from her sore breasts she was pregnant; it was always her first sign. It wasn't like they were sex fiends. Pete was eight years older than Maureen and sometimes months passed without having sex. They had discussed his problem and he'd gone to the doctor. All normal was the report. The slump happens to a lot of men in their late thirties, the doctor told them. It was a pity he hadn't stayed slumped, Maureen thought, seeing their trip to Australia move further into an uncertain future.

A week earlier, Maureen had taken the three boys shopping when a drunken ex-worker of Pete's leant into her car window. He had a knife and feigned a stab at the kids on the back seat, then looked at her and rubbed his thumb down the blade. Although he had smiled, there was something beneath the surface that chilled Maureen's blood and had left her with a constant feeling of unease. They needed to save more money.

"It's time we fixed up the flat and rented it out," Maureen said after breaking the news of her pregnancy. Pete nodded. Four bloody kids, he might move into the flat himself.

The following weekend the flat was started. George mixed the cement while Pete plastered the rough brick wall.

"You know, Boss, this working hard is not so good. I know we can make money not working so hard," George said.

Pete frowned. "What do you mean?"

"Last night my father came to me in a dream. He tell me I can trust you, Boss. When I was Little Boss Henry's age, my father make me climb the cliffs at the dam to look for Dassie piss. It is good medicine. My father was a witch doctor. That place was my homeland. Now there is a sailing club there."

"You mean Hartbeespoort Dam?"

"Yes, Boss. It is the one." George stopped mixing and sat on his haunches. "When I'm looking, I find gap in rocks, just fit me, Boss. I think lots of Dassies would piss in that hole. So, I slide inside. It is big cave. Then I see, old tin buckets and jars with lids on top. Inside these buckets are coins, Boss. Full up. They have old man Kruger's head on them. The jars have jewellery. I take some coins to show my father. He tells me to take one coin to Greek trading store to see what it buys but tells me not to tell white man where I find it. I must tell him my father give to me. I did this. The white boss says I can pick what I want in his shop. I buy tobacco and lots of sweets. When I don't say where I get the coin, he follows me home.

"My father tells the shop man he digs the coin up in our yard because he wants to grow mealies. He pay my father to dig more yard. My father dig but he knows there's nothing. It makes the boss angry and he wants his money back. Now my father tell me never go back for coins. That black mans are not allowed to be rich. That white man will steal his coins. My father mark place with two iron pegs and then he put Juju on place so no people go there. I never go back, but now my father dead and comes to me in a dream and say I should look for coins. That I can tell you so you can drive me there and you help me find it. He said you would share with me. You look after Ephraim, Boss. I know you trusting." George sat back on his haunches.

Pete stared at George, amazed. Could this be true? "All right, George, next weekend we take Madam and the kids, and you can show me."

"We still fixing house, Boss?" George's hands were sore from mixing cement.

"Yep, but get a stick and stir, man, don't use your bloody hands!"

In bed, Pete told Maureen George's story.

"You believe him?"

"I do. Why would he make up something like that?"

"Because he's lazy? He has ruined the irrigation system that serves the vegetable garden and has lost the net that covers the fig trees to keep the bats out. The pool is full of gunk, the chooks are missing, all in all he is a pretty useless gardener." On the other hand, Maureen thought, George was too smoked on dagga to make up a story like that; he wouldn't have the imagination. "There's no harm in having a look. If we find something, we could afford our holiday in Australia," she said.

Sunday was a beautiful day, perfect for a drive to the dam. Pete packed a fishing rod and Maureen packed a picnic lunch, bathers, and towels for the children. George sat in the back of the car with Henry and Liam while Gerard sat on Maureen's knee in the front. Half an hour into their drive and every window in the car wound down with heads hanging out of the windows. George's feet smelt like fresh cow manure. No one mentioned it to him. Maureen would encourage him to paddle in the dam and when they were home, she'd check Pete's shoes for an old pair so George could throw his shoes away.

Maureen found a sandy spot by the water to spend the day. The children played in the dam while Pete and George went looking for the cave. The bush was dense, baboons cavorted in the tops of trees. Yachts sailed by and people waved to the kids. It was restful and lovely. The men returned, faces thoughtful.

"The cave entrance has shifted from the blasting when the dam was extended. There's a gap that you can only get your hand in. We'll need to dig. It's quarter way down the cliff face, and it's sheer, probably thirty feet above the rocks. We need ropes."

"It's there, Madam," George said, with a lot of serious nodding. "The boss doesn't like to climb down, so I go."

Pete looked at the ground. "I don't like heights."

Maureen's eyebrows raised; she hadn't known that.

"It's why I didn't complete my flying licence," he explained.

Back at their house, Maureen and Pete had a discussion. "If you didn't go down the cliff, Pete, how do you know George isn't stringing us along, so you'll give him time off to go and look? I mean we left him there so he could visit his family and he won't be back for two days?" Maureen had listened to Dorcas ratting on George for a year and after his mother's two funerals, she didn't trust him. An image of the cliffs she used to climb in Eden as a child came to mind.

"I could climb down. You could make a rope ladder and stay at the top to make sure I don't fall or get wedged," Maureen said.

Pete looked at her, thoughtful. "As an extra precaution I could put a rope around your waist and hold the other end while you climb down."

"We'll leave the kids with Dorcas and go next Saturday."

Pete started making the rope ladder in his hangar.

18

A Lost Ring

The rope ladder was secured to a big rock and dropped over the side of the cliff. After checking the knot on the rope around Maureen's waist he walked the other end around a tree before looping it around his own waist.

"Are you sure about this?"

Of course she was sure. If Pete couldn't go down the cliff she would. Gold fever was a great incentive and a trip to Australia another one. The rope tightened around Maureen's waist as Pete lowered her over the side. She gripped the sides of the rope ladder and felt for the first rung. Rung by rung she descended, never looking at the rocks beneath. The rope around her waist slid up and tightened under her breasts.

"Pete, I'm hanging by my tits, loosen the bloody rope, I'm nearly there." Pete lay on his stomach and, foot by foot, worked the rope over the side of the cliff. The ladder just reached the ledge where the cave was supposed to be situated. Maureen's feet connected with solid ground. She looked around. The ledge was wide with no risk of falling over the edge.

"Touchdown!" she yelled. "Loosen the rope more so I can have a look around." The rope slackened and she twisted around to observe the view. Hills surrounded the dam. The water was a deep blue with a rippling surface. Immediately across from her was the yacht club and the bare cliff face she had climbed down was in full view of any passing boat. They would need to have a good story if anyone asked what they were doing.

There was plenty of room to sit. Stepping out of the rope noose, she inspected the crevice. It was her height and a bit more than her handspan wide. Maybe a small child could squeeze in sidewards once the silt was removed from the gap, but it would be risky. She dug into the hard dry earth lodged in the crevice with a trowel. Half an hour of digging got her a hole the length of the trowel. It was a job for a pick and jackhammer to break the rock and widen the gap. She stepped into the rope, pulling it up to her waist and called out to Pete. The rope tightened and she started up the ladder.

On the way out of the bush, Pete noticed dug out gullies that seemed man-made. He went over for a closer inspection. Maureen followed.

"You know what these are? They're trenches, must be from the Boer War. Could be some old bullet casings around." His eyes scanned the ground. War was Pete's thing; he had a library full of war books and the biographies of the world leaders at the time – he was fascinated by war history. "I'll look this area up."

Pete mentioned the trenches to an Afrikaans friend at work and learned about the legend. During the Second Boer War, when the British troops reached Pretoria, the Boer farmers in the area gathered their valuables and gave them to the Boer army to hide. The army was wiped out by the British, and the valuables never found. Pete wondered if the stash in the cave was hidden by the Boer army.

Pete and George went to the dam as often as they could until Pete started getting a lot of freelance work spray painting small aircraft on weekends and Maureen had to go with George.

She parked the car. They got out and were heading for the bush when a police car pulled up. Maureen didn't take any notice and then a voice shouted.

"Hey, Lady. Where are you going?" She turned; George kept walking. "Hey, you boy, I want to talk to you. Come here." Her heart rate went up. Why were they being stopped? Then she clicked. She was a white woman going into the bush with a black man – it was illegal. Her mind raced.

"Don't say anything, let me talk to him, George." She trotted back with George lagging. "Hello, Officer." He was young, not much taller than her. His eyes swept her. She noted his appreciation. He squared his shoulders and drew himself up.

"If, you'll excuse me, Lady, I would like to know where you are going with this black man?" A chill went up Maureen's spine, she forced a smile.

"We've come to find a ring I lost yesterday. I was here with my family for a picnic, and we went for a hike in the bush and I lost my engagement ring. My husband is working so I've brought our gardener to help me find it." She gave him big innocent eyes, hoping he couldn't see the throb of her heart in her throat. Cold eyes turned on George.

"Show me your pass, Boy." George put his hand up to his shirt pocket.

"It's in the car with my jacket, Boss."

The officer inclined his head towards the car park for George to fetch it. Maureen pulled the car keys from the pocket of her jeans.

"Bring my handbag while you're there, George," she might

need ID. Her voice was demanding for the benefit of the policeman. A white lady wouldn't fetch anything if she had a servant to do it for her, she reckoned.

"Yes, Madam," he said, submissively, which was unlike George. He looked scared to death but kept his eyes down, holding out one hand, clasping his wrist with the other. She dropped the car keys into his open palm.

"Officer, where should I report my lost ring in case somebody finds it? At the yacht club or nearest police station?" She gave him a flirty smile, drawing his attention away from George. Her five-month pregnancy was hidden under her loose top and jeans. The policeman blushed.

"You can give me a description and I can make a note at the station."

"Thank you. I only have an hour to look for it." She glanced at her wristwatch and frowned. "It's a single diamond in a claw setting. Not a very big diamond." She laughed. "You won't believe it, but my husband gave it to his first fiancé before I came along." The policeman rolled his eyes and grinned. It was true and she had hardly worn the thing. She preferred Australian opals to diamonds, but they were married before he gave her his ex's engagement ring. George returned with her bag and stood in her shadow.

"I hope you find your ring, Lady."

"We didn't go far but I doubt I'll find it in this bush." He tipped his cap and forgetting George's pass, walked to the police car. Maureen's body sagged.

"Come on, George, we haven't got all day," she said loud enough for the officer to hear. They went towards the bush checking the ground as they walked, listening for the police car to move off. When it did, Maureen stopped.

"Shit, that was a close one. I'm not climbing down the cliff ladder in case someone at the yacht club sees me, or the policeman when he drives back over the bridge." They had had a lucky escape. "We'll have to forget today. Did you have your pass with you George?" He shook his head.

"The boss has it to make new, Madam." They waited in the car for an hour before leaving.

There weren't any further excursions to the dam. The baby was nearly due and Maureen was still working. She had a few false contractions, but nothing had come of them, so she dosed up with castor oil to bring on the birth. There were more contractions that petered out. At her next doctor's appointment, she told him about the castor oil. He frowned.

"I wouldn't have had contractions to start with if I'm not ready to pop," she argued.

"If you're going to do that then we may as well bring on the birth and induce you. I'll book a bed at the hospital."

The inducement was cruel. The severity of the contractions was far worse than her other births and from the time they started were two minutes apart. Pete stayed with her throughout the birth, his face sheet-white and his eyes terrified orbs. It was the first birth he had attended.

"You're not getting pregnant again. I can't stand the pain," he said. The doctor left while the baby was being cleaned up. Maureen waited to be handed her child but instead a nurse came to her with empty arms.

"There are complications with the baby. Would you give permission for another doctor to attend to him since your doctor has left?" Suddenly Maureen became aware of the extra nurses in her ward and no crying baby. Every nerve in her body tingled. Pete looked at her, confused.

"Get whatever doctor you need," Maureen said, terrified. An incubator arrived in the room and the baby was wheeled out. A nurse came over and took her hand.

"The baby is in the best care," she said. "Our top paediatrician was attending a patient next door and he is looking after your son. He weighs seven pounds two ounces, that's a good size," she patted Maureen's hand. "We will take you to a ward where you can get some sleep. Tomorrow everything will be better." Exhausted and encouraged by the nurse, Maureen managed to sleep.

The next day there was still no baby. She was desperate to see him. The doctor visited and reported the baby's progress. He had hyaline membrane disease, resulting from a premature birth. Maureen's dates had been out, she'd still had two or three weeks to go. Her baby was suffering because of her. How could she have been so selfish?

In the bed next to her, a religious young Greek woman, Zoe, who had had a caesarean birth, hauled herself out of bed and got down on her knees. "You must pray for your baby," she said.

Maureen got down on her knees. Religion was something that had ended for her when she left Eden aged fifteen, but she couldn't not pray for her baby when Zoe was on her knees with stitches in her stomach. She listened to Zoe pray and tried to connect but she was a sunken ship.

The nurses wheeled in the babies for the other mothers in her ward. Listening to the cries and suckling babies was too much for Maureen, so she pulled on her dressing gown and went for a walk up the corridor. The paediatrician met her in the hallway.

"I was just coming to find you," he said, kindly. "We have had a complication during the night. Apparently, the mask that feeds oxygen into your baby's lungs came unstuck and the oxygen escaped. His lungs perforated under the strain, leaking air into the blood stream. We don't expect him to last the day. I've called in another thoracic surgeon to see if we can draw the oxygen out with syringes, but it isn't hopeful. I'm so sorry." The walls moved in front of Maureen. A firm hand caught her before she hit the floor. Arms lifted her into a chair. A glass of water was held to her lips.

"I don't know if you are religious or not but if you would like to have your child christened, we could organise that before his operation?"

Who could she get to christen her baby? They were such a mix of religions. Pete was a Catholic, she was a Presbyterian, Henry was Church of England, and Liam and Gerard were Church of Christ. They had Lutheran, Presbyterian, and Quaker godparents. It had all been whatever was available at the time. Liam and Gerard had only been christened because Henry was christened. And she had christened him in the Church of England in Sweden, because the minister had helped her.

"Would you phone my husband and get him to come in, please." It was an effort to speak. They led her back to her bed.

"What's happened?" Zoe asked after the doctor had gone.

"My baby isn't expected to live, and I don't know anyone who will christen him," she sobbed. The Catholics wouldn't christen her other children because she wasn't a Catholic and Pete never went to mass.

"I'm Greek Orthodox but I know a Catholic priest who will do it. He's a friend of ours."

Maureen didn't need to think. "Get him."

Zoe phoned her husband to organise the priest. An hour later, Pete arrived at Maureen's bedside, pale faced. He held her hand not knowing what to do. She told him about the priest.

The nurse was taking their trays of untouched lunch away when a man in his thirties, dressed in an open-necked shirt and drill pants arrived, smelling of alcohol and cigarettes. Zoe introduced the priest to Maureen and Pete.

"I'm not a Catholic, Reverend." She corrected herself, "Father." It was strange calling someone she didn't know Father. The priest waved his hand.

"That doesn't interest me. I'm only concerned about the child. You can do what you want with your faith later, if you have any." He didn't seem at all religious. What sort of priest was he, Maureen wondered?

They congregated around the incubator. A knife went through Maureen's heart. An oxygen mask covered her baby's face with tubes going into his nose and mouth, a machine pumped next to him. His hands were wrapped and secured to stop his arms flaying towards the metal objects that kept him alive. Maureen drew a shuddering breath and clutched Pete. The priest's words were unintelligible; all she could feel was Pete's grip on her arm. As they left the neonatal ward, a large x-ray machine arrived for her baby.

"He's going to be fine. I know it," said Pete. "I had the most extraordinary feeling when the priest was praying, like an electric shock going through my body. I just know the little fellow will recover. It was amazing. Nothing's ever happened to me like that before."

The paediatrician met them in the ward and spoke to Pete, advising him to take Maureen home.

"It's not good for her to be in a ward with other women and their healthy babies while hers is in intensive care. I'll phone you tonight and let you know the baby's progress," he said.

Pete packed her things, led her to the car and together they left the hospital. It was all a blur to Maureen. She was sitting at the table playing with her plate of food, unable to eat, blaming herself for her baby's illness when the phone rang. She dropped her fork and rushed to answer it.

It was the paediatrician. "I find this hard to explain," he said, "but if you believe in God then I can only say someone must be looking after your baby, because we compared the x-rays we had taken this morning against those we took after you left the hospital. The morning x-rays showed perforations and lung damage and this afternoon there was no sign of damage. In fact, and, I have to say, miraculously, your baby has improved. I can only believe he is going to recover."

Maureen grabbed hold of Pete who had been standing next to her, eyes alight and beaming. "He's improved." The moment was euphoric.

That night Maureen's milk came in and for the next six weeks she expressed her milk every day, taking it into the hospital for her child. There was enough to feed the other babies in intensive care. Her basket of clanking bottles become a joke in the ward. "The milkmaid's here," the nurses called out, laughing. It made Maureen feel proud.

19

Adoption

Baby Clement, named after his Seychelles grandfather, came home without any brain damage or the physical disabilities that the doctors had expected. And Maureen felt she owed it to the priest whose prayers she believed had saved him, to convert to Catholicism.

"I'm going to become a Catholic," she said.

"You'll have to go to confession. And Catholics don't believe in birth control," Pete grinned.

She chewed the inside of her lip and gazed into the distance as she contemplated the demands of the Catholic Church. Pete waved his hand in front of her face.

"I heard you. I was just thinking it might be a good time to get my tubes tied."

"Up to you," Pete said. Women things were just that, nothing to do with him.

A week later Pete drove her to the hospital – the procedure would be an overnight stay. The triage nurse pushed the sterilisation document towards Pete for him to give his permission. Shocked, Maureen watched him sign the right to have her sterilised. This was her body. It should only be her decision. She folded her arms and glared at the triage nurse. Oblivious, Pete signed, then picked up a newspaper and went to the lounge while they settled her in a ward.

After undressing, she got into bed. The anaesthetist arrived, read her chart, took her blood pressure, ticked a form, and handed it to her. She signed the form and he gave her a copy. When the door closed behind the nurse and the anaesthetist, she got out of bed, dressed, and collected her bag.

At the reception desk she was a mess of nerves, stammering apologies. "I'm sorry, but I can't go ahead with my operation." Red-faced, she passed the form across the desk, appalled at herself. She had four kids, what was wrong with her? The receptionist scanned the paper, then smiled up at Maureen.

"You're not the first to pull out. It happens a lot. Just sign the cancellation form and you can leave." Maureen found Pete in the waiting room. He was going to be angry she was sure of it.

"Pete," she said in a small voice. He lowered the newspaper and looked at her with surprise.

"I can't go through with it."

"Right, well, we've got that sorted. Let's go home." He picked up her suitcase and draped an arm across her shoulders. They never mentioned it again. When Maureen came to make her first confession, she didn't mention it to the priest either.

Having committed to Catholicism, Maureen was diligent, never missing Sunday mass and the children liked their catechism classes, surprising her with their fervour. After church on Good Friday, Maureen found them playing in her bedroom.

"Arms up," yelled Liam.

Gerard stood against her wardrobe with his arms outstretched while Liam faced him, holding a nail against Gerard's palm, and a hammer in his other hand.

"You can start hammering, Liam," Gerard said. Maureen shrieked as the hammer lifted. Liam turned.

"He's Jesus, Mummy."

"You can't play at being Jesus. God won't like that. What are you doing in my bedroom, anyway?"

"I cleaned the gun," Liam said, proudly. Maureen's eyes bugged.

"What!" She looked at the chair in front of the open cupboard where Pete kept his revolver hidden under his clothes.

"Daddy showed me how." Maureen sucked in her breath. How could Pete be such a moron?

"You're never to touch the gun. Never. You understand?" She rolled the whites of her eyes, a sight that terrified her children. Liam's lip quivered. Maureen ushered them out of the bedroom, then charged over to Pete.

"What were you thinking, Man? He's only six!" she yelled, hands on her hips glowering down at Pete's feet sticking out from under a wrecked Jaguar he was fixing. He wriggled out from under the vehicle.

"What if I'm not around and there's a break-in and you get hurt? I'd rather have the kids know how to use a gun to protect themselves. You told me your father taught you to shoot when you were eight?"

"It was a twenty-two rifle. I didn't learn with a revolver."

"There's terrorist activity in the area, more break-ins, rallies. The boys at the airport told me. You can't rely on George or Dorcas to help you because there will be reprisals on their families. This weekend we'll have some shooting lessons in the garden. We'll do it after mass. It's George and Dorcas's day off."

Dressed in their good Sunday clothes, having just attended

mass, Maureen and the children stood around Pete, watching him draw the figure of a man on a piece of masonite. He propped it against the tree, counted twenty paces, and handed the gun to Henry.

"You can go first." The revolver was heavy – Henry had to use two hands, and his fingers just reached the trigger. With one knee on the ground, the other knee propping the gun, he fired. The bang carried across the veldt, loud enough for the neighbours to hear. Maureen prayed they wouldn't come running over with their guns thinking they were under attack. Pete walked over and checked the target. Henry had nicked the side.

"Bit more practice and you'll do," Pete said.

Liam's fingers weren't strong enough to pull the trigger. "You can be the gun cleaner until you're bigger."

Pete handed Maureen the gun. Holding the revolver reminded Maureen of Sweden, and she aimed and fired, hitting the target in the face.

"I won't mess with you," Pete grinned. Then he shot the target through the heart. "Lesson over." He unloaded the chamber and put the gun in a shoe box.

"No one is allowed to touch the gun without asking me first. And definitely no cleaning the gun when I'm not with you," his eyes narrowed at Liam. "Or crucifying Jesus."

A few days later, Maureen went to the police station for her gun licence. An oral test preceded the paperwork.

"What do you do if you shoot a man outside your house?" the police officer asked.

"Phone the police," Maureen said.

"No. You drag him into your house so then he's a robber. Then you phone the police." Oral test over, he handed Maureen the licence.

At her next catechism class, she showed the licence to Sister Noella, her catechism teacher. The sister glanced at it and looked thoughtful. The smile slipped from Maureen's face. Was her gun licence a sin?

"I've been meaning to discuss your registry office marriage licence with you. It isn't recognised in the Catholic Church and you will need to fix that because you are living in sin which affects the children as well." Maureen was an unmarried mother again.

When she got home, she pulled Pete aside. "Did you know we're not married in the eyes of the church?"

"It doesn't worry me," Pete said.

"It wouldn't, you're a man. I'm the one that gets the reputation."

"Well arrange a marriage then, but nothing fancy."

"I'll sort it with Sister Noella. In the meantime, I've been thinking about you adopting Henry, so his surname is the same as the others?" She had held off changing his name. She had wanted to make sure their marriage was stable because under South African law, in the event of a divorce, the father got the children. Pete looked at her, startled.

"His name is Henry Bernard McKinley. He's enrolled in school under that name," she said.

It hadn't occurred to him that Henry had a different surname to his. He was his child as much as the other three. "Better do that first."

One of Maureen's friends was a welfare officer and organised the paperwork for the adoption. Maureen signed the papers, and the process began. A week on and an official letter arrived.

There was to be an inspection visit from the welfare department. Her child now belonged to the state. Maureen and Pete would be subjected to being assessed as suitable parents for Henry.

Why hadn't her friend told her about that? Flabbergasted, she showed the letter to Pete.

"I want to cancel the adoption! I wouldn't have considered it if I'd known I would risk losing Henry." Maureen gnawed her fingernails. "What if they find us unworthy, Pete?

"We're good parents, so don't worry." He sounded more confident than he felt. South African officials were strict. "Give the department a call and see what they say."

Maureen called her welfare officer and was told the process couldn't be halted. Henry already belonged to the state.

Two welfare officers arrived, a man and a woman. Their eyes missed nothing as they walked into the lounge. Maureen offered tea.

"No thank you, we just want to look through the house and the outside. Then we'll speak with the children. The woman gave Maureen an encouraging smile. Pete stood silent, angry that they were being submitted to this. Henry was his son.

The woman interviewed Henry in his bedroom while Pete was being interrogated in the lounge room by the male welfare officer. Maureen went to the toilet next to Henry's bedroom so she could hear the conversation with her son. He was asked his favourite sport. Did he like going places with his dad? What was his favourite food? Did he get smacked when he was naughty? Maureen strained to hear Henry's answers, anxiety gnawing at her gut.

"I like shooting the gun," she heard Henry say. Shit! The hairs stood up on her arms. Why had he said that? The woman's voice dropped to a murmur. Liam screamed, bang, bang, outside, as he chased Gerard. Maureen strained to hear, her brain a fog. How was she going to explain the gun?

When the interview was over, they shook hands at the door. The concern on Maureen's face caught the woman's sympathy. "Everything's in order. He's a happy boy," she said. "Your husband is his hero." After they left, Maureen poured Pete and herself a brandy to celebrate.

Two weeks later, Henry's surname changed, and the Catholic wedding was in the planning. Maureen thought about Joey – they hadn't been in contact for months. A wedding would be a good opportunity for a get-together. Then she thought about her Quaker, Dutch Reformists and Jewish friends who wouldn't like entering a Catholic church, so decided against having guests. Then she thought about the hole a party would make in her savings and decided against a party. They would have a quiet ceremony after mass, like she had done with the kids' christenings. But she would wear her nice new dress made by one of the women from her art group. It was long, cream linen, with a low square-cut neck, puckered pleat bodice and a front and back panel with an animal print in maroon and black. It looked good on her.

The wedding day arrived. Maureen wore her art dress and Pete the only suit he owned. Mass had finished but the parishioners stayed on – the priest had announced their wedding at the end of mass. Embarrassed at their unexpected audience, Maureen and Pete walked down the aisle with Henry, Liam and Gerard trailing behind while Clement sat on Sister Noella's knee sucking his thumb and rubbing the lace edge of her old bra against his nose. He called it a "goygoy". Maureen had brought it in her handbag for the car trip because Clement didn't like being in a car. Sister Noella hadn't noticed what was in his hand. Maureen tried to signal with her eyes. Clement waved the bra at her. A giggle bubbled inside Maureen which she fought to supress.

She kept her eyes down, not looking at Pete, knowing if she laughed, he would too.

The priest read a passage from the bible and then went into a monologue about marriage which lasted too long. The duty, honour and obey bit followed. The words stuck in her head as she gave the required response, irked that Pete hadn't been asked to obey her. Maureen remembered Hannah with her stopwatch and felt sorry she hadn't thought to invite her and Damien. The parishioners were asked if anyone objected to their union and Maureen was tempted to say, "I do."

After the service there was a lot of congratulating. Maureen rescued Clement and his goygoy from Sister Noella and they all went over to the convent next door where there was tea and cake waiting. It had turned into a bigger affair than Maureen expected. When they were alone and back in their own house, she and Pete celebrated with champagne.

"Mum told me she had a dream I'd marry twice," Maureen laughed.

"Can't divorce me now," said Pete. Maureen hadn't thought about that.

"I can always change my religion," she said, with a grin.

20

A Child's Enterprise

The newly-wed Catholic Mrs Pete Millar pulled into the school to collect Henry and Liam. Henry threw his school case in the car and climbed in beside it.

"What's a bastard, Mum?" His big eyes looked at her. Maureen prickled.

"I'll have to think about it. Where did you hear that?"

"Jenny used to call me a cunt but now she says her dad said I'm a bastard." Henry had never questioned the word cunt; it wasn't a word he'd heard and thought it was Afrikaans. But he'd heard his dad call people a bastard so it must mean something.

Maureen sucked in a breath. She didn't swear much, and the word cunt had never passed her lips, nor had it ever taken up space in her head. Pete swore but he never used that word. Worse was the other word because of the way it had been aimed at her son. Who was the repulsive person who would say that about her son in front of another child and to whom had he been talking to?

"Who is the child that called you those names?"

"Jenny, she's in my class. Her dad sells houses. She said you and Dad only just got married so I'm a bastard." Dear God, is that what everyone in this three-shop outpost thought?

"Am I a bastard too, Mummy?" Liam asked.

"None of you are and that's not a nice word."

"What does it mean?" Henry asked.

"Let's ask your father," Maureen said, hoping they would forget by the time they got home.

"You had better have a word with his teacher and put her straight and I'll have a word with Jenny's father," Pete said, lips tight.

Whispers and smiles greeted Maureen as she entered her office. On her desk was a bouquet of flowers and a wedding congratulations card signed by the office staff. She put her nose to the flowers and looked at the smiling faces of her colleagues.

"Gee, news gets around fast. Thank you, the flowers are lovely." Later at morning tea, the accountant sidled up to her.

"It took you and Pete a long time to make up your minds. Shocked a few here. Not me, I'm open-minded about that sort of thing." She looked at him surprised.

"What do you mean?" He was her boss and a sly creep.

"Having four kids before deciding to get married."

"We were married. We just remarried in the Catholic church because they don't recognise civil marriages." Her eyes darkened. "I'll have to tell Pete what you all think." It was a threat. The accountant threw his hands up.

"Don't blame me, I heard it from someone else. Just letting you know what people think." He looked at his watch, "I'd better get a move on, it's pay day." He made a quick retreat from the tea room. At home she related the gossip to Pete.

"Let them think what they want," he said.

"That's all right for a man," she snapped. The next day she pinned her civil marriage licence to the work notice board.

They were a bona fide church married couple for three months when Maureen learned she was pregnant again.

She was a machine. No doubt her new Catholic friends and Sister Noella would be proud of her. What would the priest say if she went to confession and said she didn't want this pregnancy? Although if it was a girl, it would be nice. Round the family off. Australia was getting further away. Her mind raced over recent events to pinpoint dates. It must have been after the pilot's farewell party. She'd had too much wine and Pete never thought of birth control. If only her body agreed with the birth control pill.

It was eleven weeks into her pregnancy and Maureen was cleaning her teeth, readying for bed after a dinner out when pain ripped through her abdomen so consuming she dropped her toothbrush and clutched her stomach, too breathless to cry out. She sank to her knees and vomited on the floor.

"Pete," her voice was just audible. She crawled to the lavatory door where Pete was depositing his dinner.

"Pete," she tried again.

"Go away," he laughed. Maureen always fooled around. Not having the strength to knock she scratched on the door.

"You'll have to wait," he giggled. The curry had gone straight through him. Maureen curled on the floor, all thoughts erased, consumed by the pain. Minutes later, Pete opened the lavatory door.

"It's your turn, but I'd give it three days before you go in there," he said. She was on the floor, face drained, hair and dress covered in vomit. He dropped to his knees, stricken.

"Take me to hospital. I need a hospital."

"Jesus, Maureen." He lifted her up and carried her to the car and then ran for the maid to stay with the children. He stopped the car at a friend's house, hooted the horn and ran to the door, jabbing the bell. Corona answered, hair in curlers, wrapped in a dressing gown.

"It's Maureen, she's collapsed. I'm taking her to hospital and need you to come with me to look after her while I drive." Corona got in the back and put Maureen's head on her lap. Foot to the floor, beeping the horn, Pete sped through traffic to the hospital.

A doctor pressed her stomach and she screamed. Morphine and a drip went into her arm. When the pain released its grip, Maureen could answer questions.

"You have an ectopic pregnancy that's ruptured. We must operate, but due to the food you've consumed we can't operate until tomorrow morning. For now, we will knock you out, so you won't be in pain. He gave her an injection and the next morning she was on the operating table. She woke from the operation with Pete at her bedside.

"I'm so sorry. God, you nearly died. I don't know what I would have done if you had died." He put his face in his hands.

"I didn't die so don't think about it. How are the kids?"

"They're fine, Dorcas is looking after them. The doctor said you probably won't have any more children now you only have one tube. It's like a car firing on one cylinder," Pete explained. The news didn't bother Maureen. The last thing she wanted to think about was pregnancy. Her recovery was quick, and she was soon back to work. Everything normal again. As normal as African life can be when a tractor comes down the driveway.

The tractor parked under the jacaranda tree near the swimming pool. A man alighted and hailed Maureen and Pete who were watching their children ride bikes through an obstacle course Henry had created.

"Sorry to bother you good folks. My name is Yannie Van der Walt." He smiled, gave a slight bow to Maureen then extended his hand to Pete. They shook hands. "I've got two acres up the road where I've planted vegetables and the tomatoes are about to ripen. I live in town and only get out here on weekends and I wondered if you folks would mind if I parked my tractor here? I don't want to leave it on the property because I found a piece of wire stuck in the ignition, and I'm worried my tractor might disappear."

"Park it where you like," Pete said, with a sweeping arm, "plenty of room here."

"Thank you and feel free to help yourself to the vegetables. The tomatoes should be ready in two weeks. Here's my phone number if you have any problems." He went back to the tractor, parked it away from the driveway and walked back down the road to where he'd left his car.

"Seems a nice chap," Pete said.

"Fresh vegetables will be nice." Their veg garden had become a crop of mealies for George. A Citroen tooted as it passed their gate. Pete raised his hand to the tractor owner.

"Why don't we go and check his vegetable garden out?" Maureen said. They walked up the road, the children following on bikes. Rows of green tomatoes, beans, cabbage and potato plants filled the plot. "I don't know how he'll keep the Bantu out of here. Tomatoes are twenty-five cents a kilo in the store."

Henry set up the card table next to his front gate, then stood behind it. Liam filled bags with tomatoes from a bucket. An African on a bicycle stopped. Money and tomatoes were exchanged. Maureen drove through the gate on her way to pick Pete up from work and spied her children. She put her head out of the car window.

"What's going on?"

"We're selling tomatoes," Henry said, proud. "Twenty cents a bag. I've got one rand." He picked up a small box and shook the coins inside. Maureen laughed at the little businessman. "I don't think Mr Van der Walt will like you selling his tomatoes. He grows them for himself. You're not to take any more and you shouldn't be going down the road on your own. Someone might steal your bike."

"Can you believe it?" Maureen said, when she picked Pete up. "The kids are flogging the neighbour's tomatoes."

"Henry's saving money for a scale electrics car set," Pete grinned. "Let him sell the tomatoes, they'll only rot on the vines or someone else will steal them."

The tomatoes proved unviable as there were never enough for Yannie Van der Walt to harvest. At the end of the tomato season, he hailed Pete in the front yard.

"I've come to collect the tractor. The vegetable garden isn't worth the effort. I've brought you a couple of bottles of wine as a thank you for allowing me to park the tractor here." Pete took the bottles and read the labels. They weren't cheap.

"That's a shame, Man, but thanks, you needn't have done

that." He saw Yannie look towards their front door and purse his lips. Pete followed his gaze to the card table, scales, kids sign and brown paper bags, leaning against the wall.

"Tell the kids they can have what's left," Yannie said with a shrug. Pete went red.

"Look, man ..." Yannie put his hand up.

"I've got kids of my own. Hope they turn out as enterprising." He walked over to his tractor, climbed aboard, and chugged off down the drive, raising his arm as he went through the gate. Pete waved, feeling guilty, knowing he was to blame for allowing the kids to have their tomato stall.

At dinner, the contraband tomatoes were delivered to the table in the form of tomato bhurtha, a spicey tomato salad. They were joined by curried cottage cheese salad and spiced chicken in yoghurt and rice. It was one of his favourite meals. He scooped the tomato bhurtha onto his plate.

"Where did you buy the tomatoes, Maureen? They look so yummy," he said grinning.

"I sold them to Mummy, she got a special price," Henry said. Pete laughed.

"I'm afraid you'll have to close the shop soon. Mr Van der Walt has given up his garden. He said the tomatoes keep disappearing."

"George pinched them," Gerard said, scared his brothers would get into trouble.

"He pinched them for our shop," Liam said. He loved George.

"It doesn't matter who took the tomatoes, it just means you won't have any more to sell. But how about eating some, Liam?"

Liam shook his head and started to cough; Gerard followed suit. They coughed until they were red in the face. Maureen frowned. She leant over and felt their foreheads.

"You kids are very hot. I think you have temperatures."

She fetched disprin and a bottle of cough mixture and gave them a dose. "I think you should go to bed. If you're not better in the morning, I'll take you to the doctor."

After a bad night of coughing, and sighting specks of blood in Gerard's sputum, Maureen took them to the doctor.

"Whooping cough," the doctor said.

"They've been vaccinated against whooping cough."

"It's pseudo whooping cough. Sometimes these diseases mutate. Liam has a swollen heart sack but I'm not going to put them in hospital because I think they're better off at home." He wrote out a script. Whooping cough was catching, they had been to Corona's place for a braai at the weekend. She phoned Corona as soon as she got home.

"What do you expect when you allow your maid to let her friends visit? Blacks have all sorts of diseases." Corona didn't ask how Liam and Gerard were, she'd been too busy giving Maureen a lesson on how to manage servants.

"Your turn to get up," Maureen said, tired from two nights of no sleep getting up to spoon cough mixture into Liam and Gerard. Pete groaned.

"What can I give them? Can't keep giving them cough mixture."

"Mummy," Gerard cried. Maureen swung her legs out of bed, and dragged herself up the hall. She picked him up and took him back to her bed. It was easier having him next to her.

She lay on her back and listened to him whoop. Please let me sleep, she begged her brain. A heavy weight pressed into her, pushing her into the mattress. The pressure was so intense she could hardly breathe. Suddenly she felt herself whirl, faster and faster she went. Nausea gripped her; she was about to sit up when a voice spoke to her. *Lie back, relax and see what happens.* She stopped fighting the sensation and then, zing! Her soul left her body. She felt incredibly light. All her burdens had dropped away.

I've got a soul, it's real. I have a soul. She was ecstatic, travelling through space never wanting to return to the vehicle that was her body. In the distance she heard Gerard cough. I must go back, it's not time yet, she thought, and in an instant, she was back in bed. The rest of the night, she lay in a state of total happiness unperturbed by the coughing child next to her.

"Pete, you'll never guess what happened to me last night," Maureen said, full of love for him, for her children, aware of the vibrant colours in her garden outside her bedroom window. She told him of her incredible experience. Pete raised an eyebrow.

"Next time tell me when you're leaving so I can get on board," he teased. She laughed. Nothing he said would change the wonderful peace she felt in her heart.

Two weeks later, Maureen's new conviction in the freedom of the soul was a great consolation for Pete, when his brother Mick rang.

"Dad's died," Mick said, distraught. "He had an ulcer that burst. Can you make it to the funeral?"

The loss of his father hit Pete hard. He had been a loving, kind dad. Pete hadn't met him until he was five years old as his father had been away fighting in Europe and North Africa with the South African army during World War Two.

"We'll leave tomorrow," Pete said.

Everything was a rush. Dorcas put out the children's clothes while Maureen packed and Pete serviced the car. The children were excited. They were going to see their Granny and stay with their favourite uncle and his wife in Rhodesia.

Pete was withdrawn, not speaking much on their trip to Salisbury. The last time Maureen had seen his father was to say goodbye to him after insisting Pete take his parents back to

Rhodesia. She felt wretched. She concentrated on the children so as not to intrude on his grief.

Tears poured on their arrival. The children watched the grown-ups with anxious faces. Maureen put baby Clement in his grandmother's arms. Somehow, she would have to make up for sending Annie away. But she needn't have worried because there was already a plan afoot for that.

"How do you manage all those children as well as work?" Ellen, Pete's sister-in-law asked after the funeral. She was a thickset woman with a jutting jaw.

"Their nanny, Dorcas, looks after them and I'm usually home by 2.30 p.m. We manage. Pete and George, our gardener, are finishing a flat at the back of our house so we can rent it out and save for a holiday in Australia." She had recently learnt they could get reduced international airfares because they worked in the aircraft industry. In fact, they could fly for the price of one adult's return ticket. Maureen had shrieked with delight when she learned of the perk and had started planning their trip for the next school holidays. "My mother was here for a visit and now I'm so homesick." Ellen looked thoughtful.

"It would be nice if Annie could have a holiday. If she's with your children, it will help her cope with her grief. Would you consider taking her back with you for a month or two?" A picture flashed into Maureen's mind of Annie holding baby Liam, sitting next to him, rocking his pram. Henry, Pete and herself all crushed into the chook pen. She dismissed the thought – they had a big house, there was more room and Maureen was not the possessive mother she had been. It would only be for two months. After that, Australia.

"I'll speak to Pete," she said.

On their way home, Annie sat in the back with the children, There were no stray goats or problems at the border.

21

The Cat

The two months' holiday for Annie that Ellen had suggested extended into a year. Annie's visit looked permanent. Maureen didn't have the heart to send her away again. She adored the children and they her. It did change the household though, as Dorcas was silent around her and George kept his distance.

George sat on the back step eating his bowl of mealy meal for lunch while he waited for Pete to bring back the paint for the flat. Liam sat next to him. George held his bowl out and Liam scooped up a lump of the porridge squashed it into a ball and popped it into his mouth.

"Liam!" Annie had seen the transaction from the kitchen window. "Don't eat mealie pap off the kaffir's plates."

"Annie!" Shocked, Maureen whirled on her mother-in-law.

"Don't call the black people names and especially not in front of the children."

"They walk all over you. You will never get their respect," Annie replied.

Maureen's lips tightened. "I don't like you calling them that. Pete doesn't do it. And if George or Dorcas give the kids something to eat, they can. They always have done."

"They'll get worms," Annie snorted, huffing off to her bedroom.

Maureen wished she hadn't told Annie about the long round-worm she had found in Liam's nappy. Worms were a constant in South Africa. Perhaps there was a season for worms in the same way there was a season for rape, according to Annie. A finding Annie shared with Maureen's luncheon guests.

"There's more cases of rape during the avocado pear season, you know." Perhaps it was true, but it caused tea stains down the front of a friend's blouse.

Another snippet of information Annie offered was the small tree she had seen in a bottle on a doctor's shelf that had grown inside a child because it had eaten a pip. Her beliefs were unshakable. Maureen knew it wasn't her fault, that Annie's mother had died when she was eight and her schooling ended when she was thirteen. But it was hard having Annie live with them. It affected her relationship with Pete, holding her back from having an argument about how he left so much up to her, always aware of Annie's presence and where her loyalties lay. Maureen fought her irritation until she started to notice the way Henry hung back from Annie.

He came into the kitchen, face miserable near tears. Maureen was about to ask what him was wrong when Annie appeared behind him.

"You can't have my cars, Liam. You'll break my cars," she mocked. Henry walked past Maureen into the lounge with Annie still following him, repeating her words in a child's petulant voice.

Suddenly Maureen was aware of the situation. It had happened before, but she hadn't paid much attention. "What are you doing, Mum? Leave him alone."

Annie looked back at Maureen, surprised. "You're following Henry around goading him."

Annie's head went back. "Am I? He wouldn't let Liam play with his dinky cars."

"I don't blame him. Liam breaks his cars. They are special to Henry; he loves his cars. I don't want you to tease him, it's unkind."

"I'm sorry, I didn't realise what I was doing. Come and have a sweet Henry." Annie kept a packet of sweets in her cupboard for the children, guarding them for special occasions.

Henry considered it, then shook his head. "No thank you," he said.

Good on you, Henry, Maureen thought. What her mother-in-law needed was friends to occupy herself with instead of picking on Henry.

"You need friends, Mum. The Catholic church has a good social circle. They aren't all Catholics, some are like you, with Catholic husbands. They run a charity group and meet up to knit and make clothes for poor black women. They collect secondhand prams, dolls and make dolls clothes."

Annie went as still as a door stop.

"Or there's the Lion's club? They go on excursions. You'd make friends," Maureen pressed.

Annie's lips disappeared. "I have my family, I don't need friends," she said.

To keep the peace between them Maureen let the subject go. If only she had Joey to discuss her dilemma with. Joey was good at solutions, just not solutions for her own situation.

169

In bed, she told Pete about his mother's response to her suggestion, thinking he might talk sense into her.

"If Mum doesn't want to, you can't make her. She's happy enough."

Maureen turned her back on Pete; it was always easy for him. If it wasn't for his mother, they would be in Australia on holiday, or permanently. She kept a watchful eye on Annie and Henry and then Pierrette Paroz came on the scene.

Pierrette was the new freelance pilot at Maureen's work. She was Swiss-French, five-foot-two and flew the helicopter for the news traffic reports. Being around Pierrette was interesting. They shared jokes, friends, wine, and Pierrette listened to her moan about her mother-in-law. When Pete finished renovating the flat, Pierrette became the tenant and Maureen's diversion from Annie.

The children took to her immediately. She buzzed the property on her way to the airport if she knew the children were home and they would charge out into the garden waving up at her, then zoom and dive bomb around the yard for an hour after she left. A few months into her stay, Pierrette suggested the children come for a ride in the helicopter.

"On Sunday I can land the chopper in the yard and the kids can come for a ride wiz me," she said.

Everyone was excited. Pete, George, and Henry put down some planks so the helicopter wouldn't sink into the damp ground. The chopper circled, blowing the figs off the trees. It wobbled from one side to the other before dropping neatly onto the planks. Pint-sized Pierrette jumped from the cockpit.

"All aboard," she said. Pete lifted his three sons, shrieking with excitement, into the helicopter and Pierrette strapped them in.

She started the engine, the blades whirled, and the machine rose into the air along with Maureen's anxiety as she watched them ascend above the trees. Henry leant out and waved. There was no door on the helicopter. Her heart went into her mouth.

"Pete, there's no door!"

"They're strapped in." Pete didn't seem worried.

Pierrette flew over the neighbour's properties and then came back to land. Maureen watched the chopper swing above the planks and gave a sigh of relief when it landed.

"Tomorrow I'm on an early shift so can I leave the chopper here for tonight?"

"That's fine with us," Maureen said. Pete nodded in agreement. Maureen could see a permanent landing strip being erected.

At five o'clock in the morning, it wasn't so fine. The noise of the chopper starting up was like a group of Hells Angel's bikies revving under their bedroom window. The children rushed outside to watch Pierrette take off. More fruit left the trees. George collected what he could sell. The day had begun too early for Maureen, and she decided to discourage their tenant from parking the chopper in the yard.

Pierrette was away for two days, flying a team into the game park to mark the elephants for a conservation study programme. On her return, she called Maureen over to her flat.

"We have a problem wiz a pussy cat. It gets into my house and pisses everywhere." She took Maureen inside to sniff. The stench was bad. Maureen set Dorcas to cleaning the flat and filled it with gardenias from the garden.

Pierrette went away for a further two days, leaving the window open. The cat was spotted in the top of the jacaranda tree next to her flat. It was a good thirty feet up and no amount of tempting would bring the cat down. Pete was at work so Maureen and the children pelted small stones up the tree to frighten it away, but it wouldn't move.

"We have to get it down or it's going to get in Pierrette's flat."

The bars on the window made it impossible for a child to get through and Pierrette had the only key to the flat.

"Henry, get your airgun and see if you can put a slug in its bum to scare it off."

It was a bad call. Henry put a slug in the cat's face. It bunched up on the limb and yowled. Maureen had to get the cat down as it was hurt. What a stupid thing to tell her son to do. She went into the bedroom and got the revolver out of the cupboard and went outside. The shot was difficult. She held the gun with two hands aimed up the tree and fired. There was a crashing noise as the cat hurtled through the branches and landed with a thump at her feet, legs kicking. She put the gun to its head, turned her face away and pulled the trigger. Too sickened to look at the cat or her children, she turned her head towards the kitchen doorway and saw her mother-in-law standing there open-mouthed. Yes, she had killed a cat in front of her children, not thinking what effect it would have on them and now the cat had to be buried. She pulled a nappy off the clothesline and dropped it over the cat.

"Get the spade, Henry." Henry ran off and returned with the spade. Maureen went into the orchard where the ground had recently been watered and tested the earth with the spade to find the softest part. She dug a hole under the apricot tree, deep enough for the cat not to get washed up in a heavy downpour.

A chorus of Our Fathers greeted the last spadeful of earth as the children arrived, Henry in the lead, a towel draped around his shoulders and the cat shrouded in a nappy in his arms. He made the sign of the cross over the cat and placed it in the ground, turned, and made the sign of the cross over his brothers, then handed them each a leaf, which they pretended to eat. Maureen said an Our Father, shovelled the dirt over the cat and left the gravesite feeling like a murderer.

An hour later, she went to fetch the children to find Liam standing at the open grave with the cat in his arms and a towel around his shoulders. He made the sign of the cross then buried the cat for the second time while Gerard got on his knees and crossed himself.

"What are you doing, for God's sake?"

"It's my turn to be the priest," said Liam, upon which Maureen dismissed her qualms on having traumatised her children for having shot the cat in front of them.

"Dinner's ready," she said and went back inside.

Since Maureen's run-in with the police at the dam, only George and Pete were hunting for gold. It wasn't every weekend, as Pete was getting more work on the weekends. It didn't seem to bother George when they went, which got Maureen thinking George might have been hallucinating on marijuana and it was all a tall story. She had tested him a few times over the months, and he had answered, "Have you ever seen me work so hard, Madam?" That had kept her going. But now, too busy with Clement and working part-time, gold was the furthest thing from her mind.

Then Pete arrived home from a day at the dam and put two iron rods on the kitchen table. "Present."

Maureen picked the two iron pegs up and frowned.

"They are the markers George's father put outside the entrance to the cave. They were buried underneath a pile of rock. George found them."

Maureen's eyes rounded. She clutched the markers to her chest. "We can go to Australia," she said.

"Well, don't count your chickens yet. We still have to dig out the coins and think about how we can sell them. There's no treasure trove in South Africa; any discovery belongs to the government." His eyes rested on the makeshift helicopter pad surrounded by scattered figs. "Although there is a way we can get it out of the country, but I need to speak to George to see if he's agreeable."

They would have to include another person. He went off to look for George to see what he thought about his idea and found him in the shed.

"Not even whites can sell found treasure in South Africa, George. When we find it, we must move it out of the country. If we told Missus Pierrette she could fly it to another country. What do you think?

"Yes, Boss." George liked Pierrette; she gave him her left-over wine when it had been open too long. He wouldn't have to give her any of his money – the boss would pay her. George was happy to let her fly the treasure out of the country. That night when Pierrette came home, they congregated on the back porch with a bottle of wine and told her the story.

Pete showed Pierrette the markers. "Digging it out is a problem, but this is proof it's there. I know I'm jumping the gun, but once we have it, we need a plan to get it out of the country. I was thinking you could fly it out and Maureen and I will cut you in on our share." One Kruger rand from that era was worth $5,000. There were three buckets full of coins, according to George.

"When you find, I will fly it to Mozambique." Pierrette said. They stared at the rusted pegs, already seeing the buckets of coins, their eyes gleaming with dreams. Pierrette would buy her own plane, set up a safari business. Pete could own an E-type Jaguar and Maureen a beautiful farm in Eden. George could have a car, a smart suit, good shoes, socks and own a shebeen.

"We'll be set for life if we pull this off," Pete said. He clinked glasses with Pierrette, while George raised his tin cup.

In the three months that followed, Pete overcame his fear of heights and along with George, threw everything he could at the cliff face, digging into the crevice with a pick and shovelling earth into the dam. But the width of the crevice in the solid rock face was only a hand's span and impossible to enter. Despondent and a pragmatist, Pete called a meeting on the back porch,

"We need dynamite to get into the cliff which won't be possible in a national park. We're out in the open where everyone can see what we are doing. Boaters notice us, they wave. Maybe we're being watched with binoculars from the yacht club? Anyway, I doubt we can buy a stick of dynamite and even if we could, I can't guarantee the coins wouldn't be buried deeper or destroyed in the blast. We don't even know if someone found them when the dam was extended. This might be all for nothing."

George stood by, hands in his pockets looking unperturbed. He was sick of giving up his weekends.

"I want to have one more try, Pete," Maureen said. "You and me. We've been at it for two years." Her voice rose. "We could poke a steel rod in the crevice to see how far it will go inside, tie a mirror to the end and see if anything is in there. Come on, one last time?" She grabbed his hand, not wanting to give up on her dream. He sighed and nodded.

The following Saturday it was raining. Pete decided they should try a less conspicuous approach to their cliff descent. It was a track he and George had discovered, along with old Boer war trenches that Pete wanted to take a closer look at.

Soaked to the skin from teeming rain, Pete and Maureen scrambled through the orchard at the back of a private property.

"We can't climb down a cliff in this," Pete said, taking shelter under a tree. Maureen had been thinking the same thing; the cliff face was slippery. She stopped and picked a guava from a tree. Bit into it. Delicious. An ear-splitting shriek made Maureen jump with fright.

"Baboons," Pete laughed. More shrieks came from a rocky outcrop behind them. Suddenly, a loud bang ricocheted through the hills.

"What was that?"

"Someone's shooting." Pete looked around. Another bang, closer, whining over their heads, thudding into a tree.

"Jesus Christ! They're shooting at us. Get down!"

Maureen and Pete lay flat on the ground while the gunfire continued. Pandemonium erupted around them. Shrieking baboons crashed through the trees.

"Back to the car," Pete whispered. They belly-crawled through the mud with bullets zinging over their heads, echoing through the rocks.

"I bet whoever it is thinks we're baboons stealing the fruit. Keep going." They reached the farm's boundary fence, crawled under the barbed wire, and made a run for the car. They reached the car, knees bleeding, hair covered in twigs and muddied from head to foot. Pete dropped onto the car seat.

"That's it! The bloody place is cursed. There's nothing there – someone else has taken it." He wanted to cool Maureen's gold fever, he had already given up.

Maureen poured two cups of tea from the thermos she'd brought, handed one to Pete and sat next to him in silence. A baboon screamed in the distance, echoing their disappointment. Pete was right. There was no treasure. Not for them anyway. It had all been a mad dream.

When they told Pierrette and George of their decision to end the treasure hunt, Pierrette shrugged. It had looked impossible to her from the start. George just nodded and went off to water his marijuana crop hidden behind the servants' quarters. Their gold hunt had come to an end.

22

Spiritual Donations

George sat on the back step with a mug of tea while Maureen fed the boxer pup, the latest addition to the family. He contemplated his tin mug.

"Madam, can I tell you something?"

"Sure, George." Maureen waited for another of George's family problems she was expected to rectify.

"I went to a meeting last night. All the boys from the farms were there. We had to go, Madam, or they hurt us and our families."

Maureen went still. "What do you mean, George?"

"The terrorists, Madam. They say we must steal white people's guns and kill them."

Maureen gasped.

"You mustn't say so to the police, or I go to gaol," he said, alarmed at her expression.

She shook her head, wondering what she should do with the information.

"I wouldn't shoot you, Madam or the children or the Boss, I want you to know that I love you all. The boy who works on the next farm will have to kill you and I would kill his boss. He's not a good boss like our boss, Madam."

The hair on Maureen's arms stood up. What was this George was telling her? There had been a lot more attacks and robberies, especially in the outer areas where they lived. Suddenly, Maureen's feeling of contentment left her. They should consider moving to Australia permanently for the children's sakes. Tonight, when she and Pete were in bed, she would tell him what George had said without the children and Annie present. Maureen felt bad for Annie. They wouldn't be able to take her to Australia without knowing where they were going to live and without Pete having a job. She would have to go back to Kenya or to Pete's brother.

"I'm not moving to Australia without seeing it first and nothing's going to happen here, the army has it under control." Pete was born in Africa – he should know. Maureen relaxed a little. "I've got to fly to Kruger National Park tomorrow to fix an aircraft that had an emergency landing, so I might be away for a few days." Maureen's brow wrinkled; she'd never been left on her own in their house. "You've got Mum, and Pierrette." He didn't mention George and Dorcas.

In the morning, Maureen told Pierrette what George had said and that Pete was going away.

"I come and sleep at your house," she said. Maureen perked up. It would be fun having a sleep-over.

"You can share my bed. It's a king size." Pierrette laughed and declined.

Pete had only been gone two days when the stone smashed through the lounge window, shattering the glass, landing at Maureen's feet. She leapt up from her chair, heart quickening.

Someone was outside. Annie was asleep and Pierrette was making them a late-night snack in the kitchen. Pierrette came into the lounge still holding the cheese knife.

"What was zat?"

"Someone's just thrown a rock at the lounge room window, smashed the glass. I'm going to get my gun."

"I will get mine," Pierrette said. She ran out the back door and headed towards her flat. Maureen's gun was under her mattress – she had moved it after Pete had left. She pulled the gun out and checked it was loaded.

They met in the shadows at the back door, both armed, Pierrette with an automatic and Maureen with her revolver.

"You go that way around the house, and I go zis way, so we look both sides. Guns loaded and pointed in front of them, they disappeared around the house. Maureen crept along the wall of the house so as not to stumble in the dark. She reached the bushes near the front door, heard a stone roll, brought the gun up, tightened her finger around the trigger.

"Step into the light or I'll shoot." A crouched figure eased forward, gun pointing.

"Who is zat?"

"Pierrette?"

"Maureen?" Pierrette moved forward into the light.

"Jesus, I nearly shot you," Maureen gasped, gun trembling in her hand.

"I nearly shoot you. You give me such a scare, Maureen." They fell into each other's arms.

"We need a drink," Pierrette said. They went inside and sat with the wine bottle until it was empty. The story went around the airport and became a good deterrent for future intruders.

Annie kept her eye on the road for any suspicious people after the scare, noting passers-by when she was in the garden. The road was only an access to four properties and mostly used by the black workers who were usually on foot.

Today, though, two trucks caught her attention. They pulled into the paddock opposite and six blacks got out and began unloading large boxes and equipment. A white Mercedes arrived with two white men. Annie busied herself in the garden to watch what was going on as another truck arrived with a group of black men standing on the back. She hurried inside to tell Pete.

"There's a lot of activity across the road. I'm worried about the number of blacks hanging around. I think you should go over there and see what's going on."

Pete went outside to have a look. "Maybe the place has been sold and they're going to build a shed or something for the new owner." He wasn't too worried. Whoever it was owned a Mercedes and there was a white man on a ladder rigging electric wires from the electricity pole.

By nightfall a circus tent had been erected. The following day, a truck unloaded stacks of chairs and another truck deposited a generator. The chairs were lined up in the tent. Voices came over loudspeakers. "Testing, one, two. Testing."

"Do you think it's a black rally to get support for the terrorists?" Maureen asked.

"It can't be an illegal gathering if white men are there," Pete said. He went outside and called to George.

"Go over the road and see what's going on. Pretend you want a job." An hour later George came back.

"It's a church, Boss." Everyone relaxed.

On Sunday a stream of cars and people walked up the road and packed into the tent.

"There has to be over a hundred black people there," Pete said looking thoughtful. "I think we should give mass a miss today with that mob around. Never know if someone sees us leave and decides to break in." The tent rocked with singing and clapping, loud enough for all the surrounding properties to hear. Maureen listened, thinking it was far more interesting than a Catholic ceremony.

"We take the chopper up for a look," Pierrette said. It was parked in the yard ready for an early Monday start. "Henry, you and Liam come, not Gerard. He must stay home. He gets sick."

She flew the chopper over the tent, swooped low, circled, and then headed off to the airport, returning to Maureen's place from the opposite direction.

"It is a monster tent," she said.

The following morning, Dorcas came into Maureen's bedroom with the wake-up tray of morning tea, singing one of the hymns that had been playing in the tent.

"You sound happy, Dorcas."

"God is going to give me money, Madam."

"How do you know that?" Pete said.

"Pastor tells me to give all my money to the Holy Spirit and he will give back twice more, so I give the Holy Spirit everything," she beamed.

Pete sat up. "Dorcas, they steal your money. You mustn't give them money. Look at their nice cars, the big tent. That's what your money pays for."

Dorcas frowned.

"No, Boss. The Holy Spirit says give more if we want a place in heaven and he will give us back twice more money."

Pete shook his head. It was useless.

More people came the following Sunday. All the seats in the tent were taken, people stood, and crowds waited outside the entrance.

"Must be two hundred at least," Annie said to Pete. "This can't be legal."

"If I report them to the cops the cops might come over here and check our workers' passes. George and Dorcas would have to warn their friends not to visit." If Pete was caught with illegal blacks on his premises, he'd have to pay a heavy fine and the offenders would be gaoled.

The tent speakers blared.

"Good man. This man has given the Holy Spirit fifty rand. He will be blessed. Praise the Lord." Clapping and cheering followed the announcement. More donations and names were announced followed by more applause. The encouragement continued from the pulpit. It went on all afternoon. Maureen couldn't get *He's Got the Whole World in His Hands* out of her head.

The following week a circle of flattened grass was the only sign the tent had been there. It was already on its way to another vulnerable neighbourhood, taking Dorcas's money with them. Dorcas came to Maureen with a glum face.

"Madam, if you pay me for one day extra, I will not have my day off this week." Dorcas shifted her feet. Eyes to the ground.

"What's wrong, Dorcas?"

"I have no money to visit my family. No money for my mother and children's school uniform, I give it all to Holy Spirit." And it hadn't been returned threefold as promised. Maureen was angry. Why had Dorcas been so gullible? She was an educated girl. The Pentecostal church used tents for black people to keep them out of the white churches. Black people's money had contributed to building the white churches. She sighed.

"I'll give you the money to go and see your family and pay the school, but you mustn't give your money to those tents again, Dorcas." Maureen gave Dorcas an extra month's pay. Dorcas clapped her hands.

"See, Madam. The Holy Spirit has given my money back like

he said." She rushed off smiling. Maureen digested the miracle and didn't tell Pete or his mother. She could do without them shaking their heads at her.

23

Refuge

A car door slammed, and an excited young voice called out for Henry. Maureen pulled back her bedroom curtain to see who had arrived. Joey's car, stacked with blankets and clothes, was in the drive. Colin tapped on Henry's window. Maureen's gut tightened. She let the curtain fall and rushed to the front door to let Colin in and greet Joey. He charged past her, running down the hall into Henry's room where Henry was changing out of his school clothes.

"I'm sorry," Joey said, her voice catching, "but I didn't have anywhere else to go." She shivered in Maureen's warm hug and allowed herself to be led inside. Maureen signalled to Dorcas to make them some tea.

Dorcas came into the lounge with a tray, eyes downcast, and put it on the coffee table in front of Maureen. Dorcas knew the signs; she had been in this situation many times in her own life. Maureen poured tea and waited, not wanting to hurry her friend.

"You can have Pete's Mum's room. She's in Kenya with his sister for a few weeks, giving us a break."

"Thank you, I'm only here for tonight. I'm going to my brother's; he lives in Bulawayo. Des was raging all night, drunk and in a fury. After he threw Colin in the car this morning to drive him to school, I raced around the house packing stuff in my car, terrified he was going to come back and catch me. I left the house all neat, so if he did come back, he would think I had gone to work. I parked in the lane by Colin's school and waited for school to finish, grabbed him and came straight here." She had a sip of tea, "I'll have to let my boss know."

Henry and Colin chased each other around the house, shrieking with laughter while Joey phoned her boss.

"Well, that's that," she said joining Maureen in the lounge. "He was very nice. He said he would give me a good reference." Her lip trembled, and she fished for a handkerchief in her bag, mopped her eyes and blew her nose. "I think he was expecting it." She dropped into a chair and put her face in her hands. A broom swished across the floor in the kitchen and the back door opened. Dorcas addressed someone in her language and the door closed. Maureen waited for Joey to speak.

"Des has been coming into my work and making scenes. I don't know how many times a day he phones me, and my boss told me if he didn't stop, he'd have to let me go. I like my job and everyone I work with. My boss suggested I should talk to someone professional if I had problems at home. He even said he would pay. But I didn't want to accept his help. I don't want to be in a situation where I owe something." Her cornflower blue eyes looked across at Maureen. "If you get what I mean." Maureen understood what she meant.

"I knew I had to speak to Des if I was to keep my job, so I made him a lovely meal to put him in a good mood and then we cuddled up on the couch watching television. I told Des my boss liked him. He doesn't really, but I was trying to ease into having to ask him not to visit or phone me so often. I told him my boss said we were going to get busier, and would I ask that he not visit me so much. Des had laughed, said it was all right. He drank a few beers and then his face started to clamp down. I know that look," Joey shivered. Maureen's heart squeezed for her friend.

"He asked me how much I like my boss. He said he thought my boss was coming onto me." Her laugh was bitter. "My boss is sixty! Des said I still thought like a poor white and I was looking for a sugar daddy. I told him that was nonsense." She started to cry. "I should never have said that. I should have put my arms around him or made a joke about old men, kissed him or something. He punched me in the stomach, threw me on the floor, kicked me, sat on top of me and bashed the back of my head on the floor. He hits me where no one can see the bruises." She held up her bandaged wrist. "I think it's broken," she said.

"After he'd beaten me, he forced himself on me." Her voice was a whisper. "He likes sex when he's violent. Enjoys seeing me in pain. Bites me sometimes." Her face reddened, "Tore my nipple." She pulled up her blouse and showed Maureen her purple nipple crusted in blood. "I can't wear a bra."

Maureen went to get up and Joey put her hand out. "We can fix it later," she had to finish her story.

"The beatings are getting worse. I'm going to my brother's because he's in the police force in Bulawayo and Des wouldn't dare come to Rhodesia. I just hope my car gets me there." She rested her head on the back of her armchair and closed her eyes, exhausted.

"Have you ever approached Des's mother about what he's been doing to you?" Joey grimaced.

"No sympathy there. I tried early in our marriage and when I mentioned Des hitting me, she said I should try not to aggravate him, that most men hit their wives and I should learn how to handle my husband."

"Well, Pete would never hit me and if he did, I'd be out of here like a shot." It was time to make sure Joey's car got her to Rhodesia and didn't become an excuse for her to go back to Des. "Come on, let's take your car to the airport so Pete can check it over." Pete had started his own business, spray painting and fibre glass aircraft repairs. "Do you think Des will know you are going to Rhodesia?" Joey shook her head.

"He'll look closer to home. I'm friends with a girl from work so he might try her first and then maybe think I came here, but I'll be on the road by then."

"In case he does we should take the kids to the airport with us, and I'll tell Dorcas and George to say they haven't seen you." Maureen looked at Joey's stacked car. "I'll follow you with the kids."

Pete's eyebrows rose when they pulled up in front of the hangar. Maureen signalled Pete to come over. His eyes softened when he looked at Joey. She wasn't wearing makeup, her eyes were red, underneath were dark shadows. Getting out of the car she gasped and clutched her side.

"What's up?" he said, already knowing the answer.

"Joey's staying with us for tonight. She's leaving Des and heading for Rhodesia. We wondered if you could check her car over to make sure she gets there?"

"Glad to, it's about time you left that bastard." Pete turned to Henry and Colin, "You kids can go and look at the planes while I fix the car." The boys ran off, eager to play pilots. "Sit over there, ladies," Pete motioned to a car seat against the hangar wall, "and I'll get the boys to make you a coffee, but I'm afraid you'll have to put up with powdered milk."

"I grew up on powdered milk, poor white, remember?" Joey said, lifting her chin. Pete whistled into the hangar and one of his workers came over.

"This is Ephraim, but we all call him Bossboy, so we don't mix him up with another Ephraim who works for me. This one is the big cheese around here, my foreman." Bossboy gave a mocking bow. "He's a cheeky bastard but he makes good coffee," Pete grinned at Bossboy and received a mock bow. They understood each other.

"How do you like your coffee, Madam?" He was well-spoken. Maureen knew that as well as Bossboy being Pete's best worker, he was also his close friend, although Pete didn't recognise that. South Africa didn't encourage black-white friendships. Pete spoke of him often and paid him well. They talked cars, loved vintage cars. Went together to look at a few in the black township, where he lived. Pete advised him if they were a good buy and how to restore them, letting him use his equipment to fix them up. Taught him how to spray paint.

Maureen and Joey waited for an hour while Pete checked the oil, wipers, tyres and brakes. He filled the tank from the airport petrol pump, then asked Bossboy to get someone to wash the car. Joey reached for her purse. Pete put his hand up.

"This is on me. I want you to get as far away from that bastard as possible."

It was early the next morning and Joey was repacking the car when Des phoned. Maureen kept her voice light and chatty.

"Des, long time no hear?"

"I know she's there," he said. Maureen felt her arms goose flesh.

"Who is here? Not sure what you mean."

"I've just got myself a gun licence and you might have a problem if I come over." He hung up.

Maureen found Pete in the bathroom. Seeing her agitation, he put his razor down. "What's up?"

"I've had a call from Des. He said he's got a gun licence and will be paying us a visit."

"Bullshit! He wouldn't have the guts," Pete exploded, wiping his face on a towel. "But tell Joey to get the hell out of here. I wouldn't put it past him to wait until we're at work and then come snooping around. The gutless bastard."

Maureen raced to Joey's car.

"Des phoned, said he's got a gun, threatened me. You've got to leave now." Maureen gripped Joey's arms, forcing her to look at her. "This is serious, Joey. Don't weaken and go back to him, you must promise me. I can't be here for you next time if you go back to him. He's unstable. And I don't want to read about you in the newspaper."

"I won't go back, I promise." They hugged. Maureen gazed down the road until the dust had settled behind Joey's car. Turning, she faced her house, nestled in jacaranda trees and surrounded by acres of pink and white cosmos. A row of pines marked its boundaries. It looked sedate, calm. All the things she didn't feel inside herself.

What was it about this country? There was so much harshness and cruelty, and incredible beauty. She found the people interesting, their culture fascinating and the animal life amazing. Yet South Africa was unpredictable from one day to the next. She loved, feared and was excited by it. But she didn't belong.

After Joey's departure, Maureen had Dorcas wash the sheets and blankets to ready the room for her mother-in-law's return, hoping to hear that Joey had arrived safely. But there were no calls from Joey that night or the next day, and Maureen didn't have her brother's number or address to ask. The only person who might know was Des and she had no intention of speaking to him ever again. There were no more phone calls from him and he hadn't visited while she and Pete were at work, which is what she had expected him to do. Joey was probably busy settling in, looking for work and finding a school for Colin. She knew that in time Joey would get in touch with her and it wasn't the last contact they would have.

George knocked on the kitchen door. "I have something to tell you Madam," he said. It was going to be a problem, Maureen knew it.

"What is it, George?"

"The girl has been stealing your things," he said. Maureen raised her eyebrows.

"Dorcas doesn't steal from me George."

"She is, Madam, I get it from her room." He held up a necklace, it was antique with a mosaic rose set in silver on a silver chain. Maureen held the necklace aloft; she had never seen it before.

"That's not mine, George."

"She find it in the bedroom after Mrs Joey left." Maureen went still. Surely Dorcas wouldn't take something that belonged to poor Joey?"

"Tell her to come and see me, now, George." Minutes later Dorcas was on the doorstep, hands clasped in front of her, face desperate.

"I didn't steal, Madam. It was left behind. I found it in the room."

"Why didn't you give it to me?" Dorcas hung her head.

"I'm not a thief, Madam. I'll bring you all my things you will see none of them belongs to you." Dorcas rushed off to her room and minutes later came back with a blanket bulging with her plates, cups, bowls, candlesticks. She put the blanket on the ground and opened it out.

"You see, Madam. This is all mine." She pointed a finger at hovering George. "He makes trouble for me; he is a bad man. You believe everything he tells you. He fools you and the boss."

George shouted at her in his language and a fight ensued. Maureen was furious. The two of them had never been friends, always having problems. Maureen was sick of it. Dorcas had kept Joey's necklace knowing she had been running from her husband – she was at fault.

"George!" Maureen shouted over them, "Leave me to speak to Dorcas and you go away." She waited for him to leave then turned to Dorcas. "I am sorry, Dorcas but you will have to find another job."

"No, Madam, please."

"Yes. Tomorrow I will give you your money and you must leave." Maureen closed the door on the crying girl. When she told Pete she had fired Dorcas, he shrugged.

"You run the house." It wasn't his problem. Maureen felt dreadful, full of regret for what she had done. Changing her mind wouldn't do any good though, as their relationship was ruined, and it was either George left, or Dorcas and she knew Pete wouldn't send George away. He'd been with him too long.

At seven o'clock in the morning, Dorcas brought in the tray with their cups of tea and put it on Maureen's bedside table. It was her usual practice. She gave Maureen a nervous look and left the bedroom. Maureen got out of bed and went into the kitchen.

"Dorcas, you are to leave today, I meant what I said. I'll get your money." Maureen fetched her purse and took out sixty-rand, two months' salary. She handed Dorcas the money. "I'm sorry, Dorcas."

"George has put a spell on you, you believe too much what he says." She left for her room. Now Maureen would have to search for a new maid. Dorcas had been with her for four years and she liked Dorcas. The children would be sad, especially Liam, who had been a baby when she'd started working for Maureen.

The new maid was called Elizabeth, she was young and cheerful with a five-month-old baby on her back and a distant relative of George. She was a good worker and the baby, named Sonny, was no problem. If he wasn't on her back, he sat on the kitchen floor banging a spoon. She could hear the objections of her friends for allowing the maid to have her child in the house. *He's not vaccinated against smallpox or other diseases. It would be a risk to your children and a distraction for the mother. The maid won't work hard with her child around.* Pete hadn't objected and Maureen didn't care.

Elizabeth worked hard, and the house was running smoothly. Then a murdered black woman was found in the veldt next door. The dead woman was unknown to George and Elizabeth and the police didn't interrogate them. The lack of interest in the woman made Maureen more concerned about living in South Africa. She had crossed an ocean into the unknown when she had come here, believing it would give her independence, allow her to work and bring up her child on her own. It hadn't quite turned out as she had imagined.

Although her marriage was going well and she felt safe with Pete, a woman had been murdered on the other side of her fence.

24

Flight Home

Smoke tunnelled into the sky. Children scattered. Elizabeth came running, breathless, Sonny clinging to her back.

"Madam, come quick! Boss, come quick!" The panicked look on her face gave wings to Maureen and Pete's feet.

"The dump is on fire, it gets over the fence," Elizabeth panted running ahead of Maureen. The dump was feet away from the servants' quarters with only a tank nearby. They were on bore water, without hoses. The garden water was pumped into a small, cemented pool and from there channelled into the garden.

"How did it start?" Pete yelled, running for buckets and blankets to wet.

"The children," said Elizabeth.

"Fuck!" said Pete. Three frightened faces stood on the edge of the tip, bamboo bows and arrows in their hands. George threw a bucket of water into the blazing tip.

"Get the bloody hell out of there," Pete shouted. He grabbed Liam. "What did you do?"

"We made fire arrows." Liam held up a stick with a nail down the end holding a piece of cloth soaked in petrol that wrapped around the end of an arrow. Henry showed me how."

"You little shits. I'm going to kick your arses till your noses bleed." It was Pete's favourite threat that never eventuated.

The veldt was dry. Flames raced towards the road and the property next-door. The neighbour came running with wet sacks and smacked at the flames. Maureen filled buckets. People passing on the road broke off branches and rushed to help, joining the line of firefighters while the children shivered in anticipation of the belting they were going to get.

Smoke filled the yard, Maureen's eyes streamed as she beat at the flames. Her hands were black from soot. There were no vibrations from kangaroos leaping for their lives but the smoke in her eyes, the smell and shouts and flaying sugarbags, brought back memories of her childhood when a fire took her parents' farm.

Eventually they gained control and put the fire out. There were nine exhausted people gathered at Maureen's back door. Pete handed out all his beer and Maureen offered coffee.

"You'll have to manage that tip a bit better," Johan Terblanche, their neighbour up the road said, his skeletal kneecaps pointing at Pete from beneath the wide legs of his safari shorts. Pete straightened; he didn't like Terblanche.

The bastard's doberman pinscher had bailed Maureen up when she had walked up the road to show his wife their new baby. The dog had let her through their front gate and then the baby, strapped to her back African style, started to cry. The dog had flattened itself in front of Maureen, teeth bared, ready to spring. Maureen had shouted for Terblanche's wife, but no one came, and she had stood like a statue in front of the snarling dog until a car came up the road and the driver had come to her aid.

"I'll keep an eye on my tip as long as you keep an eye on your dog," he said. Pete knew Terblanche wouldn't have helped with the fire if it hadn't threatened his property. Seeing them square off, Maureen walked over. The white community in the area was small and they had to keep close.

"Thank you for your help, Johan. Anytime you need assistance with anything please let us know." Johan's look made her wish she was covered in a blanket, not the drawstring blouse and shorts she was wearing. Pete coughed.

"Yeah, thanks man." He looked at Maureen. "Guess it's time we had a word with the kids."

"Fire arrows!" yelled Pete, as he brought his belt across Liam's shrinking arse. Liam screwed his eyes up and grunted as the first stripe appeared; he had two more to follow. Gerard cried and Henry watched, pale-faced. At the end of the punishment, Pete put his belt back on.

"Now, no more playing with fire. Let's go and get some watermelon." That was it and nothing more was said about it. But the fire had fanned the flames of Maureen's longing and she went to a travel agency. The result was exciting because since she and Pete both worked at an airport, they could get discounted tickets. It meant being wait-listed and hanging around the airport until the last passengers were loaded in the hope of spare seats, but it also meant half price tickets.

She waited until they had finished dinner before breaking her news. "Pete, we've got enough money saved for a trip to Australia." Maureen looked at Annie apologetically. "There's only enough money for us, Annie, but you would be all right here with Elizabeth and George to keep an eye on the place." Her mother-in-law nodded.

"You go. I'll be fine." Annie wasn't afraid of being on her own with the natives. In Rhodesia she had jammed a robber's fingers under a window as he was about to climb through, and held him there until someone came to apprehend him. Broke most of his fingers.

"Better buy the tickets then," Pete said.

Chaos ruled for the next four weeks while Maureen tore around buying gifts for her family in Australia – African ornaments and tiger's eye necklaces. She treated her children with worm tablets and bought them new clothes, laughed at Pete's attempts at an Australian accent when he greeted their friends with, "G'day, mate, how ya goin'?" She was dizzy with excitement until the day arrived.

The flight was long with four children. Exhausted, they arrived in Sydney and into the hugs of family who had driven six hours from Eden to meet them at the airport.

Fourteen years had passed since she had seen her family. Her father dithered about, all smiles, patted the children's heads, and tried to squeeze the blood out of Pete's hand. Her mother hugged her and passed her onto Splinter then gathered Gerard into her arms. She had missed her baby and now he was a little boy.

"G'day, Bubs," her sister said with her beaming smile. Maureen's insides warmed at the use of her childhood name.

"G'day, Splinter."

"Kids, this is Aunty Louise," Maureen said, giving her big sister a tight hug. The children fell into unknown relatives' arms as though they'd always known them.

"Hello Lillian, great to see you again." Pete hugged his mother-in-law, then offered his hand to Maureen's pretty sister, blushing when she reached up and kissed him on the cheek. They piled into two cars and drove Pete to Bondi for a quick look at the famous beach before heading to a hotel.

It was eight o'clock the following morning when they were on the road to Eden.

Maureen and Pete didn't have driving licences valid in Australia so despite his expired licence, and his short-term memory loss, it was Eric who drove them along with Liam and Clement. Luckily the other two children and Lillian were able to fit into the car driven by Louise.

"Why didn't I think to get an international licence?" Maureen said to Pete, gripping the dashboard while keeping a close eye on her father.

Suddenly Eric pulled to the side of the road and stopped. He pointed for Pete to see.

"Kangaroo."

"It's dead, Dad." Ignoring Maureen, her father got out of the car and signalled for Pete to follow him. Pete obliged. The bloated kangaroo was full of flies. Pete gagged and covered his nose.

"Christ, it stinks," he said, rushing for the car. Her father got into the driving seat, frowning.

"You don't have those in Africa."

The road was winding and Liam stood behind the driver's seat, watching the road over his grandfather's shoulder. He coughed then vomited down his grandfather's shirt collar.

"Caesar's Ghost!" said Eric, screeching to a stop. He eased himself out of the car, keeping his neck stiff as a board, taking care not to let the vomit leak into his singlet. Carefully removing his shirt, he shook out the chunks of vomit and wiped the back of his neck. He contemplated the shirt, unsure what to do. Pete found a paper bag and offered it to his father-in-law. The shirt went into the bag and the car boot. Maureen cleaned Liam up.

"Why didn't you say you wanted to be sick?"

"I didn't know. It just came up." It was the first time he'd ever vomited. Pete pulled Maureen aside. "Your dad is a lousy bloody driver. He's scaring me shitless."

Maureen chewed the inside of her cheek, then went over to her father. "Dad, Liam always gets sick when his father isn't driving, so would you mind if Pete drives? Just until his stomach settles." She rolled her eyes at Liam who looked about to say something. Her father blinked, stared at Liam, who on cue had another try at being sick. It clinched the deal and her father nodded for Pete to get in the driver's seat.

There were no more mishaps on the journey and Pete sped past all the kangaroo carcasses before his father-in-law tried to stop them.

Eden was a lovely sight. Maureen's heart lifted as she saw her hometown for the first time in years. Nothing had changed. The bellbirds tinkled throughout the forest. The sapphire sea gleamed into the coves. Tears sprang to her eyes.

"Look Liam, Clemmie, that's Eden, Mummy's hometown." They arrived at five o'clock in the afternoon. The old family home was missing more fence palings and the house was in bad need of a paint job. The dunny still stood by the back fence, full of bullet holes, but instead of the dunny-can it now housed garden tools. Her mother had upgraded the house and had installed an inside toilet. After they had unpacked and had a cup of tea, Maureen suggested a walk up the street to stretch their legs.

"I want the children to see where the shops are so they can go and buy themselves an ice-cream." In South Africa, her children had never ventured anywhere on their own. They strolled to the shops and Maureen showed them the ice-cream shop. They walked through town and down to the wharf, ridding themselves of cramps from three days' travelling. The children ran down the long wharf, looking at the fishing boats and men mending nets. Mount Imlay greeted Maureen from across the bay. Eden was like a sigh of relief.

"Like it?"

"Lovely." Pete said. There wasn't much else to say in the tranquillity of the moment. They walked back to her parents' house, the children rushing ahead. Pete gave a whistle to make sure they stayed in sight. Maureen put her hand on his arm.

"Let them have their freedom, there's nothing to worry about here." There was one worry though. Her father.

Next to his bed, in the back room off the landing, leant two rifles, discovered by Liam. They had labels tied to them marked LOADED. Liam picked one up taking it to his grandfather.

"Poop," he said in his South African accent, that brought a narrow look from his grandfather. "Can we shoot your gun? I've only shot with a revolver."

He aimed the gun down the long hall and pulled the trigger just as Maureen came out of her bedroom and into the hall. The bullet whizzed past her and embedded into the front door.

"Holy fuck!" yelled Pete when he heard the bang and saw Liam with the rifle.

"I didn't know it was loaded, Dad, sorry," said Liam.

"It's got a sign on it," said Eric.

"What good's a bloody sign? yelled Pete, snatching the gun from Liam. "Fancy having loaded guns around kids."

Eric's face crumpled. "Crows. They eat the plums." Seeing the confusion on her father's face, Maureen led Pete away.

"Remember, he's had a stroke, Pete."

"Jesus Christ!" Pete said. "You could have been killed."

"Unload the guns when Dad's not around and have a talk to the kids. Tell them never to go in his room."

The following day was Sunday. Maureen, Pete and the children rose early and went to mass. It was a small weatherboard church that seated sixty people at a crush. Many of the parishioners recognised Maureen from their school days. There were hugs, greetings, and introductions.

When they got home after mass, her father glowered at them. He bent to the children.

"Have you been jangling your beads, you little papists?" he said through gritted teeth. Maureen remembered too late her father's hatred of Catholics. They avoided each other for the rest of the day. She was grateful for his short-term memory loss, knowing it would soon be forgotten.

A picnic was organised for the mouth of the Nullica River. Cricket bats, balls, fishing gear and food were loaded into Splinter's car along with her children. Everyone else got into Maureen's father's car. The day was glorious.

The tide was in. It wasn't long before warm sand squeaked beneath their feet.

Louise's youngest daughter, Chrissy, took Henry, Liam and Gerard to search for shells along the beach. Maureen's boys couldn't believe they could wander off on their own. They returned eyes wide to swim up the tidal river. It was the first time they had swum in a river.

Rivers in Africa contained bilharzia, a parasitic worm that gets into the intestines and liver and can live thirty years undetected in the body causing liver cancer and other ailments. They shrieked with delight, rolling down sand dunes, chasing each other into the water, jumping off rocks and drifting on the current. Maureen sat next to Pete watching the children.

"They are loving Australia. They have cousins and freedom here. What do you think about us planning to move to Australia, Pete?"

"I'd love to move here."

Maureen's heart lifted. "I don't know what will happen to Mum though," he said. "We'll look into it when we get back." They couldn't abandon Annie.

Too soon they were on their way to Sydney to fly back to South Africa.

25

Witchdoctors

Walking through Johannesburg airport Maureen switched onto alert mode. Police were spread throughout the airport, with army personnel everywhere. At first, she wondered what was going on and then realised this was normal. They had been away just three weeks and hadn't seen a soldier the whole time they had been in Australia.

"I guess we're back," Pete said. Maureen felt the familiar prickle at the back of her neck.

The children rushed to hug Annie and then tore over to see George. Still in Australia mode, Maureen went into the kitchen and made a pot of tea and carried it through to the lounge.

"Where's Elizabeth? Why are you doing that?" Annie said. Maureen's chest tightened as she put the tray on the table. She was incompetent with the servants, again.

"I don't need Elizabeth. She's busy washing the children's

clothes. What's been going on while we've been in Australia?" Maureen poured the tea, handing a cup to her mother-in-law.

"You met Agnes, my sister from Perth. What did you think of her? Everyone said she was the prettiest in the family and had the best legs." Agnes was Annie's half-sister, the spoilt one. Maureen heard the tinge of bitterness in Annie's voice. She had been given a hard time by her stepmother.

"She's not as pretty as you, Mum and she's fatter. Big hefty legs. Kickstart a Boeing, as Pete would say."

Annie looked pleased, reached for the teapot, and topped Maureen's cup.

"I thought with you all away it would be a good time for the girl to wash the blankets." Annie's face darkened. "Someone stole the kids' blankets off the clothesline. My bet is it was a friend of George's or Elizabeth's. They had plenty of visitors while you were away. They denied it, of course."

Maureen shrugged, too jet-lagged to be hassled. It was the wet season, hot, the children didn't need blankets. The contrast between South Africa and Australia had imprinted on Maureen's eyes from the time they had returned. There had been no visible signs of poverty where her family lived in Australia but here it was everywhere. What were a couple of measly blankets in a country where people couldn't afford to send their children to school, didn't have electricity or running water in their homes, lived in hovels? A black woman couldn't even try on a dress in a shop if she wanted to buy one. Mostly they wore hand-me-downs or made their own clothes. Maureen's visit to Australia had left her engulfed in guilt. She increased George's and Elizabeth's pay.

"Madam, look what I have bought."

Elizabeth beamed with pride as she put the hand-operated Singer sewing machine on the kitchen table. Elizabeth sang a Xhosa song and stamped her feet with glee.

"It's lovely, Elizabeth." Maureen was thrilled for her. She looked closer, noticing rust around the cotton spool and the handle and scratches on the paint. It was obviously second-hand.

"I have it in the shop on layby. It takes eight months paying, Madam. Now you give me more money, I bring it home."

"What shop did you buy it from, Elizabeth? Did you buy it new?"

"The Bergvlei Indian shop, Madam." It was on the edge of Alexandria township, the black township that bordered the suburb where she and Pete had rented Mirabelle Fosdick's cottage.

"How much did you pay?"

"Sixty-rand, Madam."

She'd paid the full price for a sewing machine that was rusty. Maureen was furious with the shop.

"Your machine has some rust on it. Why don't I take it back to the shop and ask them to give you one without rust?" How could they cheat someone so poor?

Elizabeth frowned. "No, Madam. They will not change even if you ask. And you cannot go into the township to the shop. It's not safe. I can scrape the rust off. I will oil it and it will go good." She packed up the machine. Maureen wished she hadn't spoiled the new machine for Elizabeth.

The machine was kept busy. Elizabeth's toddler, Sonny, was wearing a shirt and shorts made from a dress Maureen had given her. Elizabeth made extra money sewing at night for her friend's children.

"You get material, Madam and I make you a skirt for Christmas."

Touched, Maureen decided she would buy a nice piece of material to show Elizabeth how much she appreciated the offer.

Pete and his mother laughed when Maureen told them about the skirt. "What? Don't buy good material. She won't finish the seams off properly. And she's going to make it in her room, so you'll have to give it a good wash," Annie laughed.

Pete grinned. "There wouldn't be many madams to get an offer like that," he said. Maureen decided she'd wear the skirt on Christmas day.

But the skirt didn't happen. Sonny was sick. Elizabeth didn't tell Maureen he was sick. He slept on her back while she worked, unnoticed.

Christmas arrived at five o'clock in the morning. The children opened the pillowcases on their beds and tore around the house shooting each other with cap guns. When they tired of that they built roads in the dirt outside and raced their new dinkie cars. Maureen got out of bed, wondering where Elizabeth was, as she hadn't brought their morning cup of tea. Bleary-eyed, she trundled into the kitchen.

George tapped on the door. "Madam, you must look at Sonny, he is not looking right." He motioned to Elizabeth who came in with Sonny on her back. She gave George an angry look.

"He is not so sick, Madam." Sonny's head was all that was visible above the blanket. He was asleep as usual, cheeks plump and looking normal. Maureen still had Christmas dinner to make.

"He seems fine, George."

"No, Madam." George pulled the blanket down to show her Sonny's emaciated body. Sonny didn't respond to George handling him. His head lolled back, he was thin as a bean, not the stocky little fellow of a few weeks ago. His eyes rolled back until only the whites were visible. He looked very ill. Maureen grabbed her handbag.

"He has to go to hospital, Elizabeth. Pete, you and Mum will have to organise lunch while I drive Elizabeth to the hospital." The black children's hospital was a distance away.

Entering the hospital, the noise was deafening. Parents shouted and children cried. There was no seating. Nurses ran and red lights flashed. Maureen gazed around wondering what to do when she spied the Brazilian doctor from the Catholic church. She gave a sigh of relief and steered Elizabeth towards her.

"Doctor Ramos this is my girl, Elizabeth, her son is not responding. He's been sick for two weeks now. Elizabeth can tell you." She nudged Elizabeth. Elizabeth's eyes filled up.

"He too sick, Madam doctor."

"Come in the other room and I'll examine him. There's a long waiting list but I'll see the boy now." Angry glances were thrown at Maureen from black parents. Someone shouted at Elizabeth. She was being shown privilege because she was with a white woman.

The doctor pointed to deep scratches in Sonny's head and looked at Elizabeth. "You have taken him to a Witch Doctor. These wounds are from chicken claw and rubbed in ash. This makes him sicker."

Maureen turned to Elizabeth, horrified. When she had first learned Sonny was sick, she had given her money to take him to her doctor.

"You took him to a Witch Doctor! Didn't you see my doctor?" Images of Doris dancing around a courtyard sprinkling powder flashed to mind. Elizabeth hung her head.

"Your boy has to stay in hospital," Doctor Ramos said. She looked at Maureen and shook her head, exasperated. "Traditions." The doctor sighed. "The child has encephalitis. He is very, very sick." Elizabeth started to wail. Maureen put her arm around her.

"Can his mother stay with him?" Doctor Ramos shook her head and gave a tight laugh. "This is a black hospital. There's no room. She can visit tomorrow."

"Thank you for seeing us so quickly."

"I'm glad you came. The waiting time might have been too long for him. Merry Christmas. I will see you at mass." Maureen checked her wristwatch. God, it was Christmas Day, and one o'clock already.

Dinner was on the table when they got back. Christmas hats, whistles, and roast chicken. Pete in an apron carved the chicken while Annie loaded the plates. Maureen gave him a squeeze and thanked Annie. She didn't have any interest in eating but tried to for the children's sake.

Sonny recovered and was out of hospital in two weeks. Elizabeth brought him into the house and sat him on the kitchen floor. He crawled into the pantry and dipped his hand into the bag of dog pellets and stuffed his mouth full. He smiled up at Maureen through a mash of pellets.

"Elizabeth, he's eating dog food."

"The dogs are healthy, Madam."

"Blood and bone can't do any harm," Pete said, when Maureen told him. It explained why Pete had eaten the offcuts and ox heart she'd cooked for the dog and praised her for the stew. She hadn't told him, knowing his aversion to offal. It would be a good bedtime story for him.

Days banged together, each one with its own demands leaving no gaps to relax or reminisce. If it wasn't problems with the kids, or work, it was George and Elizabeth and their extended families. Maureen realised employing one person meant inheriting their whole family.

Health problems were constant – the blacks were poor, so dysentery, malaria, bilharzia, measles were rife. But the most common problem of all was food poisoning. George had spent two days recuperating in his township with food poisoning. In Maureen's office, if anyone wanted a day off work, they got food poisoning.

Pete rocked up to find Bossboy doubled in pain clutching his stomach. Food poisoning, Pete thought. Leaning against the aircraft he had prepared for Pete to spray paint, he gasped.

"Boss Pete, I'm sick. This pain in my gut is very bad. Fighting dogs, Boss." Pete went over to him, placed his hand on his shoulder, concerned. Bossboy never complained.

"Show me where the pain is, Chief." His hand pressed the right side of his abdomen.

"It's all over my stomach but started here. Like a fire inside." Pete knew all about that pain – his appendix had ruptured when he was twenty.

"I'll bring the car over and drive you to my doctor; he's close." Pete yelled some orders to his workers then hurried to the hangar where he'd parked his car.

"Easy, Chief," he said, as Bossboy got in next to him. The doctor had been to parties and film nights at Pete's house and took the black man in straight away, free of charge.

"Severe appendicitis. You have to go to hospital; that appendix could burst." The whites of Bossboy's eyes grew – hospitals scared him. A lot of black people died in hospital, and a lot of diseases could be caught there.

"I will call an ambulance for you."

"No! I must go home, tell my family so they know where I am." He looked at Pete. "I will go next day."

The doctor frowned. "I don't advise a delay, Pete."

"My friend has a taxi," Bossboy said.

Pete's brow wrinkled. "I'll drive you to your family, Chief."

Bossboy shook his head. "No Boss Pete. I must do this."

Pete pulled ten rand from his pocket, it was all he had on him, and handed it to his friend. "That's for the taxi and don't come to work until you're fit again. I'll pay you your normal salary while you're on sick leave. The doc will let you use his phone to call the taxi." Pete raised an eyebrow at the doctor.

"The phone's on the reception desk."

Bossboy phoned the number for the black taxi service under the questioning eyes of white patients in the waiting room and then left to wait outside.

The fourth morning after Bossboy's appendix attack, a tall, beautiful, well-dressed black woman holding the hand of a young boy walked into Pete's hangar.

"Boss Pete?"

Pete turned, surprised. The hangar wasn't an area woman frequented, and never a black woman. "Yes?"

"I am Rose, Ephraim Bossboy's wife."

"Oh, how is he?"

Rose looked away and swallowed. "He's dead, Boss Pete." Her voice was just above a whisper.

"Jesus Christ! No!" Pete choked. His face crumpled and he passed a sleeve across his eyes. "When?"

"He died at home the day after you took him to your doctor. He was in big pain and he get the Witch Doctor and he died."

"Witch Doctor! He was supposed to go to the hospital. Why didn't he go to the hospital? I should have taken him. I shouldn't have listened to him." He stood slumped in front of her, full of self-recrimination.

"I came to ask you to his funeral, Boss Pete." It was a huge compliment. Pete nodded. In a daze, he wrote down the funeral details and thanked Rose for coming. Then he closed the hangar and sent his workers home, unable to deal with the familiarity of his workplace without his friend.

It was evident to Maureen how much Pete regarded Bossboy. He kept to himself in the garage and hardly spoke, other than to say he would be going to the funeral on the weekend.

"I'll come with you," Maureen said.

Pete shook his head. "No, it's in Soweto. It's not safe."

Maureen could have gone though as Bossboy's family gave Pete an escort, and treated him like family. Pete paid Rose a salary for four months. It was as much as he could afford. Bossboy became Pete's rule of thumb, always using him as a measure for his other workers to live up to, telling them he was the best worker he'd ever had, that he was irreplaceable.

26

Botswana

It had been six months since Maureen had last heard from Joey and out of the blue she arrived. The car rolled to a quiet stop under the big jacaranda tree. She didn't get out. Sitting behind the steering wheel, she watched Colin race towards Henry and Liam in the front yard. Surprised to see Joey, Maureen ran out to greet her.

"Maureen, I'm sorry," Joey hung her head. Maureen's heart nearly broke at the sight of her friend. Heavy eyed, a cut lip, bruises. It explained why Maureen hadn't heard from her. Joey had been too ashamed to let her know she had gone back to Des.

"Oh, God, Joey. Come inside." Seeing the suitcase on the back seat, Maureen opened the back door and dragged it out, then pulled Joey into her arms.

"It's just for tonight."

"Are you going back to your brother?" Joey shook her head.

"I don't get along with his wife. My neighbour has a holiday house in Vereeniging, I'm going to stay there."

"You have to see a lawyer, Joey. You can't keep going on like this. If not for yourself, what about Colin?"

Joey looked away. It was fruitless talking; they had been through this before. She carried Joey's suitcase into Henry's bedroom. He and Colin would share the couch bed in the lounge.

Annie put her head around Henry's door. "I thought I heard voices?" Joey looked at Annie and flushed. There was an awkward silence.

"This is my friend Joey, Mum. She's staying the night. Would you mind checking on the children?" Maureen's eyes signed her mother-in-law towards the door, hoping she would catch on. To her relief she saw recognition dawn – they had discussed Joey in the past.

"Welcome, Joey. Excuse me while I see to the children." She closed the door and left.

"How is it going with her?" Joey asked. Maureen threw her hands open.

"She's a good granny and tries to keep out of my way, but it would be nice not to have to share Pete and the kids. Selfish, aren't I?" Joey's problems were far worse than hers. Remembering the necklace, she changed the subject.

"I've got something for you. Last time you were here you left a necklace." Maureen's chest tightened with remorse at the thought of Dorcas. "You settle in while I go and get it."

"It was a gift from my aunty," Joey said, turning the necklace in her hand. It's not worth very much." More guilt filled Maureen. The necklace had cost Dorcas and herself a lot.

"Leave your things and let's go and have a cup of tea."

"Curtains look nice," Joey said walking into the lounge room, her face clouded. "I'm really sorry, Maureen."

"Don't worry about me, I just want you to be safe."

213

Pete drove through the gate and sighted Colin playing soccer with Henry in the front yard. He sighed. He would love to throttle Des.

"Hello Joey. Lovely to see you." He went over and gave her a gentle hug aware she might have injuries.

"Des reported your film nights to the police," Joey said.

"Kind of him. At least he saved me a lot of money in grog." He had always suspected it was Des who had stopped them.

In the evening, mindful of the children and Annie, Maureen kept the conversation light while they watched television, sharing news about their trip to Australia. Pete did an imitation of Eric's Australian drawl, making Joey laugh.

"The kids loved Australia," Pete said. "It's such a free, safe country. The people are friendly and helpful, there's no army conscription. I'm hoping we'll settle there one day."

"You're lucky," Joey said. "Well, I'm off to bed, it's been a big day. I'll be leaving early in the morning."

They had breakfast and Maureen walked Joey to her car. "Please don't go back to him, Joey. You can't keep doing this. I don't want to read about you in the newspapers."

"I won't go back, promise." She put out a pinkie and Maureen hooked her finger in Joey's. Hadn't they done this before?

"Whatever you do, please phone and let me know how and where you are. It's excruciating wondering if you're all right."

"She'll be back," Annie said after Joey had left. "She won't be able to support Colin without help." It was true, a child changed everything.

A phone call from Australia pushed Joey from Maureen's mind and threw her into a panic of excitement. Sarah her childhood friend was coming to see her. They had gone to school together in Eden and later Sarah married a Norwegian boy and moved to Norway and eventually Sweden. She had been with Maureen in Sweden when she was pregnant with Henry and going through all her dramas. Maureen owed her a lot. Annie was going to visit her brother in Port Elizabeth so they could use Annie's room.

"Definitely not," Annie said. It was her room, the only place she could retreat to when she felt in the way. Pete had agreed with his mother. Maureen wished she hadn't asked. She went over to Pierrette's to moan about Annie's lack of support.

"They'll be here for three weeks so I can't put Sarah in the lounge for that long, there's no privacy. I can borrow stretchers for the two children, but I can't put an eight-year-old girl in with the boys."

"I will make my trip home to Switzerland the same time your friend comes so she can use my flat."

Maureen clapped her hands. It was a perfect solution. "Fabulous, you can have a month's free rent."

"I have ze cheapest rent already and sometimes you feed me. At work they joke about my cheap rent, and I was thinking to pay you more, so you will not give me free rent while your friend is here."

It was true, Maureen had never thought to put Pierrette's rent up. She loved having her in the flat. Pierrette had been there two years already and was one of the family, buying birthday and Christmas gifts for the children, listening to her moan about Annie.

"Pierrette's going to let me use her flat." She was already planning their itinerary. Pete smiled at Maureen's excitement.

"That's nice of her. What about taking Sarah to Mashatu Lodge?"

Mashatu was a game park in Botswana that belonged to Air Safari, the company Maureen worked for. Part of her job was to organise flights for the company's VIP guests and to arrange their accommodation at the Lodge. Mashatu bordered Rhodesia and South Africa. It was also a route for the guerrillas who were trying to reclaim Rhodesia from the illegal white government. Pete's brother was the resident manager and game ranger at the lodge – Maureen had gotten him the job.

"It's the off-season and they're renovating so there won't be any guests," said Pete. "I'll phone Mick and organise it with him."

"We would have to make it a long weekend. Take the Kombi." Pete's latest acquisition was a new Kombi and he had made sure to discuss its purchase with Maureen, the same as he had done with the Ford Maureen drove, remembering the fight they had had over his Peugeot when they lived at the chicken coop.

In the following weeks, Maureen could hardly contain her excitement. It was eleven years since she had seen her friend.

They recognised each other immediately. Sarah still looked the same, but her son, Mickey, was now twelve. The last time she had seen Mickey was in Sweden. Now he had a little sister, Fleur, four years younger and the image of Sarah.

"Four kids? I can't believe it," Sarah laughed, looking at Maureen's brood exploding around her. "I'm glad it worked out for you."

"A bit different from the television actress I thought I was going to be," Maureen laughed. She had accepted her lot although she would have liked a bit more romance. Pete usually approached her in bed with the question, "Do you want a bit?" or "How about I throw a leg over?" She could have taught him bed manners but didn't in case he thought she'd shagged a lot of blokes. But she hadn't.

"You're going to stay in my tenant's flat, so it will be nice and quiet. I'll give you a couple of days to settle in and then we're going to have a weekend in a game lodge in Botswana. Pete's brother runs it. We'll see lots of elephants."

Sarah was thrilled.

It was a noisy six-hour drive to Mashatu with six children in the Kombi and for once, Pete was happy to stop for everyone to pee. It gave him time to rest his ears.

They parked under a carport on the side of the Limpopo River and watched while two Africans loaded their belongings onto a wooden platform suspended from a rope beneath a steel cable and pulley, fifteen feet above a river teeming with crocodiles and hippos. The men signalled to two men on the opposite side of the river and the platform was hauled across. It swung from side to side, its cargo sliding. Once it was unloaded it was pulled back to collect Maureen and three of the children. They were instructed to sit down and hang onto a knee-high rope handrail. The platform swung into the air and rocked across the river. All Maureen could see were the rapids beneath. It took two more trips, and everyone was safely on the other side. They had all been terrified.

Mick drew up in a Land Rover towing a small trailer. Henry, Liam and Gerard threw themselves at him. He swung them into the Land Rover, laughing.

"Good to see you, man." Pete said, slapping his brother on the arm. Mick grinned.

"Ellen says welcome. She's down at the trading store. I'll settle you in and we'll meet in the bar for a beer."

"This is Sarah, Maureen's Australian friend, she lives in Sweden."

Mick shook hands with Sarah. "Welcome to Botswana. Better get everyone on board before we lose the light. Gets dark quickly and I don't want to be out late." He leant towards Pete, lowering his voice. "There's been some terrorist activity in the area." Thick grass switched the side of the Land Rover as they drove to the lodge.

It was typical of most African lodges. Exotic plants exploded along the pathway to an archway entrance of purple bougainvillea that led onto a wide verandah under a pitched thatch roof. The verandah was enclosed in thin chicken wire to deter inquisitive monkeys. The lounge was large, with a big central fireplace built from river stone, and thick black beams crisscrossed the high thatch roof. It had white walls and polished stone floors. In the bedrooms, mosquito nets hung from the ceiling. Each room opened onto the verandah and stretcher beds were in a line along the verandah for the children.

Mick's wife, Ellen, arrived and they all sat down to a dinner of roast venison, with fresh fruit salad served by a waiter in a white uniform with a red sash across his chest and a red fez.

"We'll leave early in the morning, it's the best time for spotting elephant," Mick said. He turned to the children. "You will have to keep very quiet. No talking in the Land Rover or you might startle an elephant and we don't want them stampeding us. If they do, we'll be as flat as the bread on your plate." The children's eyes popped.

The night was chilly, so Maureen zipped the children into their sleeping bags. "I won't lock my bedroom door so if you want to go to the toilet come to our room and wake me up, I've got a torch." All the rooms had them in case the generator failed.

A mosquito net hung above her bed to keep the blood suckers out, so she left her bedroom window open for the fresh night air. After the long journey over corrugated roads and a few glasses of wine at dinner, it didn't take Maureen long to fall asleep.

In the middle of the night, she woke to strange noises outside her window. She lay and listened, considered waking Pete but decided not to disturb him after driving all day. Maureen felt for the torch next to the bed, switched it on and crept to the window. The sight that met her eyes was astonishing. Lit by moonlight, the garden was full of zebra. Putting her hand through the window grille, she trailed her fingers along the back of a zebra feeding on the grass beneath the window. It flicked its tail and continued munching, then lifted its head and breathed into her face. She stood motionless at the window in awe, as she watched the creatures graze. This was a moment that could never be repeated in her lifetime, a moment that bonded her with Africa. So consumed by the experience, she didn't think to wake Pete or the children. When clouds blanketed the moon, erasing the vision, she went to bed and lay listening to the sounds of Africa until she fell asleep.

Frightened voices woke her before dawn. Liam and Gerard stood in their sleeping bags at the end of her bed. Gerard was crying and Liam was babbling.

Pete sat up. "What's up, Buddy?"

"We were sniffed. Something very big sniffed us." They had scrunched down and pulled their sleeping bags tightly over their heads. "I don't want to sleep on the verandah, Daddy," Liam said.

"That's okay, Buddy. It was probably just an inquisitive monkey." But to reassure the kids, he got out of bed and dragged their stretchers into the room. When it was light Pete went to investigate what had disturbed the children and saw a large bulge in the chicken wire next to the children's beds. He looked closer. Pieces of hair were caught in the netting as though an animal had rubbed its face on the wire. Large paw prints marked the damp earth next to the verandah.

Mick approached to call them for breakfast and Pete motioned him over, pointing to the paw prints.

"Take a look at this! Shit! The kids had a visitor last night. It looks like a leopard."

Mick stepped off the verandah to inspect the prints. "Leopard for sure. We lost a dog two nights ago to a leopard."

Pete looked at him, incredulous. "Why didn't you tell us? This bloody chicken wire won't hold a leopard back. One swipe and its gone. It could have taken one of the kids!" Pete contemplated the wire in a fury. "They can sleep in with us and I'll tell them it was a monkey, so it doesn't spoil the holiday." It wasn't a good start.

A rifle rested across Pete's knees while Mick drove Maureen, Sarah, and the children through the game park, easing around corners over rocks and through mud.

"Now, quiet everybody, absolutely no talking," Mick warned. They followed a trampled track through long grass and popped out into a clearing right in the middle of a herd of elephants. One of the children squealed in fright. A trunk went up and sniffed the air. Giant ears flapped and heads turned towards the matriarch elephant to see what the disturbance was. She swung her trunk and stamped her foot. Maureen's heart jammed in her throat; Pete's finger went to the gun's trigger. Mick put the jeep in reverse and let the engine idle. No one moved. And then like a silent grey cloud, the matriarch turned and drifted into the bush with her tribe behind her, hardly disturbing a leaf.

Maureen let her breath go. "They caught our scent. We won't see them again today, so I suggest we go down to the river and find some hippo. Anyone get a photo?" No one had. But cameras were ready for the giant heads that came up out of the water to observe them.

"Never get between a hippo and the water," Mick said. It was a message soon forgotten when they came to spread the groundsheet under a thorn tree and have lunch. Lunch was cold chicken, salad, bread rolls, beer and cordial. The children went to the river's edge to paddle.

Pete jumped up and pulled them away from the water. "Don't go in the water it can make you sick."

Sarah laughed, thinking Pete was joking.

"You can get bilharzia, it's a disease caused by a parasitic worm and there could be crocs," he said.

Sarah tensed, looking around. "Is there anything that isn't dangerous? she asked.

"We've got a gun," Maureen said.

On their second and last day at the lodge, a monkey stole Gerard's blankie, a piece of blanket edged with satin that he carted everywhere. He chased it across the lawn, crying.

"You are too old for your blankie, Gerard. The monkey wants your blankie to keep its baby warm. You've got Ratty now." Ratty was a failed attempt at a knitted teddy bear Pete's mother had made. Ratty was Gerard's special friend. If Gerard annoyed Liam, Liam would smack Ratty to make Gerard cry.

"Come on buddy, don't cry," said Mick. "Hop in the jeep with Mum and we'll go to the trading store for an ice cream." He looked around the other eager faces. "Okay, you can all get in." Maureen went with him to keep the children under control.

The trading store was a corrugated iron building with groups of Africans laughing and talking outside. A few skeletal dogs roamed around, noses to the ground.

"Everybody out," Mick yelled. The children charged towards the store with Mick and Maureen following. He entered the door and stopped, then leant over to Maureen and spoke in a low voice. "Don't look at the two Africans with dreadlocks at the counter, just buy the ice creams and get the kids out to the jeep as quick as you can."

Prickles went up the back of Maureen's neck. Henry walked over to the men with dreadlocks and stood next to them, examining the pictures of ice creams taped to the chest freezer. Maureen sauntered to the counter and removed her purse from her handbag. She forced herself to smile at the children's excitement, ignoring the two men. Meanwhile Mick sorted through a stack of garden tools, picking up a spade and weighing it in his hands. The children pointed out the ice creams they wanted and Maureen beckoned to the nervous shop assistant behind the counter.

"It is five-rand, Madam."

"Thank you," Maureen said, handing the money over and the ice creams around. "Now, back to the car you lot."

The two men spoke to each other in undertones and cast a furtive look in Mick's direction. They pushed past the children, leaving the shop ahead of Maureen. She could feel the sweat trickle down her back. Were they waiting for them outside?

Mick came over, still holding the spade. "Come on, let's go," he said, hustling the children in front of him.

From the doorway, he could see there was no one outside. The two men had disappeared and the crowd outside the shop had dispersed. He propped the spade against the door and strode to the jeep and the gun inside. Maureen held the children's ice creams while they climbed in the jeep.

"Everyone, lock your doors," Mick said.

Maureen didn't have to be told. She'd already pushed the locks down on the passenger doors. Mick started the engine and they sped down the road.

"How did you know they were terrorists?" Maureen whispered to Mick.

"They were wearing army issue boots. They are from Rhodesia. I've seen them hanging around the store before. I'm going to drop a word to the South African army after you leave."

"Don't say anything to Sarah, I don't want to spoil her holiday," Maureen said.

On the last night of their holiday, they sat in front of the fire having drinks and toasting the future for peace in South Africa and Rhodesia.

"I don't see any war going on. I thought from Maureen's letters you were all carrying guns and people were attacking houses," Sarah laughed. "I find the black people friendly."

"South Africa is very complex; you have to live here to know what's going on," said Mick. "When you're on holiday, you go to game reserves and tourist places where rich people go. You don't see the real country or experience the fear of not knowing what the future will be for white people when the blacks take over. Which they will," he said.

The fire crackled and they sipped their wine as night closed in.

27

Escarpment

Following the success of their Botswana trip, Maureen crossed her fingers for the next event she had planned for her visitors.

The mine site was on the opposite side of Johannesburg, an hour's drive away. They arrived at the entrance and were ushered into the pavilion by a well-built black man wearing a feathered head dress and a beaded breast plate over his bare chest. They joined a small crowd in front of a group of African dancers. The dancers were lined up in front of them, half crouched, pangas – short-curved swords – raised, also in headdresses and breast plates with shorts and black gum boots. Their voices harmonised. They stamped their feet, then went still, giving a blood curdling yell and charging their white audience with knives raised. Everyone jumped back.

A dancer's face stopped inches from Maureen's. She could see white saliva in the corners of his mouth, the anger in his eyes.

She held his gaze and didn't flinch. Inside, her chest squeezed. As suddenly as they had charged, they whirled and stamped their way back into the centre of the arena, shaking the ground as they went. They dropped their knives, lined up, and lifted their voices in lovely harmony, then drummed their gumboots with both hands in a rhythm that got everyone stamping. It was exciting and ominous, as though heralding something to come.

"Scary," Sarah said, with a nervous giggle.

They hate us, Maureen thought.

Her next outing for Sarah was the musical, *Ipi Ntombi*. It was experimental theatre with a black cast performing African music for a white audience. The response had been unexpected, receiving rave reviews despite Apartheid.

The music coiled inside Maureen and flowed through her body. She loved every minute of it.

After the show the car wouldn't start. "Bloody Pete," she cursed, "he never charges batteries."

Sarah was short, and always wore high heels. She struggled behind the car to push it, while Maureen sat in the driver's seat trying to kick the motor over. The performers from the musical came out of the stage door and, seeing their plight, told Sarah to get in the car and they would push. The motor kicked over, and Maureen roared off down the road, waving and yelling thanks. It was generous of them to help white women when their own people couldn't sit in their audience.

At work a week later, Pete clasped his chest and doubled over in pain. He staggered towards his car and drove to the doctor.

Doc Smith, their usual doctor, was away, and Pete had to see the new doctor in their area. A religious man and a member of the Dutch Reform Church, he was known to write bible references on his scripts. He hooked Pete up to his heart monitor and read the results.

"You're having a heart attack. I'm going to call an ambulance you must go to hospital right away."

"I don't need an ambulance. I can drive myself," Pete said.

"No. You might collapse and have an accident." Ignoring Pete's protests, the doctor called the ambulance. Annoyed, Pete refused to get on the stretcher and climbed, unassisted, into the back. On his arrival at the hospital, he was met by an orderly with a wheelchair who he waved aside.

"I can walk, man."

The ICU nurses stared at Pete as he walked into the ward, face beaded in sweat, doubled with pain.

"You are the only case that's ever walked in here," a nurse said, helping him into bed and hooking up a drip.

When Maureen arrived, he was sitting up talking to a man tangled in tubes in the bed beside his. She walked over and waited for him to finish telling his famous joke. The patient's eyes crinkled, and a corner of his lip lifted above the tube that went down his throat. He gurgled in response and an alarm went off. A nurse rushed over and pulled a curtain around his bedside, cutting Pete off. He sat back, spied Maureen, and held out an arm with a tube.

"Surprise!" he said, with a grin.

Next to the rest of the inert patients in the ward, Pete appeared normal, the healthiest person in the ward.

Maureen let out a sigh of relief, she hadn't known what to expect. "God, I thought you were dying." She sat in a chair beside him.

Pete smiled, happy to see her. "I feel all right. Still have some pain in my chest area but that's all."

"I was so worried, the doctor said you were critical in intensive care."

"The doctor said I was having a heart attack, but I think it's from the bloody curry ball I ate at work. Thing is I can't leave here until he says so."

Maureen peered at him; he didn't look like he'd had a heart attack. Nothing like her Aunt Maggie had looked after her heart attack.

"Hazel at the airport only asked me this morning if we wanted to take Sarah to visit her brother's farm in the Cape. They live just out of Knysna. She's leaving the day after tomorrow and said we could follow her. Imagine if we had gone and you'd had a heart attack on the trip?"

"You should still go. I'm fine. It would be a shame for Sarah to miss out and you haven't seen the Cape." Maureen frowned; she could imagine what Pete's mum would think if she went on holiday with her friend while Pete was in hospital.

"In fact, I insist you go. Leave Henry and Liam with Corona so they won't miss school and take Gerard and Clement. I'll be out of here in no time. I've sent a message to Doc Smith to come and see me here. I don't trust this new guy. He made me ride in a bloody ambulance. My car is still at his rooms. Take it to the boys at the airport and get them to check the oil and the tyres. It's 1145 kilometres to Knysna, a two-day trip. Sarah can help with the driving."

It occurred to Maureen that Pete was giving her orders from an intensive care bed in a room where none of the other patients were even capable of speech. He looked normal and it was a great opportunity for Sarah to see the country but what they didn't know was that Sarah didn't have a driver's licence and Maureen would have to drive the whole way.

The night before leaving, Maureen dropped Henry and Liam off at her friend's house.

"You be good for Corona. I won't be away long," she kissed them both. Henry turned his face away, so her kiss glanced off his cheek. He wanted to go too. Corona's promise to visit Pete in hospital gave Maureen the guilts. What wife would leave her husband in intensive care to take her friend on a holiday? But this wasn't any friend, Sarah had helped her in Sweden; she owed her. And Sarah hadn't tried to dissuade her from going, she had been all for it.

Maureen packed the car, debated over the gun and then put it in the glove box.

"What are you taking that for?" Sarah said, looking nervous.

"We might hit an animal and have to put it out of misery," Maureen replied. That wasn't the only reason she felt safer with a gun. She strapped Clement into the children's seat between Sarah and herself. Gerard and Sarah's children got in the back. Maureen handed Sarah the map. "I've marked the route to keep an eye on the towns we pass through."

The first day on the road was uneventful and apart from meerkat sentries sitting on posts, they didn't see much game. They passed through a few shanty towns, weaving their way between cattle, chickens, and thin children with outstretched hands, but made good time. It was evening when they reached a motel. Maureen was exhausted. Her back ached and her eyes stung from staring at the road. She let the children run around the motel garden to stretch their legs before calling them in for dinner and flopping into bed.

Seven a.m. and they were on the road again. The small towns flashed by Maureen, with dirt roads and stray goats making it impossible for her to take in the scenery. She parked under a group of thorn trees so they could have a pee and eat lunch. Meerkats watched them from high mounds in the Karoo Desert. It was hot and dusty. Sarah cleared up while Maureen got the kids in the car. The car made a few attempts to start and failed.

"Bugger! I don't believe it. It can't be the battery, it's new." She got out and lifted the hood, unscrewing the cap to check the water. A small hose leading from the spout had come off, otherwise the water level was good. The battery terminals were all in place. Oil fine, fan belt intact. She turned the motor again and it fired up. "Thank God," she said.

Two bushmen, wearing flaps of cloth hanging from a leather strap around their hips, hailed them as they passed. Maureen slowed for Sarah to take a photo. They spied zebra in the distance. The day disappeared and night closed in as they wound their way up the escarpment.

Maureen hugged the side of the rock face to allow enough room for oncoming traffic. It was a sheer drop on the other side of the road.

They were near the peak of the escarpment heading for the town of George when the motor died.

"Shit!" Maureen turned the key off, rested the motor and then tried to start the car again. The motor made two more failed attempts before it stopped responding. She looked at Sarah. They couldn't stay here all night. The road was narrow, an oncoming car could hit them. Road traffic had been scarce. It wasn't school holidays and not many took this mountain route.

"I'm going to hitch a ride into town. It's at the bottom of the escarpment on the other side of the mountain. If I take Mickey and carry Clement, someone should pick me up." On her own they might not stop, or they might with another purpose in mind. "Will you come with me Mickey?" He could run for help if she was attacked.

"Yes, sure." He got out of the car, too young to consider the risk. Maureen collected Clement from the baby seat.

"If anyone stops and asks if you need help, tell them I'm walking ahead and to pick me up. The gun is in the glove box if they try and break into the car. Will you be all right with the kids, Sarah?"

"Hurry back," Sarah said, full of apprehension.

Maureen lifted Clement onto her hip and left the car. Without a torch she had to rely on moonlight and the brilliance of the stars. Over the top of the escarpment they walked, keeping as close to the edge of the drop as they dared. A night hyrax gave a blood curdling scream.

"What was that?" Mickey said, drawing close.

"It's a small animal with a big voice, it won't hurt you." Pete's love of the bush had taught her a lot. The next sound made the hair on her arms stand up. A cough. The sound of the leopard echoed along the valley. She muttered some quick Hail Marys and shifted Clement to her other hip, walking faster. Way below she could see a glimmer of lights. The town.

She heard a car approaching from behind and waved her arm. It slowed, the passenger looked at her, then sped past. Panic gripped her. God, what if no one picked them up? A truck came along, its brakes filling the air with the smell of burning rubber. She moved into the road and waved her arm, desperate. It stopped beside her, and the driver leant across the seat and opened the passenger door. She pushed Clement in and then climbed up after him, Mickey following.

The driver gave her a hard look. He hadn't realised she was a white woman. "Where are you going in the night, Madam?"

She looked at the driver; he was light skinned but must be a coloured if he'd called her Madam; there had recently been riots in the Cape.

"My car broke down. You must have passed it back there. I need to get to a garage."

"The garages will be closed."

"Then a place where I can telephone." Silence sat between them. The motor whined and the cabin smelled of burning brakes as the truck edged its way down the mountain. They hadn't been in the truck long when Mickey started to squirm beside her.

"I need a pee," he said.

"Why didn't you go when we stopped?"

"I didn't want to do it then," he moaned.

Jesus Christ! What was she going to do? She would have to get the truck to stop. Would the driver wait? "I'm so sorry, but my boy needs to pee, can you stop, please?"

"This is a dangerous place to stop, very steep."

She heard the annoyance in his voice, but to her relief he stopped the truck. Mickey got out.

"You get out too," the driver said. "I will get someone to come back for you." Reluctant, Maureen got out of the truck with Clement. The truck moved off leaving her helpless in total darkness in a dangerous area with two children. What an idiot! Furious with herself and Mickey, she rounded on him.

"You stupid boy, why didn't you pee before we got in the bloody truck?" In the distance she heard another cough. "Hear that? It's a bloody leopard." She wanted to frighten the shit out of him.

In the dark, their progress was slow. They felt their way along the edge of the road, eyes straining in the dark. Rounding a tight corner, Maureen was suddenly hit by a blast of headlights. Blinded, she stopped. The car was going the wrong way, but she waved in the hope it would stop and get her help. But it passed by. Minutes later the vehicle returned, drew alongside her and a woman put her head out of the passenger window.

"Get in. We passed you going down the hill, saw you carrying a baby and thought you might be in trouble, so we came back up."

Maureen could have dropped on all fours and kissed her feet. They clambered in the car. "Thank you, thank you."

"Is that your car on the other side of the escarpment?"

"Yes, we broke down. My friend is there with two children waiting for me to get help."

"Bad place for you to be walking. You would have to walk through the coloured area before you got into town. I'll drop you at the nearest hotel where you can phone your people."

It was a godsend. By the time Maureen reached the hotel it was eight o'clock at night. She had been on the road thirteen hours and was exhausted.

The receptionist welcomed her and directed her to the telephone where she put a call through to the farm. Hazel's brother answered. They had expected her hours ago and were worried something had happened. He would pick them up and take her back to the car, but the farm was another hour away and she would have to wait for him to get to her. Maureen ordered drinks for Mickey and Clement and a coffee for herself, which the proprietor refused payment for.

"You can sit in the foyer and wait for your friend," he said, waving his hand towards two comfortable armchairs. Grateful, Maureen sank into soft luxury, Clement in her arms while Mickey sat in the other chair. It was hard keeping awake, but she didn't want to be asleep when Hazel's brother arrived, nor could she sleep with the monster headache hammering the back of her skull, which she felt she deserved for leaving her husband in hospital a thousand kilometres away. Why did she jump into things without thinking it through? Hadn't her Swedish experience taught her anything? She was saved from any further self-recriminations when her host walked through the hotel doors.

"Maureen?"

"Yes. Oh, thank God. I'm sorry you had to come and get us. The engine turns over and dies but the battery is new so it couldn't be that and I checked the water and oil. The only thing I can think of is water in the petrol," she babbled. He had a kind face.

"David," he shook her hand and stared at the child in her arms, perplexed. "Let's go and see to your car." He led the way to his Land Rover.

They came over the top of the escarpment and Maureen pointed to her car on the side of the road, squeezed against the cliff face.

"I'll drop you off and go further down so I can turn around," David said.

Maureen got out, Clement in her arms. She tapped on the car window. "Sarah, it's me. Sorry it took so long. Bet you thought I wasn't coming back until the morning." Maureen looked at her friend and smiled, exhausted.

Sarah unlocked the car. "I knew you would come back tonight."

"Anyone stop and ask if you needed help?

"I waved them on. I was too scared to unlock the car."

"You have the gun?"

"Yes, but I would have shot the children and then myself if someone had forced their way in," Sarah said, grim-faced.

Maureen stared at her in disbelief – she wasn't joking. Once she was in the car, she moved the gun under the driver's seat without Sarah seeing and made a note never to trust her with the gun or the children. David pulled in front of them leaving his lights on high beam. He lifted the bonnet and looked at the motor. Maureen stood next to him, waiting to hand the spanners.

"It's too dark I can't see. I'll have to tow you. I'll need you to steer your car and use the brakes. It's steep and I don't want you banging into the back of me. The others can come in my car."

Maureen fought to keep her eyes open, braking when the towrope slackened as they descended the escarpment, steering when they swung too wide on the sharp corners. Free of the mountains, the gravel road straightened out and they gathered speed, the Land Rover churning dust into Maureen's car, stinging her eyes and making her nose leak. This was the worst road trip of her life and she swore if anyone else visited her she would pay their bus fare or lend them her car to go sight-seeing. When they reached the farm, it was one o'clock in the morning.

"We'll talk tomorrow," Maureen's hostess said, after helping her get the children to bed. Maureen was asleep before she could say goodnight."

28

Soccer Game

The farm was idyllic, a Cape Dutch house surrounded by snow-capped mountains with fields of wildflowers and butterflies. Maureen placed her deck chair next to her car and dropped into it, lying back to let the sun seep into her body while David checked the motor. She didn't want to see the inside of a car for a week.

First turn of the key and the car started. David let the engine idle while he investigated the problem. The radiator hose had come off and water was squirting all over the electrics shorting the motor. It was cheap and easy to fix.

"You can get a hose at the garage in Knysna when you go shopping with Hazel," David said.

Knysna was on the sea and reminded Maureen of her home-town, Eden. They could have been in Australia. African culture wasn't as visible in the Cape as it was in Johannesburg and

Durban. There were more whites and coloureds, and despite the Cape's mountainous beauty, Maureen wondered if she wouldn't have been better off taking Sarah to Zulu Durban.

They visited Oudtshoorn and watched the ostriches race. People paid for rides on the backs of the huge birds. A ranger demonstrated the ostrich's long throat by gripping its neck halfway down and pushing something large into its mouth until it swallowed. The object went down its throat until it reached the ranger's hand and then he squeezed it back up for it to regurgitate. Maureen felt sorry for the animals and didn't enjoy the park. The car drama had dampened her holiday. She worried about Pete and thought about Henry and Liam in school and was happy when it was time to return to Johannesburg.

The trip back was quicker, and Maureen was more prepared. The children all did a pee when they were asked, scared the car would break down.

She tooted the horn to announce their arrival as she drove through the gate. Henry and Liam came running with Pete walking behind them. Relieved at the sight of Pete, she pulled up, happy to be home with her family, exhausted from the long drive. She got out of the car and gave the children a hug and then Pete. "You look good," she said.

"I didn't have a heart attack. That quack of a doctor's equipment wasn't working properly and the pain in my chest was from my liver, caused by bilharzia. They put me on a drip and filled me with poison to kill the bilharzia which made me pretty sick for a couple of days and then I came good."

Maureen looked closer at Pete, noticing the pallor of his skin, and felt bad she hadn't stayed with him. Next time she'd put her family first.

"Did you have a nice time?"

"I phoned Corona and left messages for you?"

"You didn't leave me a number to call you back."

George sauntered up the drive to unload the car.

"We've got television," Henry said bursting with pride.

Pete gave a wide grin. "It's black and white, got it second-hand to keep the boys occupied while you were away."

Another stab of guilt went through Maureen. Pete had wanted a television when it first came to South Africa, he had been waiting two years, but she'd insisted on saving their money for a holiday.

They sat down to watch *Haas Das we Nuuskas*, a rabbit and mouse newscast. Sarah and her children laughed at Henry and Liam fighting over positions in front of the television. So much fuss over the only children's show on the television, which was in Afrikaans and only Pete and Maureen's children could understand.

"Only one station?"

It wasn't the first time Sarah had been astounded at Africa's backward lifestyle. Maureen didn't have a vacuum cleaner or a floor polisher, the maid used a broom and skated on brushes to polish the floor.

"They break everything," Pete explained.

She believed him after their first outing to the snake park, when Maureen had left a roast in the oven with instructions for the maid to turn the oven down. Instead, the girl had taken her afternoon tea break and when they had arrived home, George was waiting outside the kitchen, smoke billowing around him. He had pointed at the smoke.

"The girl didn't turn the roast off," he said, folding his arms.

But he hadn't either. He'd left it burning for Maureen to see. She had to throw the roast and the roasting dish away.

"I don't think I could live here," Sarah said, watching the Afrikaans programme with the enthralled children. "It's too backward. I've had a fabulous time but I'm ready to go home next week and relax." She liked an organised life; it was too unpredictable here. "It will be nice to go to bed and not worry about being murdered," she said, happy to leave the blue skies of Africa to don the skis of a Swedish winter.

Saying goodbye to Sarah was hard. She had brought a piece of Eden to Africa and her departure left a sag in Maureen's shoulders and a longing to see her family in Eden. But Pete wasn't getting much work and money was tight.

Pierrette's return and the introduction of her new Australian boyfriend, Bluey Carmichael, lifted Maureen's spirits. Bluey hailed from Horsham in Victoria and was a veterinarian working with the white lions in Pretoria Zoo.

It was hard feeling gloomy around Bluey. His cheerful grin and "G'day, mate," made her smile, and she liked that Henry always ran for his cricket bat when he saw Bluey visiting Pierrette. Their romance didn't last but Bluey and Pierrette remained friends and he continued to visit Maureen and Pete for a beer and to boast to the kids about his cricket prowess.

"I'm batting next Saturday so I'll take you to see how Aussies play cricket. Aussies can beat the South Africans one-handed," he teased.

"No, they can't," Liam said.

"I'll prove it next Saturday if you want to come and watch me play." He grinned at Maureen. "Is that all right with you, Mum?"

"As long as you're not driving with a six pack between your legs." It was a habit of Bluey's.

"I'll be a good uncle."

Saturday couldn't come fast enough with the children ticking off the days on the calendar. They were dressed and waiting when Bluey arrived.

"Stay for dinner tonight," Maureen called after him as she and Pete waved the kids off. He tooted the horn in response.

Late that afternoon, three devastated children pushed past Maureen leaving a sheepish Australian to explain himself.

Bluey shook his head. "Out for a duck, never happened before. I don't think the kids will ever forgive me." He couldn't forgive himself.

After dinner and twelve beers later, he recited all eight stanzas of *The Man from Snowy River* while he blubbered into his beer. "I'll have to make it up to the boys, they were so disappointed." He thought for a moment and then raised eyes that matched his red hair. "Tell you what, come to my place next Sunday for a barbie and I'll have a surprise for them."

Unaware of the furthering of her children's education, Maureen sipped wine next to Bluey's thick green-scummed pool and talked to his latest girlfriend while they waited for the boerewors to cook on the barbeque. Pete and the children were in the adjoining paddock.

The children kept a safe distance, watching Bluey and his helpers restrain a big bull. When the bull was completely immobile Bluey brought out a large pair of what looked like iron tongs with curved snippers on the ends. He slipped the snippers over the animals' prominent testicles and snapped them shut. A bellow from the animal and a mighty kick followed. The restraints were let go and the knackered bull took off. Bluey picked up the bulls' balls and handed them to Henry.

"Here you go, boys, stick those on the fishing rods over there and have a fish in the pool. I've got trout in there." He was making up for the cricket disappointment.

Three white-faced young boys fished with the bull's bollocks for twenty minutes without any luck. Tired of fishing, they pulled the balls off their hooks and dropped them on the ground where they were immediately gobbled up by Bluey's dog.

The following week, Gerard recited the incident at show-and-tell in his classroom and Maureen's parenting skills were whispered about for weeks while the vet and his reputation got away scot-free.

Although Johannesburg only had two seasons, the wet and the dry, Maureen's children had a lot more.

"Mummy, the flying ants are here," Gerard yelled, rushing past her to retrieve her squash racket while Liam and Henry ran for their tennis rackets. Racquets swinging, they raced outside and into a cloud of ants rocketing up out of the ground and began their game of termite tennis to see who could hit the most towards their opponent. Although Maureen dreaded having to scrape the ants off their clothes and wash them out of the boys' hair, she let them kill as many as they could. The buggers were eating her house. She could hear them in the door frames.

Pete wasn't concerned. "The house is brick, what are they going to eat?" he'd said.

If he wasn't worried, then she wasn't going to be. The cost of getting rid of them would have come out of her holiday savings.

Soccer season began at the end of ant season and they were having a kick in the front yard. Henry booted the ball over the fence in the path of two young African men. One of them caught the ball on his foot and demonstrated some fancy footwork, passing the ball back and forth to his friend before booting it back over the fence to the boys.

"You're good," Henry said. The men saluted and continued up the road. The children knew them – they had been customers of Henry's tomato stand. They were also security guards at Ethnor, the pharmaceutical company at the end of the road where the school bus stopped.

"See you tomorrow after school," Liam yelled after them.

Hands were raised in response.

The following day, Henry and Liam got off the bus and entered Ethnor's gate, their shortcut home. The two young African security guards who had kicked the ball waved them through the gate.

"Hello McDonald, hello Wilson," Liam said. He loved black people.

"Hello Liam, hello Henry." The guards' grins were big.

The boys put down their school bags and talked about their soccer game. McDonald smiled; he and Wilson played for the Moroccan Swallows, a renowned black soccer team. They discussed soccer moves and feigned a few kicks.

"Why don't you come and play with us at my house?" suggested Henry. "We can play on the front lawn – it's as big as a pitch." The deal was done, and Henry and Liam made their way home, passing the tractor man's dead tomato plants still clinging to stakes. Henry booted a stone, disappointed he hadn't made enough for the Scalextric set. "We can be professional soccer players and make money, Liam."

Liam nodded, he was good at sport, they both were. Gerard was also looking promising for a five-year-old.

At dinner, Maureen only had half an ear to Henry's chatter about McDonald and Wilson coming to play. Friends from school, she thought. The next afternoon she met their friends.

"Mummy, McDonald and Wilson are here to play soccer with us," Henry said, rushing into the kitchen.

"Tell them to come in."

"They don't want to. You have to come outside." Henry jumped from one foot to the other, waiting for her. Giving the beef stroganoff a stir, she put the lid on and followed Henry outside.

There were two black men in their early twenties, handsome

in their soccer club jumpers and soccer boots. Flustered, Maureen was suddenly aware she was shoeless and wearing a kikoi – the bright coloured cotton wrap she'd bought in Kenya – not the usual attire for a madam.

"My name is McDonald, and this is Wilson, Madam." They gave a slight bow. We have come to teach your children how to play soccer, Madam." Polite and well-spoken, McDonald looked her in the eye.

"That's very nice of you," she dithered. Was she expected to pay them tuition fees? Pete was tinkering in the garage, maybe he knew about this and had forgotten to mention it? The children jumped around the two soccer players, eager to start their game. She watched the young men follow the children up to the front lawn where white stones marked out the playing field and then she went to find Pete. "Did you know about the soccer game, Pete?"

Pete came out from under his car. "What game?"

Maureen proceeded to tell him about the game on the lawn and the two young men who had come to play soccer with the children.

Pete laughed. "We'd better go and watch." He put his spanner down, grabbed two chairs from the porch and carried them up to the field. He raised his hand in greeting and set the chairs down. "I believe there's a game on?"

McDonald picked up the soccer ball he had been bouncing on his foot and tucked it under his arm. "Yes Boss." The two men stood to attention, watching Pete's reaction.

"Which one of the kids conned you into this?" Pete laughed.

McDonald relaxed. "We are the guards at Ethnor. Henry and Liam get off their bus and come through our gates to walk home. They asked us to play a game with them."

"I'm a rugby man, too much fancy footwork in soccer." Pete didn't add he thought soccer was a poof's game. He turned to

Gerard. "Go and see what your mother's doing, tell her she's holding up the game." Gerard ran off.

In the kitchen, remembering what they used to do in Eden when there was a footy match, Maureen was cutting up oranges. She put the segments on a plate and made a jug of orange juice. These went on a tray with a glass for each of the players.

"What's going on?" Annie said, coming into the kitchen.

"The children's friends have come to play soccer."

"You don't mean those blacks?" She looked aghast. "They could be terrorists."

Gerard ran into the kitchen.

"Mummy, Daddy said you're holding up the game."

"I'm coming right now." Ignoring Annie's tutting, Maureen picked up the tray and followed Gerard. She put the tray on the ground and sent Gerard to call everyone over.

"These are refreshments," she grinned at the young black men's looks of surprise. "This is what we do at footy games in Australia so help yourselves. I'm sorry I don't have cake."

"Thank you, Madam." They put their hands on their hearts.

"Thank you for giving up your time to teach the children soccer." There was something ridiculous about the whole thing that made her want to laugh.

She settled in the chair next to Pete while the players sucked on oranges then pitched their skins into the garden. Pete stood up and gave a piercing whistle. The players ran to the middle of the field. Gerard threw the ball between the two captains. McDonald and Henry against Wilson and Liam. Pete yelled, clapped and whistled praise for each player and when he fell off the chair laughing at Liam scoring for the wrong side, the visitors laughed at him. Although the young black men were highly regarded players amongst the black people, Maureen's family were their first white audience.

At the end of the game the boys waved them off and Maureen thought it would be the last she saw their soccer visitors. But three weeks later Air Safari had merged with another company and Maureen lost her job.

29

A Partner

The loss of her job was devastating. They had a mortgage to pay, and she longed for Australia. It seemed that every time her dream of returning to Australia was within reach, her ship sank. Downhearted, she and Pete discussed their predicament.

"There's no work at the airport. Why don't you try Ethnor, it's just up the road and you can walk there?" Pete said.

She had thought of trying Ethnor but remembered that her neighbour, Terblanche, was the personnel manager and she couldn't think of anything worse than asking him for a job. "I would be interviewed by Terblanche and he's such a sleaze."

"Think of it as an interim job until something comes up at the airport," Pete said.

Maureen grimaced and, after Pete left for work, she phoned Terblanche for an interview.

Instead of walking the children's route through Ethnor's

grounds, Maureen drove in the main gates. McDonald greeted her at the car window.

"McDonald? I forgot you worked here." He pointed to the small office at the gate.

"We both do. Wilson is in there, Mrs Millar." It was the first time a black person had called her anything but Madam.

"Can I ask what your purpose is?" He smiled.

"I'm coming for a job interview with Mr Terblanche." At the sound of her neighbour's name, McDonald's mouth turned down.

"I hope you are successful. He has a bad dog."

"Yes. It menaced me once. My husband told him he should keep it chained up." McDonald nodded in agreement.

"Go through, Mrs Millar and good luck. Just beep your horn when you come back, and I'll open the gate."

Terblanche greased her with a smile, eyes appraising. "I can't believe you've had four children, Maureen."

Something curdled in her stomach. She put her reference letter from the airport in front of him. "I was the General Manager's secretary and public relations officer. I organised all the functions for our VIP guests. That included Mario Andretti." She dropped the name, knowing Terblanche followed motor racing.

Terblanche leapt up from his chair. "Come and meet Dan Boorman, he's looking for a secretary."

Half an hour later Maureen blew her car horn at the gate and McDonald rushed out.

"Success?" he said in a hopeful voice.

"I start next week."

"I will reserve parking for you and get you a pass card."

"I'll probably walk to work, McDonald."

"I will get it for you anyway. Say hello to your little skellums," he said, grinning. He drew himself to attention. "I was going to

246

ask you Mrs Millar, if you had spare rooms in your servants' quarters that Wilson and I could rent?"

An image came to Maureen of the dank, small concrete rooms without electricity next to the garbage tip and the lavatory where a little girl had fallen through the seat. If it hadn't been for Henry, she would have met a terrible death drowning in the cess pit. Maureen was filled with shame. These young men were more fitted to living in the flat Pete had fixed up, but she knew Pete wouldn't allow them to live there because it was too close to their house. He wouldn't want unknown blacks visiting the men. George would also object and cause more problems.

"We don't have spare rooms, McDonald, we use them as storerooms." It was true – Pete's mother's belongings were stored there. "Anyway, it's not good enough for you, there's no electricity."

"Wilson and I can fix it up and we can use lanterns, Mrs Millar."

Maureen was feeling pressured. She would like to help them with accommodation – the black township where they lived was a long way from their work.

"I'm sorry, McDonald but I don't think we can help you." She bit her lip and looked at him regretfully.

"It's all right, Madam," he said. There was something in the way he said Madam that stung. Maureen mumbled a goodbye and left, cursing Apartheid. Later she told Pete.

"We can't have them, it would be illegal," said Pete. "They know we can get into trouble if they stay here, so don't feel bad."

What he said made her feel a bit better about disappointing the nice young men.

Not long after Maureen started her new job, Pete was approached by Mitch Flynn, the swimming pool millionaire. Mitch had a plane stationed at the airport and was interested in buying into Pete's business. Since Bossboy's death, Pete had let things slide.

The new partnership refuelled his enthusiasm. Mitch had a professional sign made with the company name and had it installed above Pete's hangar. He advertised in aircraft magazines and printed leaflets to leave in flight offices. Under his guidance, Pete bought new equipment putting his business in debt for the first time.

Seven months later Pete sat in the lounge, his head down and hands between his knees. "I've failed us." His partner had used him as a tax dodge and Pete was bankrupt.

Maureen put her arms around him. "You'll find something else; we can manage for a couple of months." She ran their bank account and was a good saver. There was the money for Australia they could use.

"I'll speak to some of the guys whose planes I've looked after and see if they have something going."

A month went by, and Pete had to take out an overdraft. Pierrette mentioned their plight to Bluey.

Bluey turned up with a live goose under his arm. He had too many, he said. And the following week he had too many hens, then he had too many eggs and vegetables that he didn't know what to do with. Bluey kept them in food until Pete found a job.

He started work as the sales representative for an international metal spray company. It was his first job in the business world, and he liked it.

"We've been invited to a restaurant with my boss and his wife. He wants to meet you."

Maureen wanted to make a good impression for Pete. She bought a new dress, a black mini that sat nicely around her curves, grateful that having babies hadn't spoiled her figure. Her dark hair was short and feathered around her face. She wore her favourite Masai earrings made from copper and pieces of turquoise that Pete had bought for her when they were going out in Kenya. Last were her black stilettos. Pete whistled when he saw her.

The boss stood as they approached the table, motioned them to their seats and made the introductions. Pete's boss and his wife were in their late forties, friendly and relaxed. Pete told jokes and his boss reciprocated. Maureen added a funny story about her father. The evening was going well.

At first, Maureen didn't notice the pressure on her foot under the table, and then she sat back and lifted the tablecloth to see what it was. The boss's foot tapped on top of hers. Not wanting to alert his wife or Pete, Maureen pushed her chair back and bent down pretending to pick up the table napkin that she had let slip off her lap. "Dropped my serviette," she said, with a laugh, then tucked her feet under her chair, not looking at his boss. Pete wasn't going to get any promotions through her.

She thought how Joey would enjoy the story; they hadn't spoken in a while. She had moved again and said she would let Maureen know her new phone number as soon as she was settled. That was three months ago. Her silence was concerning. Maureen put Joey out of her mind and concentrated on charming the wife of Pete's boss.

The company sent him to England on a six-week-course. Pete was enjoying his new career, particularly when he read in the business section of *The Daily Mail* that Mitch Fynn had gone bankrupt.

"Serves the bastard right," he said. It wasn't a good time to be in the aircraft business. The boycotts against Apartheid were hitting South Africa hard. Aeroplanes were a luxury item. Pete would have struggled, whereas now, for the first time, they had a steady income and if Pete became sick, they were covered. There were also other possibilities – the company had a branch in Melbourne.

Having newfound security meant Maureen could afford to put four-year-old Clement in a kindergarten. He was lonely without his school-going brothers.

But kindy wasn't to Clement's liking. He wanted to be at home – if not with his mother, then with Elizabeth the maid. Every morning he stacked on a turn and Maureen persevered, hauling him out of the car at kindy, sure he would get used to it.

Then a call came through to her office from the head of the kindergarten.

"Did you collect Clement early today?"

What was the woman talking about? "No. Why?"

"I'm just checking because the children have all gone inside for their rest and he's not with them." She gave a titter. "He's probably still outside somewhere. Don't worry, I'll get someone to look for him and call you back."

It was half an hour before the next call came through. "Could you check if Clement is at home? We're thinking he might have asked a parent to take him home."

"He's missing? Are you saying you have lost my son?" The whole place was behind a six-foot wire netting fence, how could they lose him? She couldn't phone home. Annie was with her brother in the Cape for a month and Elizabeth was afraid of the telephone and wouldn't answer it.

"I'm leaving my office and going home now." In her panic, she hung up on the kindergarten. "My child's missing," she called out to her boss as she rushed for the door. She took her high heels off to run home, cursing she hadn't brought the car. At the gate she started yelling for Elizabeth and George. They hadn't seen Clement.

"Look everywhere," Maureen screamed. She ran into the bedroom he shared with Gerard. One bed was made, the other was a heap of blankets. She lifted the blankets on Clement's bed to find him curled underneath, asleep. The breath went out of her body. She dropped onto his bed. "Thank you, God." She didn't wake him.

She phoned the kindergarten. They had found the spot where he had crawled under the wire fence. The kindergarten was eight kilometres from his home. How he knew which way to walk flummoxed Maureen. Questioning Clement later, he told her he was walking home when a kind man had stopped his car and picked him up. The man told Clement he knew him and that he used to live down the road from them. The man didn't come into their driveway, he just dropped the four-year-old off at the gate. Not knowing who he was, Maureen couldn't thank him, but it terrified her to think Clement would get in a stranger's car.

It was the last time Clement attended kindergarten. From then on, he stayed home with Elizabeth and played with Sonny.

30

Heartbreak

It was a peaceful Saturday afternoon. The children were having a game of war in the garden and Annie had just finished knitting a jacket for Clement. Pete was outside tinkering with the crashed XK120 Jaguar he had bought to rebuild and Maureen was going through her cordon bleu cookbooks for recipes.

The phone shrilled. It was her friend, Corona. "Have you seen the paper?"

"No, I haven't bought it. We're just having a lazy day."

"Joey's dead. Colin too. He shot them both. It's on the back page of the newspaper."

The words skewered into Maureen's body, the pain so intense she doubled over clutching at her stomach and screamed. "No! God, no!"

Alarmed, Corona started to apologise. She'd relayed the information as though it was the latest gossip with no idea of the impact it would have, but Maureen didn't hear her. The phone dangled from the receiver as she rocked on the floor. Hearing her scream, Pete and Annie rushed to her.

"What's happened?" Pete had never seen Maureen in such a state and didn't know what to do.

"I knew he would do it. I knew it. I saw it in his eyes at our party. Oh, God, Pete, he killed Joey and Colin, shot them. It's in the newspaper." Her prediction had come true. "I told her," she sobbed.

"Jesus Christ!" Pete pulled her up from the floor and held her in his arms. The children watched their parents and Gerard started to cry.

Annie rounded them up and led them into the garden. "Stay outside until I call you." She went into her room and collected a bag of sweets and handed them out to the children. She made Maureen and Pete a cup of coffee and retreated to her room to give them time on their own.

In the yard, Henry picked up his toy gun and aimed it at Liam. "Bang you're dead, Colin," he yelled.

Still in shock, Maureen rushed outside and shouted at the children. "Stop that game. What are you doing?"

The children skulked off. Afterwards when Maureen had recovered, she was full of remorse. Colin was Henry's friend. It was probably a child's way of dealing with such shocking news.

Pete drove into the village and bought the newspaper, reading it first to see if Maureen would be able to cope with the story before he took the paper home.

There had been a big argument. Pete could visualise the event. Des attacking Joey. Joey running outside and grabbing Colin to escape to the neighbour.

"Come back here or I'll shoot you," the eyewitness, her maid, reported him saying.

Pete could see the terror in Joey's eyes, her fear for Colin. She would do as Des told her; she always had.

"The madam turned around, her nose was bleeding. The boss aimed his gun at her. 'You wouldn't,' the madam said. He shot her in the face. Her boy saw his mother shot and ran, and then his father shot him in the back. After the killing the boss went inside his house and shot himself through the cheek."

Pete made a bet that Des hadn't intended to kill himself; he would have been scared and done it to gain sympathy. It was a pity the bastard hadn't blown his brains out, Pete thought. There was to be a post-mortem. Des was in custody. Folding the newspaper, Pete decided to wait for Maureen to get over the shock before giving it to her to read.

Two weeks on and Maureen had managed to pull herself together. She still had the funeral to deal with and decided the children were too young to go through something so gruelling. There was no doubt she would be a mess on the day.

It was a sober gathering at the Dutch Reform Church. It was an overcast grey day, and inside the church was like a black cavern. The only colours were the school uniforms. Colin's whole class was there. A bent woman, body angled over a walking stick was helped inside – Joey's grandmother.

Maureen sat on the right-hand side of the church, two pews from the front, between Corona and Pete. She didn't know anyone else there yet the church was full. She guessed some of Joey's old work colleagues were present. She saw a handsome fellow in the front pew and guessed it was Joey's brother from the likeness. Maureen drew a shuddering breath and swallowed. She wanted to bawl her eyes out even before the service had started.

The organ heralded the beginning of the service. The predicant raised his hands for everyone to stand. A hymn, familiar to

Maureen, began, but her head was too muddled to remember the words. Nor could she take in anything that was said about Joey.

The first coffin was carried down the church aisle. On its top was a ring of red roses with a photo of a smiling Colin, inside lay a little boy without a future, and next to it schoolboys marched. Their young primary school faces were sombre in their task. People coughed, grunted, moaned. Maureen's hands could barely hold her hymn book; she felt sick. The coffin was placed in the front of the church and then the second coffin came down the aisle.

Joey's brother, stone-faced, walked at the front of the coffin. An animal moan came from the grandmother in the front pew. She fell backwards into her seat and two people leant to attend her. Maureen closed her eyes and sobbed, unable to control herself.

Then a commotion occurred at the back of the church. People turned to look. A breeze of whispers reached Maureen so she turned. Two policemen stood at the back of the aisle with Des handcuffed between them. Maureen's knees weakened and she clutched Pete. How dare he come here! The murderer. She was suffocating with fury. Pete felt her shaking beside him and put his arm around her shoulder.

"What's he doing here?" Corona hissed beside her.

"I hope he's in agony. I hope he remembers and regrets what he's done every day for the rest of his life." Maureen stared straight ahead, refusing to acknowledge his presence, shivering at the thought he'd once threatened her family. He had killed three people – one when he was twelve. She tried to concentrate on Joey, remembering the first time they had met at the parent-teacher night at the school. Joey had rolled her eyes after the headmaster's pompous speech and whispered the Afrikaans word for idiot. They had laughed. Joey could imitate his accent to perfection and sometimes Maureen had to leave a meeting to stop from laughing. She choked at the recollection.

She remembered the day they had gone shopping in Vreededorp, a poorer part of Jo'burg, and bought the material for her curtains. First, they went for a coffee in one of the narrow cafés that sold everything from coffee to bags of rice and mealy pop. They had squashed into a table against a peeling wall, feeling conspicuous in their smart clothes against a clientele in mended hand-me-downs. They had had a Koeksister plaited donut each, licking the sugar lemon syrup that dripped down their fingers and drinking a coffee that increased their heart rate. After the café they had walked down the narrow streets looking at the sun-faded materials packed in shop windows. A roll of purple jersey had caught Maureen's eye.

"Look, that would pick up the purple in my Casa Pupa, what do you think, Joey?" Everything had to show off Maureen's beloved Casa Pupa.

Joey's small shapely lips had pouted in thought. "It's a big room with high ceilings so it would probably take the colour but I'm not sure about jersey being the right material. It tends to stretch."

"I love the colour." Maureen had never considered the interior of any home she'd lived in before. "I can see it with my black slatted lounge chairs and orange cushions."

The shop assistant had flinched. Holding the fabric against Maureen Joey had said, "If it doesn't work as curtains it would make a nice suit."

Joey had looked so relaxed and pretty that day. Maureen promised herself she would never take down the purple curtains in her lounge room.

The moan of the organ brought her back to the flower-covered casks at the altar. The pall bearers lifted them onto their shoulders, Colin behind his mother's, his classmates following, white-faced after the ordeal. Maureen waited for the last of the mourners to reach her before joining the exit line behind the coffins. She didn't want to see Des's sorry wounded face; he didn't deserve any pity. Fortunately, the police had removed him during the final hymn.

Des appeared in the newspapers again. He had received ten years in prison for both murders with the sentences to run consecutively. Maureen knew a South African prison wasn't a good place for an inmate, particularly if one of their victims' brothers was in the police force and Joey's was. She wished Des a nightmare incarceration.

31

Lunch Guest

Maureen was grateful for her promotion, although it wasn't glamorous or exciting keeping track of veterinary stocks. It was boring, but she liked the move to the laboratory and learning a new job. Working with new people helped take her mind off the loss of Joey.

A young Indian employee from the mailroom put a letter in her in-tray and smiled, then walked past her and threw an envelope at Caroline, sitting next to her. The envelope landed on the desk and fell to the floor. The mail clerk carried on walking. Caroline picked up the envelope.

Caroline was a coloured and Ethnor didn't discriminate. They were an international company following international guidelines and under Ethnor's roof, all races worked together and had equal opportunities. However, what they couldn't do was change the prejudice of their employees.

The Indian workers in the mail room wouldn't accept Caroline. Coloureds were a lower class than Indians and they objected to delivering her mail. In the lunchroom they had removed the spare chairs at their table so Caroline couldn't sit with them. The whites allowed her to sit at their table, but she always sat at the end, with empty chairs in-between and she was never invited to join their conversations.

None of this had been obvious to Maureen. She hadn't worked with coloureds prior to her promotion and she hadn't used the lunchroom, preferring to walk home for lunch instead. The box of veterinary samples she had picked from the stock room had to be packed. She put the tray of samples on Caroline's desk. "Caroline, can you take this to the mailroom and get the clerk to pack it please."

Caroline lowered her head. "I can't, Mrs Millar."

Maureen frowned. It was urgent. "Why not?"

"They won't pack for me."

An image of the thrown envelope stilled Maureen. "Take it and I'll follow you."

Reluctant, Caroline picked up the tray and walked down the hall, with Maureen a distance behind her. She entered the mailroom. The two mail girls didn't see Maureen. Stopping what they were doing, they stood in front of Caroline, arms folded. "What do you want?"

Caroline put the tray of samples on their table. "Mrs Millar needs this to be packed, it's urgent."

One of the girls picked up an empty box and threw it at Caroline. "Pack it yourself, we don't work for coloureds."

Maureen stepped into the room and picked up the box. "You will pack this," she said, putting the box on the counter. "Caroline is my assistant. She also works for my boss. Do you want me to tell him about this?"

The girl picked up the box. "I will pack them for you, but not her," she indicated Caroline with her chin.

Maureen flushed with anger. "We'll see about that. Come on Caroline."

Her boss leant his elbows on the desk and tapped his pen. "It's not right, I know, but we can't change how it is. All the staff in the mailroom are related, one gets the other a job. They would walk out rather than feel subordinate to a coloured, and they'll probably target her even more now that she's made trouble for them." He frowned. "It would have been better if you had left things as they were."

Maureen left her boss's office with a burning hot stomach. South Africa was giving her ulcers. At lunchtime, she went to look for Caroline and saw her sitting at the end of a table with four empty chairs between her and the other occupants. So as not to embarrass the girl any further, she went over and whispered an invitation in her ear.

Caroline picked up her lunchbox and said loud enough for the whites at her table to hear. "Yes, I would like to go to your place for lunch, Maureen."

Heads turned and shocked eyes looked at Maureen, full of disapproval. It would be the end of her popularity. One of the women, Lila, gave her a wink of approval. "Better than eating with the bitches in the mailroom, or at the end of our table, hey Caroline." Noses lifted around her. "See you after lunch," Maureen said leaving the lunchroom.

Clement ran to the door and threw his arms around Maureen. "This is my youngest, Clement," she said to Caroline, bending down to hug her excited child. Behind him, stood Annie. Maureen hesitated. "And this is my mother-in-law, Mrs Millar."

Annie's tongue searched the inside of her cheek as she levelled a look at Caroline.

"Caroline and I work together," Maureen said with a bright

smile. "I've brought her home to have lunch with me. Do you want to join us, Annie?" She hoped not.

"I've eaten and I have some handwashing to do," Annie said stiffly, walking off. Good, thought Maureen. She had been scared Annie would join them and make Caroline uncomfortable.

It hadn't fazed Pete when she told him later. His only concern was that it might affect her at work and in a roundabout way it did.

A problem with the Product Returns Book was causing Maureen a headache. There were more credits than returns on a veterinary product. She approached her boss about the discrepancy.

He waved her away. "Sign it off," he said. It was her efficiency on the line. When the auditors asked for her ledger, she drew their attention to the figures that didn't correspond. A quiet investigation occurred; no one had ever bothered with the unaccountable rohypnol drug before. Without realising it, Maureen had drawn attention to the disappearance of a dangerous drug. Over the following weeks, her work began to find its way onto Caroline's desk, leaving Maureen twiddling her thumbs. Worried, she decided to have it out with her boss. He had been ignoring her.

But there was one other thing she had to attend to first. The pregnancy test she had just peed on was positive. She stared at it in disbelief and tried a second test with the same result. Her plan to discuss her job went out the window; she'd lose it anyway. She drove home in a daze, parked and locked the car. Liam and Gerard leapt out from behind a tree in front of her shrieking with laughter, their heads and bodies dripping in egg yolks, slime, and bits of eggshell. The stench made her gag.

"What are you doing?"

Gerard fell on the ground giggling. "Rotten eggs, we found rotten eggs." Liam tried to pull him to his feet and fell on top of him. They clutched at the tree and tried to stand, both hysterical. Maureen hoisted Gerard to his feet, and he vomited down the front of his shirt. The sour smell of regurgitated alcohol hit Maureen. Her children were drunk!

"George!" Maureen shrieked. George came running. "What's going on? These kids are drunk!"

"Yes, Madam. And they found the chicken eggs you thought I took;" he folded his arms. "Very old eggs, Madam."

"Bugger the eggs. How did they get drunk, man?" Her fingers bit into the arms of her two children.

"From the box with the tap in the fridge, Madam."

"Shit!" All the alcohol was locked away except the cask in the fridge. Why hadn't Annie noticed what they were doing? Or Elizabeth? Maureen dragged her two spewing children into the house and shoved them at Elizabeth.

"Please, give these monsters a bath and soak their clothes in a bucket." She rounded her eyes glaring at the sorry children. "After your bath you go to bed."

Maureen stamped down the hall to her mother-in-law's bedroom. "Do you know what those little buggers have done?"

Annie looked at her with red eyes. "I know, I found Gerard hiding in the cupboard where I keep the sweets, his mouth was full of them. He said 'Fuck off, Granny!'" She caught her breath and a tear rolled down her cheeks.

A laugh threatened Maureen, which she quickly turned into a cough. She mustn't laugh, she was angry. "Oh, Annie, he was drunk, he didn't mean it."

Annie's face switched from sad to shocked.

"He and Liam got into the wine cask in the fridge and apparently they found some rotten eggs which they were throwing at each other. I've just chewed George out for not stopping them."

She had a gardener, a maid and her mother-in-law, and yet the kids ran wild. How would she cope with another child? She would never manage in Australia.

"They're drunk?" Annie's face went from forlorn to prim. "They need a good belting."

"They'll get one," Maureen promised.

The boys were too sick to get a hiding. Vomiting and headaches were punishment enough as far as Maureen was concerned. She left them inert in their beds with a bucket between them and spent the rest of the afternoon wondering what Pete's reaction would be to her pregnancy news.

"You can't be! You've only got one tube. The doctor said it wouldn't happen. Five kids?" he stared at her, incredulous. "Can't you do something about it?"

His response triggered an old memory of her time in Sweden and her eyes became coals.

Seeing the look on Maureen's face, Pete felt sorry for his reaction. He put his hands up. "Look, it's your call, I'm happy with whatever you decide." His job was earning enough to keep the home going. Children, maids, shopping, cooking were up to her – the income from her job was never counted.

"Then get used to it," she said. He always seemed to think it was her fault when she fell pregnant. "This baby might be a daughter," she said.

"You can't blame Pete; he has a lot of mouths to feed," Annie said.

Maureen whirled. She hadn't realised their conversation had been overheard. "I've helped him with that. I've worked from the time we got married. I haven't stayed at home and held garden parties like his friends' wives. If you remember, I went to work at your suggestion when Liam was only five months old, and I haven't stopped since."

"Mum, this has nothing to do with you," Pete said.

His mother looked stricken; it was the first time Pete had taken her to task in front of Maureen.

"I didn't mean anything by it." She hadn't, but Annie had always felt unwanted in Maureen's home. Perhaps she should feel grateful for the new baby. At least a baby meant they wouldn't be rushing off to Australia. That was her greatest fear.

Nothing more was said about the new baby and Annie began knitting a wonderful layette. At seven months' pregnant, Maureen put in her resignation and Caroline took over her position. There were no more lunches with Caroline.

Number five was her easiest birth. A girl! Lilly. Maureen was thrilled. As she cuddled the bundle in her arms, she thought of Joey and how pleased she would have been to know she'd had a little girl. Now her family was complete. Tomorrow she was having her remaining tube tied before she left the hospital. What went on with her body was nothing to do with a priest or being Catholic or Pete, and it galled her that he still had to sign a permission form for her procedure.

The first night home from hospital, she was sitting on her bed feeding the baby when a line of cars entered the driveway and parked under the large tree in their front garden. Hearing doors slam and loud greetings, Maureen peeked through her curtains. People were entering her courtyard, with bottles tucked under one arm and loaded plates of food in the other.

Pete came into the bedroom. "I've invited a few people to wet the baby's head," he said.

Maureen groaned. "I'm so tired, Pete."

"They won't stay long." He thought she would have been pleased.

Eighteen people raised their glasses to her as she entered the lounge, her sodden bra packed with pads to stop milk leakage. She played the hostess, greeting everyone with an enthusiasm she didn't feel. The oven was on warming sausage rolls and quiches and women tripped over each other in her small kitchen, hunting for cutlery, serviettes and plates. Maureen laid the dining table, found a bottle opener and raised her glass of water to well-wishers. In two hours, it would be feeding time again and all she wanted to do was go to bed, but the party had started to swing.

She pulled Pete aside. "I'm going to bed. I need sleep. Make sure they all leave by ten o'clock." Her exit went unnoticed.

In the morning Henry, Liam, Gerard and Clement stood next to her as she changed the baby's nappy. They stared in awe.

"Her dickie's been sliced off," Gerard said.

"Girls don't have a dickie," Maureen said.

"How do they pee?" Liam asked.

Henry walked out of the room snorting. Liam knew about their dickies, he knew where babies came from, he had told Henry. It didn't bother Henry that his informant was his eight-year-old brother. Maureen made a note to get Pete to tell them about the birds and bees.

Lilly was christened in the Catholic Church. Her godmother was Sister Noella – it should have been Joey – and Bluey was the godfather. After the ceremony everyone went back to party at Maureen and Pete's. Pierrette emptied her wine stock into Pete's bar.

Bluey was well under the weather when he yelled out to Maureen, "Hey Maureen, watch my beer I need to crack a darkie."

She whirled, glaring at him. "It's okay, only Aussies know what I mean," he laughed and headed off to the lavatory. He came back and wobbled towards Sister Noella, removing the glass from her hand. "Let me fill that for you."

"I only drink cordial," she said.

He bowed, chivalrous. "Your wish is my command." He bore her glass to the bar with a grin, filling it with cider and ice cubes.

After the first sip her eyebrows rose in appreciation.

"It's an Aussie apple cordial, all the way from Australia." He didn't mention the alcohol content. The beer flowed while Bluey remained attentive to Sister Noella's glass. He recited *The Man from Snowy River* for her; she clapped, her eyes sparkling.

"How about you get out of that habit, and we make babies?" he said, with a cheeky grin.

Noella's eyes rounded. Maureen was too stunned to speak. She frowned and shook her head at him.

He ignored her. "I wouldn't mind taking that habit off."

There was a sudden lull in the conversation around them. Maureen grabbed Bluey's arm to yank him outside and give him a good talking to when Sister Noella started to laugh. She dribbled and choked on her cider cordial and couldn't stop herself laughing. Days later, she told Maureen that Bluey was her favourite person.

32

Changing Neighbours

A new house was being erected on the property where the church tent had once been pitched. According to George, the builder, his wife and six-year-old son were living in the garage while it was being constructed.

Maureen knocked on the open garage door thinking the child might play with Clement while his brothers were at school. The woman was standing with her back to Maureen stirring a pot on the stove and didn't hear her knock. She knocked louder. "Excuse me," she called out. There was still no response. "Hello," Maureen shouted. The woman had to be deaf. She would get George to find out more about them and maybe drop a note in their letterbox. She turned to go.

"Hello." A young voice greeted her from a dark corner in the shed. He was sitting on the floor pushing a truck along a chalk road beaming at Maureen and Clement. Jumping to his feet the child went over to the stove and tapped his mother's arm. His hands made rapid movements and then he pointed to Maureen in the doorway.

Bugger! thought Maureen. The woman motioned Maureen to come inside and made some unintelligible sounds. Maureen opened her hands, helpless, not understanding what the woman was trying to say. The child interpreted for her in Afrikaans. Maureen shook her head answering in English. The woman picked up a pad and pencil and wrote something in Afrikaans. Maureen pointed at the message and shook her head then wrote: I only speak English. They smiled at each other, helpless.

Maureen looked at the little boy's eager face and tapped the truck in his hand, pointed at Clement and made a sound like a truck pretending she was driving it. She pointed at the boy and up the road towards her own house. "Can your boy come and play?"

There was a flurry of hands, and the mother shook her head. The child looked disappointed. His mother pointed to Clement, and her own house. Then wrote 'hier' on her note pad.

It was close enough to English for Maureen to understand. God, what had she gotten herself into again? She could see Pete rolling his eyes. "Will you play here for a while, Clement? I will come and get you when the boys are home from school."

Clement frowned at the ground. The woman came over with a piece of chocolate cake and his face brightened. He reached for the cake and Maureen laughed ruffling his hair. She tapped her wristwatch and held up two fingers, then nodded to the woman and left.

The children were playing outside when Maureen came back to pick Clement up. She leant over and opened the car door. Clement hopped in the car and waved goodbye to his new friend. He had had a nice afternoon.

At eight thirty the next morning there was a knock on Maureen's front door.

"Who's that? Don't they know it's Saturday?" Pete said, tweaking a curtain aside and peering out.

"Who is it?" Maureen asked.

"Don't know, never seen them before."

Maureen craned around Pete. It was the deaf lady from down the road, with her husband and son. "They're the people building the new house. Clement's been playing with her little boy. She's deaf."

Pete dropped his head and looked at her from under his eyebrows. "What have you got yourself into now? Don't involve me," he said.

What was she going to do? How could she entertain them on her own? She couldn't speak Afrikaans and Pete wasn't going to help her. Elizabeth opened the front door and yelled over her shoulder, "Madam."

Maureen cursed under her breath and went to meet her visitors. "Come in," she said. The husband didn't answer, he signed to his wife. God, couldn't he speak either? She motioned them to come inside. Annie poked her head into the lounge and quickly disappeared.

Maureen heard her call out to Pete and heard him reply. "Don't call me, I don't want to know them." Shame flooded Maureen. How mean of Pete. Red-faced, she looked at her caller and mimed writing a note.

"My name is Corbus, and my wife's name is Nellie," he spoke English haltingly. It dawned on Maureen that he must have heard and understood Pete. Her insides cringed. How could she salvage this? She pointed to the lounge.

"Please, come in and I'll get us a cup of tea."

"No tea, thank you. We didn't come to visit, I came to explain why my son, Willy, can't come here to play with your boy."

Relieved that he could speak English Maureen led them towards the lounge and sat down. "My wife has epilepsy and blacks out. One time she fell on the stove and burnt her arm badly." He signed to his wife, and she lifted her arm to show Maureen her scars. "Willy has to watch his mother, so she doesn't have an accident." Maureen's heart went out to the little boy with such a big responsibility. There was an exchange of hand movements between Corbus and his wife, then Corbus nodded. "She says I can tell you what happened to make her like this if you want to know?"

"Yes, I would like to know."

Corbus took his wife's hand. "When Nellie and her brother were small, they had a nanny. But her mother was hard on the nanny and one day they had a big argument, so the nanny paid the mother back by poisoning the children. Nellie's brother died and she survived, but it left her deaf and mute and with epilepsy." Maureen's hand went to her mouth.

"The house I am building is for another family and so we are not here for long. We would like your children to come and play with Willy while we are here, but Willy can't visit you and leave his mother." He held his wife's hand the whole time he was speaking.

Maureen swallowed the lump in her throat. What would she do if someone poisoned her children? She felt terrible for wanting to avoid her neighbours and angry with Pete for being mean. "Of course, the children can play at your house."

"Playing with your children will help Willy learn English. He cannot go to school because he has to watch his mother, so we teach him at home."

There was a shuffle in the hallway. A determined glint came into Maureen's eye. "Excuse me, I think my husband's back, you must meet him." She went into the hall and saw Pete leaning against the wall.

"Pete," she shouted, "we have visitors I want you to meet. Come in the lounge." Pete pulled a face. They eyeballed each other. "Did you hear me, Pete?" she yelled.

"All right," he muttered, following her into the lounge. He had a good heart but just needed a kick in the arse sometimes. Pete shook Corbus's hand.

"Nice job you're doing on the house," Pete said, embarrassed he had been overheard.

"What a good man," Maureen said, after they had left. "Poor woman. Imagine being poisoned by your nanny. I wonder if they ever caught her?" Maureen realised how easy it would be to disappear. She had never asked Elizabeth her surname or where her family lived. She knew nothing about her.

The children enjoyed playing at Willy's place. Marcela and Lola joined in. There was always chocolate cake and homemade ginger beer. Maureen didn't entertain the parents; it was too hard with the language differences, and they were never asked to the garage. When the house was completed, the children said sad goodbyes and watched for the new arrivals.

"Those boys go to my school," Henry said, as they passed the new house where a furniture van was being unloaded. "They are twins, and they're mean." He didn't wave, and Maureen didn't stop to invite them to play or to introduce herself to the parents. But it wasn't long before the twins were in their front yard kicking a soccer ball with Henry and Liam.

"Rooineks," Pete said, when he heard their accents. It was a derogatory Afrikaans name for the English. The word meant rednecks and came from the sunburnt necks caused by the British soldier's inefficient pith helmets during the Boer war. Pete hadn't forgiven the British for not allowing him to work in

England even though he held a British passport. His passport was considered second class because he was born in a British colony even though he'd fought for them during the Mau Mau uprising in Kenya.

Pete's reaction was good enough for Maureen. She didn't want any more complications in her life, or Pete rolling his eyes at the people she brought home. Most of the time he liked them, and it was just some of their partners that were a bad fit. She ticked off the ones whose relationships hadn't lasted, and she'd had to help by babysitting while they dealt with their personal issues.

There was Julie, who nailed her husband's best silk suit to the floor when she discovered his affair. Rita, who made her husband sit on their kid's potty and mash his poo after swallowing his false eye. It was the way he made sure his houseboy didn't take a sip from his brandy glass when he went to the toilet. Rebecca, who had sneaked off for a dirty weekend with her pilot lover in a stolen aircraft from Pete's hangar. Then there were the girls from the escort agency when she had lived at Mirabelle Fosdick's. There were others that had come and gone, like Angela, whom she didn't want to think about. Maureen had reported her to child welfare for the dreadful abuse of her six-year-old daughter. She didn't add Joey to her list. They had been such close friends and it hurt too much to think about her. Ticking some of them off in her mind, she thought Pete did have a point, but he couldn't say her friends were boring like some of his were.

The Rooinek parents of the twins weren't to be escaped though. It was England versus South Africa in the front yard and Henry scored. The twins laid into Henry, pushing and punching. They were taller than him, more aggressive and bullies. Henry had always been a candidate for bullies.

"Liam!" Henry, yelled, as a fist collected his face.

"Rooineks," Liam shouted running inside.

Henry saw the back of Liam disappear into the house. He was done for. Gerard too small to help, although he tried.

A moment later Liam roared out of the house brandishing a carving knife and charged at the twins. The twins screamed and started to run. Undeterred, Liam chased them down the road, ready for the kill. The twins locked themselves in their house and that evening Maureen and Pete met the parents, Sandra and Trevor.

Maureen settled them in the lounge and Pete went to fetch beer. The twins stood next to their parents, arms folded, eyes daring Liam while Henry gave an account of the twin's aggression.

Returning with glasses and beers from the fridge, Pete scrutinised the parents from the corner of his eye to see if they were oddballs, secretly proud of Liam for standing up for his brother, even if he had used a knife.

Liam stood in front of his accusers, chin up.

"This little kid?" Trevor looked at his twins, a head taller and four years older than the runt accused of chasing them with a knife.

"He called us Rooineks," one twin spluttered.

"He's a bloody Rooinek himself," said his father.

"We're not bloody, Rooineks," said Pete, outraged. "I was born in Kenya."

Maureen looked at the two men and then at the Rooinek wife and motioned with her head towards the kitchen. "Wine?" Her guest nodded. Maureen filled two glasses and they went outside; this little farce was all up to Pete. "Been in Africa long, Sandra?"

"Six months. Trevor has a twelve-year-old daughter, and his ex is a bitch and after more alimony. She can't get him here and there's more opportunity for us than England. I don't know what all the Apartheid fuss is about. I think it's a good idea the blacks having their own townships and ruling themselves."

"They're not in charge of themselves. They don't have rights.

The police are always hassling them, checking passes to see if they are allowed in an area. Blacks can't swim at white beaches, try a dress on in a shop, go to a white hospital, have jobs where whites are their subordinates. The cleaner at my bank has a science degree. Black children have to travel miles to school, often on foot." Maureen hadn't realised she was so angry at all the injustices the blacks had to suffer. There were so many it would take all evening to list them. But she wasn't black. She was living a comfortable life and she wasn't doing anything to change the system, only going by her husband's motto, 'When in Rome.' Sandra's ignorance had given Maureen pause for reflection.

"Your husband was born in Kenya. That's a black country. Does he feel the same?" Sandra asked.

"We don't discuss politics." She wasn't going to get mad at Pete because of this woman. "We're thinking of moving to Australia."

Apart from attending a housewarming at Sandra's house, Maureen kept her distance.

33

Immigration

Pete walked in the door, looking around to make sure the children and the servants weren't within earshot and spoke to Maureen. "Make an appointment with the Australian embassy, we're leaving."

"What's happened?" It had to be something big to rattle Pete.

"Last night Anika was robbed and raped by three bantus."

Anika had taken over the job of Aero Club manager and lived in one of the airport cottages. She was twenty-four years old. Maureen gasped. She knew Anika, had worked with her in the office before she became manager of the club. "Is she all right? Who found her? Did they catch her attackers?"

"Apparently, she went home after a function and caught three blacks ransacking her cottage. They attacked her, held a knife in her mouth while they took it in turns to rape her. She ran into the club naked and screaming. Johannes covered her with a blanket and called the police. She's in hospital, off her rocker, poor girl. I was thinking how it could have been you when I was away." Pete shuddered and looked at Maureen. A decision had been made.

It was sickening. Africa had become too violent. There was no future here for her children. If they stayed, Henry would be conscripted into the army and Maureen would never forgive herself if anything happened to her children.

It was a four week wait for an appointment with the Australian Embassy in Pretoria. The time dragged.

They grouped in front of the immigration officer: Pete, the children, and Maureen. 'Bring back a Britain' had been the slogan when she'd left Australia. It was a joke only meant for single Australian women when they left the country. Well, she was bringing one back even if he was only on a second-class British passport. The children had all been registered as Australians at birth. The immigration officer had a strong Aussie accent.

"You don't need to immigrate, you're Australian and Pete can enter Australia as your spouse. He can get citizenship after six months if he wants and he can change that useless passport." The officer tossed it in front of Pete with a laugh.

"Of course, as an expat you do know there's no immigrant assistance for you. That means no cheap accommodation, health assistance, low interest bank loans, or government support that's available to other immigrants. You're on your own." The officer looked sorry.

It took a moment to sink in. As an expat having lived overseas for sixteen years, Maureen would be moving to a country with a higher cost of living, and with five children. The only money they were allowed to take out of South Africa was ten thousand dollars. Their house would fetch a lot more than that, but the Government would freeze their money. They could only spend it in South Africa if they came back on holidays.

Owning a house in Australia would be out of the question for a few years, and Pete would be arriving without a job. But none of this dampened her ardour. She had always coped, and she would do so again. It was all a matter of booking a flight and leaving whenever they were ready.

But there was one hitch – Pete's mother. "I think we'll have to leave your Mum behind until you find a job, Pete?"

Pete frowned, thoughtful. "Couldn't she stay in Eden with your family?" An image of Eric popped into his mind. He was a weird old boy. Pete remembered the compass his father-in-law had given him and taken back when Pete had stood up to leave before the old boy had finished one of his monologues. Waiting for him to finish a story was like fly-fishing. He pondered every word before pulling it to the surface. He remembered some of his comments about women. *"I could mount that sturdy legged heifer."* God! What if the lecherous old sod took a fancy to his mother? Lillian didn't have a problem, she knew how to cope with the old boy, but his shy mother wouldn't have a clue. And she wouldn't have a pension to live on and he wouldn't have a job, nor did he know which end of Australia they would live in. Pete's conscience was torn.

Returning home, they sat down to discuss their embassy interview with Annie.

Annie showed a brave face. She couldn't imagine her life without the children, especially darling Lilly who climbed out of her cot and crawled into her bedroom in the mornings. When would she see her grandchildren again? In her bedroom she cried herself to sleep, and the following day wrote to her daughter in Kenya, her son in Botswana and her brother in the Cape, looking for a place to live.

It was her brother who offered her a home with him. He lived alone. Everything was set for Pete and Maureen's departure.

Their house went up for sale and they gave most of their furniture to the blacks. It would cost too much to take their furniture and store it in Australia when they didn't know where they were going to settle.

Pete found George a gardener's job and Elizabeth found one for herself. There was a farewell party at a friend's and phone calls to all the oddballs Pete had eventually lowered his newspaper to greet. Maureen thought about the sixteen years she had been away from Australia. So much had happened, good and bad, and she didn't regret any of it. Africa would always be a part of her. It had given her and Henry Bernard a new start. Some of the best times of her life had been in Africa. She would miss it. It had taught her a lot about herself, filled her with laughter and sadness. Perhaps it was prophetic that the only departure date available to them within their three-month plan was 1st January 1980. New Year's Day and a new beginning for Maureen.

When she said goodbye to the first house she had ever owned, Joey's curtains still hung at the windows.

Acknowledgements

I raise a glass of shiraz to toast the editors of Spinifex Press, Susan Hawthorne, Renate Klein and Pauline Hopkins. Three wonderful women who kept me focused and working during the lockdown years of COVID. Pauline, you have a great memory and keen eye.

My second toast is to thank writer, Jennifer Williams who read the first draft of *Africa's Eden*. I always find it scary handing over the first draft and wondering how it's going to be received. Jennifer's feedback and guidance was invaluable.

There's also my son, Stuart, who after reading my manuscript tried to justify his naughtiness as a child, escapades that influenced my novel. And I thank the friends who gave me encouragement – you know who you are.

Other books available from Spinifex Press

Lillian's Eden
Cheryl Adam

With their farm destroyed by fire, Lillian agrees to the demands of her philandering, violent husband to move to the coastal town of Eden to help look after his elderly aunt, despite his ulterior motives. Juggling the demands of caring for her children and managing two households, Lillian finds an unlikely ally and friend in the feisty, eccentric Aunt Maggie who lives next door. In this humorous yet rich and raw novel, Cheryl Adam shows us the stark realities of life in 1950s Australia, and pays homage to friendship and to the rural women whose remarkable resilience enabled them to find happiness in the most unlikely of places.

A sparkling debut novel, reminiscent of Ruth Park and Kylie Tennant.

Lillian's Eden is a garden full of stolen roses, family secrets and ambivalence. It's also home to one very attractive snake. I couldn't stop reading till I found who got cast out.

—Kristin Henry

ISBN 9781925581676

Out of Eden
Cheryl Adam

Pregnant, abandoned and homeless, Maureen battles to survive a Swedish winter until help arrives in the form of a mysterious woman with a veiled past. With the prospect of being deported, Maureen learns who her real friends are, especially when she faces investigations due to her links to a suspected criminal.

Meanwhile in Australia, Maureen's family is scrambling to support her after the health of her unscrupulous father declines and he depends on the clever intervention of his estranged family members to salvage both his dignity and finances.

In this engaging, rollicking yet poignant sequel to *Lillian's Eden*, we see Maureen's ambition to explore the world encounter its harsh realities, and her mother Lillian using her resourcefulness and intelligence to tackle the ongoing family dramas at home.

This is a novel about women in the world in the 1960s, in Australia and abroad, and their resilience and capacity to manage their lives at a time when others want to take that independence and decision-making from them.

Out of Eden is an engaging story of a resilient mother and daughter who defy the conventions of their era. Cheryl Adam is a natural storyteller with a comic gift who succeeds in capturing the feel of the 1960s and its uneasy transition between the stifling conformity of postwar Australia and the move into the new freedoms of the 1970s. It also features that rare thing, a lively and unsentimental portrait of a truly good woman.

—Amanda Lohrey, author of *The Labyrinth*

ISBN 9781925950267

*If you would like to know more about
Spinifex Press, write to us for a free catalogue, visit our
website or email us for further information
on how to subscribe to our monthly newsletter.*

Spinifex Press
PO Box 105
Mission Beach QLD 4852
Australia

www.spinifexpress.com.au
women@spinifexpress.com.au